INVEST

To Live, to Love, to Last

By Peter J. Briscoe

Invest, to Live, to Love, to Last.

ISBN: 9789082904109

January 2024

Published by Compass –finances God's way,
European office, Amersfoort, The Netherlands

www.compass1.eu
www.compass1.org

Bible references

Verses are taken from The ESV® Bible (The
Holy Bible, English Standard Version®). ESV® Text Edition: 016.
Copyright © 2001 by Crossway, a publishing ministry of Good
News Publishers. The ESV® text has been reproduced in
cooperation with and by permission of Good News Publishers

All other verses are taken from THE HOLY BIBLE,
NEW INTERNATIONAL VERSION®, NIV®
Copyright © 1973, 1978, 1984, 2011 by Biblica, Inc. Used by
permission. All rights reserved worldwide.

Verses identified as (NLT) are taken from he Holy Bible, New
Living Translation, copyright © 1996, 2004, 2015 by Tyndale House
Foundation. Used by permission of Tyndale House Publishers, Inc.,
Carol Stream, Illinois 60188. All rights reserved. Verses identified as
(TLB) are taken from The Living Bible, copyright © 1971 by Tyndale
House Foundation. Used by permission of Tyndale House
Publishers Inc., Carol Stream, Illinois 60188. All rights reserved.

Table of Contents

Content summary

Part 1: Money with a mission

What is the mission of investing as a financial disciple? The Lord gave us three commissions. To work the earth, to love God and our neighbour and to make disciples. How does investing contribute to these three aspects of our commission as a disciple of Jesus?

Part 2: Starting on a journey of investing

Using an analogy of a journey by car to reach our goal, we will look at what we need to reach our preferred destination safely. We will look at setting our investing goals, the risks involved and how to prepare for the journey

Part 3: Your investment vehicle

Which type of vehicle will we choose in which to invest? What are some characteristics of the vehicle, some specific risks involved, and how can this investment impact our mission? What is a Biblical perspective on each investment type?

Disclaimer

This book does not give specific financial advice but merely offers a Biblical approach to investing as a financial disciple and an overview of general investment opportunities, together with their risks and impact.

The content provided in this book on investing as a Christian is for informational purposes only. It does not constitute personalised financial advice; the author is not a licensed financial advisor. The book intends to offer a general understanding of principles and considerations for Christian investors, considering values and biblical perspectives.

Any decisions made based on the information presented herein are at the sole discretion and risk of the readers. It is strongly recommended that readers seek guidance from qualified financial professionals and conduct their own research before making any investment decisions. The author and publisher disclaim any liability for financial losses, damages, or adverse outcomes resulting from actions taken based on the contents of this book.

Compass - finances God's way organises study groups on various topics around money management as a financial disciple. Joining such a group can give you a space to pray with fellow believers, seek God's heart on financial decisions and share experiences.

Foreword

By Dr. Alexander Matijevich, Senior Partner, Bibelfinanz, financial advisors, Nürenberg, Germany. (bibelfinanz.de)

In Christian literature, books on biblical financial principles lead a shadowy existence. This is despite the fact that Jesus frequently spoke about this topic in his sermons and parables. Obviously, Jesus felt an important need to discuss this sensitive topic with his followers. Christian circles today only share this heartfelt desire to a limited extent. A biblical approach to finances is hardly ever discussed in churches. When money is discussed, it is often focused on the cheerful giver, saving in times of scarcity or legal regulations.

Peter Briscoe takes us into a completely different field of biblical financial teaching in his book "Invest – to Live, Love and Last."

Why should it be a matter of course for every follower of Jesus to be a faithful investor? What are the spiritual challenges that Christians face when investing? What impact beyond returns and costs can Christians achieve as small and large investors?

With his writing, Peter hits the pulse of time, as many Christians are unsure how to manage their assets responsibly. Beyond the standard answers from banks, investment companies and financial advisors, are there perhaps completely different ways and standards that should be observed when investing from a biblical perspective?

Join Peter on an exciting journey of discovery through the investment world. Peter uses the metaphor of a car journey to give even investment novices a clear understanding of all aspects of responsible investing. The book is rounded off with a biblical look at various asset classes of the present day: How do they work? What should be considered with these assets and where are the particular risks? What positive impact can Christian investors achieve with them? And what does the age-old Bible say about these 21st-century forms of investment?

Whether you are an investment novice or an experienced asset manager, this book will change your perspective on investing and realign it with biblical principles. As you read it, I wish you God's wisdom and courage to apply his biblical truths to your life. God bless you on this journey!

Introduction

I have written this book with some reservations. I am not a financial advisor and have never worked for a financial institution. However, I have been a disciple of Christ for almost 60 years, seeking to follow Jesus in every area of my life. Money affects virtually every area of my life, and I have been studying, learning, and applying what the Bible has to say about handling money for well over 30 years.

Many years ago, a wise mentor said, "Peter, show me your bank statements, and I will show you what your priorities are. You say that following Jesus is the most important goal in your life, but if this is not reflected in the way you are allocating your finances, then you are deluding yourself." He was basing this on Jesus' statement, 'Where your treasure is, there shall your heart be also.' (Matthew 6:21) Your heart follows your money.

This not only refers to spending money but also to investing. I have invested in stocks, mutual funds, start-up businesses and retirement funds. I must admit that I have been a reluctant investor and have experienced changing fortunes in my financial investing.

Remember 9-11? On my very first venture into the stock market, I invested about €20,000 into a mutual fund in the spring of 2001. The first signs of the fund's growth were very positive until September. Then, the unthinkable happened. Almost 3'000 people lost their lives in terrorist attacks on Washington and New York. This changed the world and the financial markets. The fund lost a serious amount of money as shares plummeted. It took me about six years to get my original investment back.

In 2018, my stock portfolio took another hit, and it took me another four years to get that investment back.

However, there were some successes along the way, like an investment in an Egyptian tech start-up, which yielded a good return with the added value of getting a company started, which is having an impact in Egypt for Christ. I invested in starting my own business, which enabled me to be a 'tentmaker' for many years. Another wonderful investment was in a Christian non-profit start-up dedicated to helping people get out of debt. This investment in people is, I am sure, reaping eternal rewards!

As I am writing this, I realise that I have a sizeable investment in a company whose goals and services I later realised that I shouldn't be supporting as a Christian. I will get out of this position as soon as I can. This shows a predicament we, as financial disciples, are facing.

Many of us invest through retirement accounts or funds managed by others, so we don't know where our money is being utilised. This raises a question: If we believe that it all belongs to God, should we trust unknown institutions with God's money and not know how it's being used?

If we care about certain values, we might find out that our investments support companies which go against those values, doing harmful things or mistreating people. Realising this can make us rethink our investment choices based on our Christian principles.

On a larger scale, this uninvolved investing can put money where it doesn't align with what society really needs. For example, investing heavily in gaming, weapons, or media companies may not reflect our true desires for a healthy society due to concerns about mental health and relationships.

To fix these problems, we need more transparency and thoughtful decisions in investing. Considering our values and how they match our investments can lead to better choices that have a positive impact on the world. We should actively invest in businesses that align with our principles and support a better future for everyone.

If we believe that we'll be held accountable for how we live our lives and our stewardship of God's resources, it becomes clear that God won't primarily be concerned merely with financial success. Instead, He'll ask about our love for Him and service to others. So, we should focus on meaningful relationships and the positive impact we make on people's lives, as these are what truly matter to God.

Why invest?

Is investing an activity which disciples of Christ should be involved in at all? Is it scriptural? As in many cases, the answer depends on your motivation. Anyone investing because of greed (Luke 12:15), to get rich quick (Proverbs 23:4-5), or to massage his or her ego (Proverbs 29:23) is not participating in investing as a disciple. On the other hand, those who are acting as good stewards as described in Jesus' parable in Luke 19:12-27 or those who are saving for future needs such as college or retirement (Proverbs 6:6-8) are participating in biblical investing. In the end, it all depends on our attitude, which is ultimately judged by God. Remember, "All a man's ways seem innocent to him, but motives are weighed by the Lord." (Proverbs 16:2).

The Parable of the Talents (Matthew 25:14-30) illustrates our stewardship responsibility:

1. Each of us has varying abilities to manage what God has given us.
2. Doing nothing is poor stewardship.
3. We will be held accountable for how we manage the assets entrusted to us.
4. We are expected to do something with what He has provided to help it grow.
5. Investing is the way to help financial assets grow, and this can take many forms (even if it is just earning interest at the bank). We all may not be able to get the best return, but we should do what we can.

I would suggest, from the message of this parable, that all believers with surplus funds, above those which are needed for short- and medium-term needs, should be investing.

As a Christian, there are several reasons why you might consider investing:

The Bible teaches about stewardship, emphasising that everything we have, including our financial resources, ultimately belongs to God. Investing responsibly and wisely can be seen as a way to manage God's resources effectively and make the most of the blessings He has given you.

Investing can help you secure a stable financial future for your family. By building wealth through investments, you can provide and leave a legacy for your loved ones.

As a Christian investor, you have the opportunity to direct your investments towards companies and initiatives that align with your values and promote positive change in the world. Impact investing or supporting businesses with ethical practices can be a way to be a good steward of your resources and make a positive difference.

By growing your financial resources through investments, you may have the ability to contribute more significantly to charitable causes, missions, and organisations dedicated to spreading the Gospel and helping those in need.

Investing can empower you to be more generous and charitable. As your investments grow, you have more resources available to support and care for others in your community and beyond.

Investing can be a way to prepare for retirement. By investing wisely, you can have a source of income and stability in your later years, freeing you to focus on serving God and others without financial worries.

As a Christian investor, you have the opportunity to engage with the financial world and business community, demonstrating godly principles in your dealings and encouraging ethical practices and fair treatment of others.

It's essential to approach investing with a balanced perspective, understanding that it comes with inherent risks and rewards. As a Christian, prayer and seeking guidance from wise counsel can help you make investment decisions that align with your faith, values, and long-term goals. Remember that your ultimate purpose as a Christian investor is to glorify God in all aspects of your life, including how you manage and utilise your financial resources.

I believe there are three fundamental Biblical reasons for investing.
1. To further God's work (Acts 4:34)
2. To provide income for family needs. (1 Timothy 5:8)
3. To meet long-term goals for future needs. (Proverbs 6:6)

Your faithfulness in handling money is a key to opening the door to living as a dedicated disciple! Jesus was clear and gave us a standard to live by - trustworthiness. "If you have not been trustworthy in handling worldly wealth, who will trust you with true riches?" (Luke 16:11) Can He depend on me to invest money for His purposes in His way?

Money management is not merely a technical exercise but especially a spiritual discipline. Following Jesus in our financial life should be a significant topic of learning for all believers.

The way we allocate our money is a direct reflection of our heart's priorities. How we choose to use money provides a window into the soul.

Impact Investing

Impact investing as a disciple of Jesus is embracing the belief that everything ultimately belongs to God. He is genuinely concerned about the principles, methods, and reasons guiding our investment approaches.

Unlike traditional investing, where the primary focus is solely on financial gains, investing as a financial disciple aims to make an impact on pressing global challenges, such as poverty, climate change, healthcare access, and education, while still achieving competitive financial performance.

As investors, we are invited by God to collaborate with Him in fostering the well-being of humanity. Since the dawn of creation, God designed us to be caretakers of the earth's resources with purpose, enthusiasm, and ambition. He entrusts us with ideas, aspirations, and financial resources to influence the world and bring honour to His name.

INVEST TO LIVE, LOVE & LAST

By directing capital towards God-given goals with sustainable, socially, and biblically responsible initiatives, impact investing plays a crucial role in driving positive change and creating a more sustainable and equitable world.

As disciples of Christ, we desire to centre our lives around God and allow Him to guide every aspect of our existence – from our parenting and leadership to our acts of service and spending habits. What if we could align all our investments with God's values and priorities? By doing so, we can have a meaningful and positive impact on the world.

Recognising that God is the ultimate owner of everything, we understand that the responsibility of managing capital isn't solely ours. It is a comforting realisation that money is entrusted to us for stewardship, with the purpose of bringing glory to God and contributing to the betterment of the world. God's ownership extends to all aspects of our lives, including the way we approach investment strategies, and He deeply cares about the motives, locations, and reasons behind our financial decisions.

Peter J. Briscoe
Leiden, The Netherlands
January 2024

Part 1: Money with a Mission

Investing as a financial disciple comes with a unique set of principles and values that go beyond just financial gain. One of the most significant aspects of responsible Christian investing is having a clear mission and purpose. This mission serves as a guiding light, ensuring that investments align with your beliefs and values.

First and foremost, having a mission when investing as a Christian helps maintain a spiritual, moral and ethical compass. The Bible places a strong emphasis on living a righteous and virtuous life. Investing with a mission allows individuals to avoid investments in companies or industries that go against their beliefs. For instance, Christians may choose to avoid investing in businesses involved in activities such as gambling, pornography, or weapons production, which they view as incompatible with their faith. This deliberate approach to investment ensures that one's money is not being used to support or profit from activities that contradict Christian values.

Furthermore, being on a mission in Christian investing encourages stewardship. Christians believe that they are stewards of God's resources, and this includes their financial assets. Investing with a mission prompts individuals to consider the impact of their investments on society, the environment, and the well-being of others. They are more likely to seek out investments that promote social responsibility and sustainable practices, thus contributing positively to the world.

A mission-driven approach to investing also helps Christians to avoid the pitfalls of greed and materialism. The Bible warns against the love of money and the pursuit of wealth for its own sake. By having a clear mission that emphasises responsible and ethical investing, Christians can prioritise values such as generosity, charity, and helping those in need. This allows them to strike a balance between financial success and their spiritual well-being.

Moreover, investing with a mission provides a sense of purpose and fulfilment. It allows investors to feel that their financial decisions are contributing to a greater good, which can be deeply satisfying. Knowing that your investments are aligned with your faith and values can bring a sense of peace and contentment, even during times of market volatility or economic uncertainty.

Chapter 1. First - Invest yourself!

"To be invested with" originally refers to the act of granting or conferring someone with a particular authority, power, responsibility, or a special quality or attribute. It carries the idea of bestowing or entrusting someone with a certain role or status, often accompanied by a formal ceremony or ritual.

The term "invest" in this context has its roots in the Latin word "*investire*," meaning "to clothe" or "to dress." In medieval times, when feudal lords granted a fief (land) to a vassal, they would symbolically clothe the vassal with a piece of their own clothing, signifying the transfer of power and authority over the land. This practice evolved over time, and the phrase "to be invested with" took on a broader meaning beyond the feudal system. When a bishop was installed in his office, it was said: "he is invested," meaning to give authority and power to someone.

Today, "to be invested with" is commonly used in a metaphorical sense, denoting the granting of authority, responsibility, or trust to someone in various contexts, such as in politics, business, or social institutions. For instance, a leader might be "invested with" the power to make decisions on behalf of a group, or a person might be "invested with" the responsibility of managing a project. It carries the sense of being officially and formally given a role or duty.

The financial meaning of the word also descends from Latin, but it entered English via Italian in the early 17th century, as people invested money in trading companies. In Italian, '*investire*' developed a special sense fabricated from the notion of "clothing" money in a new form.

That use was attached to the English word invest, which eventually came to refer to a commitment of money to earn a return. This financial sense of ' to invest' was first mentioned in the early 1600s by the East India Company in connection with trading.

"Having left with us in goods and monies to be invested in commodities fit for England ... to the value of 4000 li." [1]

When individuals or institutions invest, they commit their money and 'clothe' others with power and authority to use the funds in various investment vehicles to grow wealth, preserve purchasing power, or achieve specific financial objectives. Each of these investment options comes with its own risk profile, potential for returns, and time horizon.

As disciples of Jesus, we are accountable to God for the way in which we use the money which He has trusted us to use. One of the foundational principles of investing as a believer is that the Father is the Provider of the money we have in our power to use. He trusts us to manage His money for His purposes and in His way.

Therefore, we need to be very careful in whom we invest God's money - clothing finances with delegated authority and power to use the funds in our name and ultimately in God's name. We cannot necessarily look to invest the funds in the most profitable way with the least risk and highest liquidity. First and foremost, we should be asking the Lord the most important question; "Lord, what would you want me to do with your money?"

We are God's strategic capital investment, and as disciples of Jesus, we are called to 'invest ourselves' in Christ - to 'put on' Christ and become invested with His power and authority.

Invest yourself ... in Christ Himself ... and His mission.

"And all who have been united with Christ in baptism have put on Christ, like putting on new clothes." (Galatians 3:27)

In the Bible, the phrase "clothed with Christ" is found in several passages, particularly in the writings of the apostle Paul. It conveys a powerful metaphorical image that represents the transformation and identification of believers with Christ. Here's an overview of what the Bible teaches about being "clothed with Christ":

Being clothed (invested) with Christ implies a deep, personal connection and identification with Him, united with Christ in a spiritual and practical way. This identification occurs through professing faith in Him, accepting His sacrifice, and surrendering your life to follow Him. Surrender to the will of the Father characterised the life of Jesus and so must also define our lives. When investing, we should, first of all, surrender our will to His. "Thy will be done, on earth as it is in heaven."

Being clothed with Christ means to put on His identity, clothe ourselves with His character, build up His Body, the Church, and help fulfil His mission.

When a person embraces faith in Christ, they undergo a radical transformation. They receive a new identity and are seen through the lens of Christ's righteousness rather than their own shortcomings. This new identity is symbolised by being clothed with Christ. It signifies being enveloped in His righteousness and living in accordance with His teachings. When investing funds, we need to discover His teachings on using our money - His way.

To be clothed with Christ also means to embody His character and virtues. As followers of Christ, believers are called to emulate His love, compassion, forgiveness, humility, and other qualities. Clothed with Christ reflects the process of sanctification, which is the ongoing work of the Holy Spirit in believers' lives. They are renewed in their minds, their attitudes are changed, and their behaviours align with Christ's teachings. They are encouraged to let go of their old self and to "put on" the virtues of Christ, allowing His nature to permeate their thoughts, words, and actions. "Since God chose you to be the holy people he loves, you must clothe yourselves with tender-hearted mercy, kindness, humility, gentleness, and patience." (Colossians 3:12)

This brings us to ask ourselves, "Does the way our funds are invested reflect the character and nature of Jesus?"

Another aspect of being invested with Christ is the idea of unity and well-being among believers. Regardless of their background, ethnicity, wealth, or social status, all who have put their faith in Christ become part of the universal body of believers. This unity is symbolised by the common clothing of Christ, transcending human differences and emphasising the shared identity and purpose found in Him. Building the Body of Christ also means using resources for this very purpose and sharing, promoting mutual well-being.

Lastly, being invested with Christ means being available to utilise all we have under our control, our time, talents, and treasure, to help fulfil His mission for us. I believe that this can be described using the three commissions known as the Cultural Mandate, the Great Commandment, and the Great Commission.

The Threefold Mission of Investing as a Disciple

Investing ourselves with Christ - putting on His identity, His values, and His mission, should define how to invest - in His way, for His purposes.

When asking, "Lord, what would you have me do with the money you have trusted me to use?" I believe His answer would start with the three commissions He has set out in His Word. I suspect very strongly that He would reply - "Well, I have told you. Look after my creation, love me and your neighbour and make disciples." These three commissions have profound consequences for investing as a financial disciple.

The first commission, known as the Cultural Mandate, is derived from the start of human inhabitation of our earth, where God commands Adam and Eve to "be fruitful and multiply, fill the earth and subdue it, and have dominion over the fish of the sea, over the birds of the air, and over every living thing that moves on the earth." (Genesis 1:28)

This mandate emphasises human stewardship over creation, encouraging believers to care for and develop the world around them. It implies that humans are co-creators with God and have a responsibility to cultivate and enhance the earth's resources, culture, and society.

The second commission, known as the Great Commandment, is found in Matthew 22:37-40 and Mark 12:29-31. It is a teaching of Jesus, who summarises the essence of the entire law by saying, "You shall love the Lord your God with all your heart, with all your soul, with all your mind, and with all your strength, and you shall love your neighbour as yourself." This commandment highlights the importance of love for God and love for others as the foundational principles of Christian living. It calls believers to prioritise their relationship with God and to demonstrate compassion, kindness, and care for their fellow human beings.

The third commission, known as the Great Commission, is recorded in the New Testament in Matthew 28:19-20. Jesus, after His resurrection, commands His disciples to "Go therefore and make disciples of all the nations, baptising them in the name of the Father and of the Son and of the Holy Spirit, teaching them to observe all things that I have commanded you." The Great Commission emphasises the mission of spreading the teachings of Jesus and making disciples of all nations. It encourages believers to actively share the message of salvation, lead others to faith, and support their growth as followers of Christ.

These three commissions give us a three-point plan for investing as a financial disciple. Invest to live, invest to love, and invest to last.

Let's look in the following chapters at how this works in practice.

Chapter 2. Invest to Live

The Lord blessed us by giving us our very first commission to "be fruitful and multiply and fill the earth and subdue it and have dominion over the fish of the sea and over the birds of the heavens and over every living thing that moves on the earth." And God said, 'Behold, I have given you every plant yielding seed that is on the face of all the earth, and every tree with seed in its fruit. You shall have them for food.'" (Genesis 1:28,29)

The word used for 'subdue' is the Hebrew '*kavash*'2, which means 'to bring under control.' Adam was to cultivate the resources God gave to him in Eden and was put to work to multiply these resources for more people to enjoy. We are physical beings in a physical world, and God blessed Adam with all the physical resources we need for life.

However, as we know, Adam chose to disobey God and was expelled from Eden, with tough consequences. His stewardship of creation would be fraught with problems. "Cursed is the ground because of you; in pain, you shall eat of it all the days of your life; thorns and thistles it shall bring forth for you; and you shall eat the plants of the field. By the sweat of your face you shall eat bread..." (Genesis 3:17-19)

After being expelled from Eden, Adam became a farmer. "The LORD God sent him out from the garden of Eden to work the ground from which he was taken." Every farmer understands the art of investing - the art of accepting a risk with the potential of reward. He can eat his seeds, sell his seeds, or sow some for a future harvest. This requires wisdom and discipline.

A new kind of economy emerged, in which we find not only plants and livestock but also instruments manufactured out of iron and bronze were developed. (Genesis 4:22) A more complex society in cities began to emerge. People still needed to eat and to find ways to use the resources the earth offered to sustain and develop their lives together.

Later, God re-confirmed His cultural mandate to Noah after the flood in a covenant in which He promised to sustain life. "Every moving thing that lives shall be food for you. And as I gave you the green plants, I give you everything. Be fruitful and multiply, increase greatly on the earth and multiply in it." (Genesis 9:3,7)

Therefore, all the resources He has given us are to be used to sustain life and promote well-being for all people. This is our first criterion for investing.

The Bible gives us an insight into the fulfilment of creation, showing us a world teeming with people from every nation praising God. They are no longer in a garden but a city with foundations, walls, gates, tree-lined streets, iron, gold, domesticated animals, and trading ships (Isaiah 60, Revelation 21). This development of creation from a garden to a city filled with people and their cultural elements is the conclusion of God's mandate to fill the earth, subdue it, invest in it, work it and care for it. Even though God's creation at the beginning was perfect and full of resources, it was not as complete as God intended it to become.

I believe that God intended right from the beginning that human beings would develop the earth with multiple products of our hands to make life good. We are God's creative hands and continue his creative work, building, by grace, on the foundation of His perfect and abundant creation.

Investing surplus

Over time, correctly stewarding what creation has offered to us and employing our God-given skills and talents will lead to a surplus as resources are multiplied.

"And the LORD will make you abound in prosperity, in the fruit of your womb and in the fruit of your livestock and in the fruit of your ground, within the land that the LORD swore to your fathers to give you. The LORD will open to you his good treasury, the heavens, to give the rain to your land in its season and to bless all the work of your hands. And you shall lend to many nations, but you shall not borrow. (Deuteronomy 28:11-12).

The Hebrew term translated as 'abound in prosperity' is '*yatar*'3, which means a surplus of that which is good, more than enough. This describes a situation whereby people have far more than they require for their needs. Once harvested, the surplus needs to be stored, and in the ancient economy employing commodity money, stored goods represent both reserves and investable funds. Thus, it would be a natural progression for the Hebrews to graduate from being successful grain producers to becoming grain traders – and eventually grain bankers. This is why we read that the Lord's abundant blessing would cause His people to lend to many nations (Hebrew: '*goyim*', usually a reference to non-Hebrew people), which would cause them to become economically powerful and a blessing to the nations.

Therefore, as the Lord allows us to prosper, His norm is that we should become lenders and not borrowers, investing our surplus to bless many and helping them sustain and develop life.

Allocating our resources for life

Managing resources over time to facilitate growth is crucial for fulfilling the creation mandate. Investing plays a pivotal role in enabling individuals to adhere to this mandate from God. Notable instances illustrating how investing helps humans to carry out this mandate encompass actions like setting aside funds to procure seeds in preparation for spring planting, mobilising funds to acquire mining machinery for extracting iron and copper ores, young families seeking loans to purchase homes, and communities issuing bonds to erect schools.

Finance serves as the mechanism that strategically allocates resources toward future growth. It empowers those with the highest potential to augment resources in the upcoming period. Subsequently, it shares the gains with those who provided spare resources that would have otherwise lain idle. The absence of investment would confine people to living hand-to-mouth, solely relying on daily acquisitions or the personal accumulations of previous days. Humanity's remarkable economic progress across centuries owes its existence to the practice of investment. The flourishing of humanity would only be attainable with the interplay of lending and investing.

God's directive encompasses the cultivation of His creation and its careful preservation. The inherent timespan of borrowing and lending underscores how investing fosters a forward-looking mindset in decision-making. Those who secure mortgages for homeownership often exhibit greater responsibility in maintaining their properties than short-term renters. Conversely, practices that are unsustainable face hurdles in obtaining financial support. A lumber company depleting forests rapidly over a few years would need help finding lenders. Additionally, finance facilitates capital enhancements that curtail the excessive utilisation of natural resources. For instance, a city can acquire funds to expand its public transit system, optimising carbon resources while affording retirement earnings to municipal bond investors.

The Lord granted us resources to uncover, develop, and harness. He guides us to engage with these resources productively. The yields of our toil are meant to be shared for the collective welfare. Finance serves as a conduit for realising our roles as industrious labourers, effectively leveraging the resources bestowed upon us and generously distributing the abundant fruits of our efforts.

In essence, finance transforms the circumstances of human existence into channels for honouring God, stewarding creation, and upholding justice and love. When contemplating the divine intent behind the financial aspect of His creation, we must comprehend how finance can be harnessed to express love for our fellow beings and advance equitable and just interactions. If financial dealings lack fairness and compassion, we deviate from God's intended purpose for the financial facet of His creation.

We shouldn't relegate any facet of God's creation to secular realms; rather, we should acknowledge the entirety of creation as subject to His sovereignty and power. He extends an invitation to redemption, beckoning us to return under His authority within His Kingdom.

I have often asked myself if I should be investing in things of this world, which has drifted so far from God's original intentions and is positively hostile to Christ. The apostle John stated forcefully, "Do not love the world or the things in the world." (1 John 2:15a)

A wonderful challenge and promise that Jesus gave us is to "seek first the kingdom of God and his righteousness, and all these things will be added to you." (Matthew 6:33) 'All these things' which Jesus talked about in His sermon, refer to all we need to sustain us for daily living, without the need to worry about it.

This gives us two immediate goals for investing: to advance His Kingdom, His righteousness and His right way of living. I believe that when Jesus talked about God's kingdom, He was not just referring to the spiritual kingdom but also the material kingdom - both of which belong to Him.

At the very centre of Cristian life is the prayer, "Your will be done, on earth as it is in heaven." This means that our return on investments will bring justice out of oppression, hope out of marginalisation, sharing out of individualism, and healing out of brokenness.

Seek first His Kingdom and His righteousness.

God actually has two Kingdoms. The Kingdom of God (or of heaven), which Jesus introduced by saying, "the Kingdom of God is in the midst of you" (Luke 17:21) and the natural kingdom which God created and which He sustains, also called the common or natural kingdom. As investors, we are called to invest in both.

When the children of Israel were banished to Babylon, we read in a letter from Jeremiah how the Israelites were to conduct themselves in that strange and faraway land. This must have come as a great surprise to the Israelites when they were instructed to build houses, plant gardens, get married, and have children, to multiply and not decrease. In other words, they were to live peaceful lives and pursue their ordinary cultural activities and invest in this foreign land. They were also encouraged to "seek the welfare of the city where I have sent you into exile, and pray to the Lord on its behalf, for in its prosperity you will find your prosperity" (Jeremiah 29:7)

So how, then, are we to live and invest?

In Al Wolters' book *Creation Regained,* he makes the point that Christians are reformers, seeking to restore something that's been tarnished, acknowledging that it was once *good.* "Humankind, which has botched its original mandate and the whole creation along with it, is given another chance in Christ; we are reinstated as God's managers on earth. The original good creation is to be restored."4

Firstly, Christians should pursue investing surplus funds not with any sense of superiority but with the spirit of love and service towards others. We have been justified in Christ in order that we may love and serve our neighbour, for this is the fulfilment of the law. (Romans 13:8 – 10)

Secondly, we are called to critically engage in our economy. While we seek to treat all people with love and generosity, we must remain awake and perceptive to the many ways in which sin has corrupted human culture in this fallen world. Paul stated, "We destroy arguments and every lofty opinion raised against the knowledge of God and take every thought captive to obey Christ." (2 Corinthians 10:5.) Paul acknowledged that living in the common kingdom means that "We are engaged in spiritual warfare for though we walk in the flesh, we are not waging war according to the flesh. "For the weapons of our warfare are not of the flesh but have divine power to destroy strongholds." (2 Corinthians 10:3,4) We need to realise that the ethic in the common kingdom is rebellious to the things of God and to be on our guard against the philosophy and empty deceit that seeks to take us captive. (Colossians 2:8)

Third, we are called to invest in worldly organisations with a deep sense of detachment, realising that our true home and hope are in the world to come. We are encouraged to seek the things that are above, not on the earth, because our life is hidden in Christ. We are to seek not to lay up treasures of the Earth but to lay up treasures in heaven. (Matthew 6:20) We must realise that one day this common kingdom will pass away, and we must not seek success and glory in this present age but instead seek to please God – to renounce ungodliness and worldly passions, and to live self-controlled and godly lives in this present age, waiting for our blessed hope, the appearing of the glory of our great God and saviour Jesus Christ.

Importance of stewarding creation

As disciples of Christ, the call to care for God's creation is not only a moral responsibility but also an essential aspect of our faith and belief. From the very beginning of the Bible, in the book of Genesis, God appointed humans to be stewards of His creation, giving them dominion over the earth and its creatures. This divine commission reflects God's intention for us to protect, preserve, and responsibly manage the natural world.

The Bible is replete with references emphasising the importance of caring for God's creation. Psalm 104 beautifully depicts God's intricate creation, and it highlights the interdependence of all living beings on Earth. As stewards of this marvellous creation, we are entrusted with the task of safeguarding and nurturing the environment, ensuring that it flourishes for future generations.

At the heart of Christianity lies the commandment to love our neighbours as ourselves, and this principle extends not only to our fellow human beings but also to the broader community of life on earth. Caring for God's creation is an act of love and compassion towards all living creatures, recognising their intrinsic value as part of God's grand design.

Additionally, practising environmental stewardship aligns with the biblical concept of justice and equity. The consequences of environmental degradation, such as climate change, disproportionately affect vulnerable populations and marginalised communities worldwide. As Christians, we are called to address social and environmental injustices and work towards creating a more sustainable and just world.

Caring for God's creation is an act of gratitude for His abundant blessings. Nature provides us with resources like clean air, water, food, and shelter, sustaining our lives and enhancing our well-being. When we engage in sustainable practices and advocate for environmental conservation, we demonstrate our thankfulness for God's provisions and demonstrate proper stewardship of the gifts He has bestowed upon us.

Moreover, by caring for God's creation, we bear witness to His love and goodness to the world around us. Our actions speak volumes about our faith, and being responsible stewards of the environment can be a powerful testimony of God's love for all creation.

Let us remember that caring for the environment is not solely an environmental issue; it is a profound expression of our faith and obedience to God's commandments. As we engage in environmental stewardship, may we continuously seek His guidance and grace, knowing that in caring for His creation, we draw closer to His heart and purpose for our lives.

The questions we have to ask ourselves, as investors, are … "Are my investments working to care for the environment, to serve people so that they can enjoy all the earth's resources have to offer and bring glory to God?

This leads us seamlessly into the next commission on investing - to love God and our neighbour,

Chapter 3. Invest to Love

The second great commission which we have received is the command to love God and neighbours, as described in Matthew 22:37-40. "You shall love the Lord your God with all your heart and with all your soul and with all your mind. This is the great and first commandment. And a second is like it: You shall love your neighbour as yourself. On these two commandments depend all the Law and the Prophets."

Jesus is basically saying that everything we have been taught in the books of the law and the prophetic books is based on this commandment to love. This commandment to love God with all our heart, soul, and mind, and to love our neighbour as ourselves is at the core of discipleship. This love is not merely an emotion but a principle that should guide our actions and decisions, including how we handle our finances. Viewing investments through the lens of love means considering how our financial decisions impact other people, both near and far.

Investing money from a biblical perspective goes beyond seeking personal gain and financial success. Investing with a mindset grounded in love and compassion can lead to a transformative approach to financial stewardship, one that aligns with the teachings of Jesus and seeks the well-being of others.

One of the central themes in the Bible is the call to care for the poor, the marginalised, and the vulnerable. Throughout the Scriptures, God's heart for justice and compassion is evident, as He calls His people to defend the cause of the oppressed and provide for those in need (Isaiah 1:17, Psalm 82:3-4). Investing with a love-driven approach means seeking out opportunities that promote ethical and sustainable practices while avoiding companies or industries that exploit or harm others. It means supporting businesses that prioritise fair labour practices, environmental responsibility, and social impact.

Investing with a stewardship mindset also means using our resources to make a positive impact on the lives of others. It means seeking out investment opportunities that contribute to the betterment of society and the well-being of all people, not just the few.

Investing with a love-driven approach means guarding against the allure of excessive wealth and placing our trust in God rather than in riches. It means using our financial resources to bless others and promote the common good, rather than becoming consumed by the pursuit of wealth for its own sake.

By aligning our investment decisions with principles of love, compassion, stewardship, and an eternal perspective, we can use our financial resources to make a positive impact on the world around us. As we seek to invest in ways that honour God and benefit others, we become agents of change and transformation, bringing God's love and light to a world in need.

It would therefore appear that if we are looking for ways in which to invest our surplus, we need to ask ourselves, "Will this investment contribute to loving God and my neighbour?" In fact, loving my neighbour is a prerequisite to loving God.

"If someone says, 'I love God,' and hates his brother, he is a liar; for he who does not love his brother whom he has seen, how can he love God whom he has not seen? And this commandment we have from Him: that he who loves God must love his brother also." (1 John 4:20-21)

Genuine love for God should naturally result in love and compassion for others.

This great command to love God and our neighbour follows on closely from the first great commission to be fruitful and multiply and fill the earth and subdue it. When considering investing, the financial disciple will look for projects and enterprises which promote both sustaining and flourishing of people, while developing resources for those people to utilise with regard to the sustainability of the earth's resources.

Loving God

Loving God when investing is to stay connected to the heart of God. I often have to ask myself, "Am I truly seeking the heart of God in all my financial decisions?" This does not come to us naturally!

I like the example of David, who was a man after God's heart. The Lord said of him, "I have found David, son of Jesse, a man after my own heart; he will do everything I want him to do." (Acts 13:22).

The answer to why David was considered a man after God's own heart is found right in that verse: David did whatever God wanted him to do, to honour Him in all he did. Investing to love God is earnestly seeking His heart and following His ways, which are totally different from the ways of the world.

Despite his imperfections and mistakes, David demonstrated a genuine love for God and sought to align his life with God's principles.

When David was preparing to build the Temple, he invested in buying real estate, what is now the Temple Mount, from a man named Araunah. He invested great wealth in building the Temple. "With great pains, I have provided for the house of the LORD 100,000 talents of gold, a million talents of silver, and bronze and iron beyond weighing, for there is so much of it; timber and stone, too, I have provided." (1 Chronicles 22:14)

In today's money, the total of the offering David made to build the Temple is estimated to be about a billion and a half dollars! "I have provided for the house of my God, so far as I was able" (1 Chronicles 29:2).

Why did he invest such huge wealth in the Temple? Because His heart was right there. You can tell this from his songs. "LORD, I love the house where you live, the place where your glory dwells." (Psalm 26:8). Remember the principle from Matthew 6:21? Where your treasure is, your heart is right there!

David described his life mission in Psalm 22:4. "One thing have I asked of the LORD that will I seek after: that I may dwell in the house of the LORD all the days of my life, to gaze upon the beauty of the LORD and to inquire in his temple."

Investing after God's heart? The Temple is now formed by the Body of believers. Invest there!

The Bible provides guidance on how to honour God with our investments, emphasising wisdom, integrity, and a focus on eternal values.

Firstly, seeking wisdom is paramount in investing as a disciple, as we work out our relationship with God in a practical way. Proverbs 3:5-6 reminds us to trust in the Lord with all our hearts and lean not on our own understanding. This means seeking God's guidance through prayer, seeking advice from wise and godly mentors, and conducting thorough research before making investment decisions. By seeking wisdom, we acknowledge that God is the ultimate source of knowledge and insight.

Secondly, investing as a disciple emphasises integrity and ethical considerations. The Bible is clear that we should not exploit or take advantage of others for personal gain. Proverbs 11:1 states, "The Lord detests dishonest scales, but accurate weights find favour with him." Therefore, investing in companies and ventures that engage in honest practices, promote fairness, and contribute positively to society can align with God's values.

Additionally, investing as a disciple encourages a focus on eternal values. In Matthew 6:19-21, Jesus teaches us to store up treasures in heaven, highlighting the transient nature of worldly wealth. While financial gain is not inherently wrong, investing with a broader perspective that considers the impact on the Kingdom of God can bring a sense of purpose and fulfilment. This can involve supporting causes that promote justice, care for the vulnerable, and advance the Gospel.

Ultimately, investing in a way that loves God involves aligning our financial decisions with biblical principles. It requires seeking wisdom, demonstrating integrity, focusing on eternal values, diversifying investments, and recognising that our resources are ultimately entrusted to us by God. By honouring God in our investment practices, we can use our financial blessings to make a positive impact on the world and advance His Kingdom.

Here are a few practical considerations when investing money with a view to the application of loving God with all your soul and with all your mind.

- Consider investing in faith-based organisations, charities, or mission-oriented projects that work to spread the love of God and make a positive difference in the world. These investments can support various causes, such as missionary work, humanitarian aid, education, and community development.
- Seek opportunities that contribute to the expansion of God's kingdom on Earth. Invest in churches, ministries, or organisations focused on evangelism, discipleship, and spiritual growth. These investments can have eternal significance by supporting initiatives that bring people closer to God and His teachings.
- Beyond investing, prioritise giving generously to support charitable organisations and those in need. Allocate a portion of your income to tithing and giving to causes that resonate with your heart and God's teachings on giving.
- Explore impact investing, which prioritises both financial returns and positive social or environmental outcomes. Impact investments can range from supporting clean energy projects to investing in affordable housing initiatives that benefit disadvantaged communities. By investing with a focus on societal impact, you can demonstrate your love for God by helping others and caring for His creation.
- Choose investment opportunities that align with your Christian values and promote ethical and responsible practices. Look for companies or funds that prioritise environmental sustainability, social justice, fair labour practices, and positive community impact. Many financial institutions now offer socially responsible investment options that can help you invest in line with your faith.
- Lastly, be mindful of avoiding investments that contradict your faith and values. Steer clear of industries involved in activities like gambling, alcohol, tobacco, or other harmful practices that may harm individuals or the environment. Taking a stand against unethical

investments can be a tangible expression of your love for God and your commitment to following His teachings.

Investing after God's heart means putting the priorities of the Kingdom of God first. He promised that if we put the interests of His Kingdom first, together with His righteousness, we need never worry about our basic needs. (Matthew 6:33) My paraphrase would read, "Your first priority in investing is to get to know the heart of God, to obey His leading and to align all you do with His principles." This is what discipleship is.

I can invest in my own spiritual growth by investing in conferences, books, courses, training, etc. I can also invest in others to help them grow in their relationship with God and develop a lifestyle which pleases Him.

This gives us some excellent questions when evaluating possible investment opportunities.

- Will it contribute to establishing God's rule over the hearts of men and women?
- Will it help people to develop a godly lifestyle?

Loving your neighbour

The biblical command to love can inspire investors to invest in companies that prioritise their employees' well-being and development. This can involve investing in companies that offer fair wages, benefits, and opportunities for growth, as well as those that foster a culture of inclusion and respect.

It can also inspire investors to invest in companies that make a positive impact on the communities in which they operate. This can involve investing in companies that prioritise corporate social responsibility, including those that give back to their local communities through charitable donations, volunteerism, or other initiatives.

Investing in ethical practices loves our neighbour when we invest in companies that prioritise ethical business practices, such as transparency, integrity, and accountability. This can involve investing in companies that have strong governance structures, as well as those that prioritise environmental sustainability and social responsibility.

Loving our neighbour can also move investors to invest in companies that are focused on innovation and improving people's lives. This can involve investing in companies that are developing new technologies or products that address pressing social and environmental challenges, such as climate change, healthcare, or education.

Finally, the principle of loving our neighbour can motivate investors to use their investment returns to support charitable causes and organisations. This can involve investing in socially responsible funds that donate a portion of their returns to charity or using investment returns to support causes that align with their values and priorities directly.

Investing, at its core, is a practice deeply intertwined with social aspects that extend far beyond financial gains. While the primary objective of investing is to grow wealth, the way individuals allocate their capital can have profound societal implications. Here are some e social dimensions of investing.

- **Job Creation**: When investors provide capital to companies, they contribute to job creation. As businesses expand, they hire more employees, thereby reducing unemployment rates and improving the overall socioeconomic conditions of a region. Responsible investing, in particular, can have a positive impact by directing funds towards companies that prioritise fair labour practices and job growth.
- **Innovation and Progress**: Investment often fuels innovation. Companies that receive funding can develop new products, services, and technologies that enhance society's quality of life. This innovation can extend to areas such as healthcare, renewable energy, and education, addressing pressing social challenges.
- **Wealth Distribution**: Investing can either worsen wealth inequality or help lessen it. When done responsibly, investing can allocate resources to companies that focus on equitable wealth distribution and social impact, such as investments in affordable housing or community development projects which can directly benefit marginalised communities. For instance, investing in a micro-finance institution can help alleviate poverty in underserved communities.

- **Corporate Responsibility:** Investors, especially institutional ones, have the power to influence corporate behaviour and can engage with companies on issues like sustainability, diversity, and ethical governance. This engagement can pressure businesses to adopt more socially responsible practices, ranging from reducing their environmental footprint to ensuring fair treatment of employees.
- **Community Development:** Local investments can have a direct impact on communities. Investing in local businesses and projects can foster economic development, create jobs, and improve the overall well-being of the community. This not only benefits investors but also strengthens social bonds and community resilience.

Investing is a powerful tool that can shape society in profound ways. Whether through responsible investing, impact investing, philanthropy, or engagement with corporations, investors have the capacity to contribute to the betterment of the world. As individuals and institutions increasingly recognise the social aspects of investing, there is growing potential for capital to be a force for positive change in our interconnected global society.

Chapter 4. Invest to Last

The third of the great commissions the Lord gave to us was just before He ascended into heaven. His last words to His disciples were to challenge them to carry on the work which he started. This commission is based on the first commission to go and multiply - not only in a physical sense of bearing children but also spiritually with spiritual children - to make disciples, who will make disciples.

Jesus challenges us in Matthew 28:18-20 "All authority in heaven and on earth has been given to me. Go therefore and make disciples of all nations, baptising them in the name of the Father and of the Son and of the Holy Spirit, teaching them to observe all that I have commanded you. And behold, I am with you always, to the end of the age."

This is a great investment - helping people become disciples who will help others become disciples, and an investment that will last until eternity!

Invest in making disciples.

If we are not teaching people how to handle their finances in God's way, then we are omitting a large part of His teaching. We need to preach, teach, and model financial discipleship.

Following Jesus in our financial life should be a major topic of learning for all believers. A Bible-based teaching programme will have a huge impact on spiritual growth; it is an essential, if not critical, path to discipleship. Compass offers a wide range of material to help learn, apply, and teach Biblical financial principles.

We need to make financial disciples due to the serious problems people are facing. These include:

1.   Idolatry, as we worship at the altar of materialism, bolstering ego and cluttering our lives with stuff we don't need and, in many cases, can't afford.

2.   Materialism leading to a lack of contentment and a restless existence, always being on the move for more and never experiencing true fulfilment.

3.   Marriage tension and breakdown as couples fail to communicate about how to handle money issues.

4.   Church budgets suffering and people not experiencing the joy of generosity because of a lack of giving.

5.   Anxiety, lack of freedom, and strained relationships under the burden of debt.

6.   Additional problems arising from gambling, stealing, cheating on taxes or expenses, and a variety of other negative behaviours the Word teaches us to avoid.

7.   Our culture is adrift with myths about money and its power and influence. We are led to confuse our self-worth with our net worth.

The church may be the only remaining place where the issues can be discussed in non-market terms. Today's pastors and leaders must be prepared to articulate, teach, train, and encourage their people toward a biblical perspective regarding money and possessions. The financial and spiritual well-being of many people are at stake.

Using financial situations to disciple people.

Here are a few of the many investing principles Jesus used to teach His disciples very important lessons.[5]

1. Jesus referred to investing in jewels and treasures to illustrate the importance of investing in the Kingdom of God (the parables of the treasure hidden in the field and the valuable pearl: Matthew 13:44-45)

2. He talked about capital, investments, banking, and interest to emphasise our human responsibility to make use of God's gifts wisely and responsibly in the parable of the talents, (Matthew 25:14-30) and the parable of the ten minas, (Luke 19:11-27)

3. He discussed money lenders, interest, and debt cancellation to illustrate the importance of love and appreciation to God for cancelling our debt of sin (Luke 7:41-43)

4. He spoke of building barns to store grain for the future, while neglecting to store up spiritual treasures as a very foolish decision (the parable of the rich fool: Luke 12:16-21)

5. He used wealth, dividing up the estate, irresponsible spending, and a change of heart to illustrate repentance and forgiveness (the parable of the prodigal son: Luke 15:11-32)

6. He used questionable financial management and debt reduction to illustrate that sometimes, people are wiser in their worldly realm than honest followers of Christ are in the spiritual realm (the parable of the shrewd manager. He encouraged us to use money to make friends and influence people for a specific purpose. (Luke 16:1-12)

7. He contrasted a rich man who died and went to hell with a poor beggar who died and went to heaven to illustrate how wealth and what it can provide may harden our hearts against spiritual truth (the parable of the rich man and Lazarus: Luke 16:19-31)

Making friends with false mammon

Jesus gave a one-sentence explanation of the parable of the so-called "Unrighteous Steward" – a parable we find really difficult to understand. I am thankful that his explanation was clear. "And I tell you, make friends for yourselves by means of unrighteous wealth, so that when it fails, they may receive you into the eternal dwellings" (Luke 16:9).

Jesus is saying that we are to use money, behind which is an inherently unrighteous power, to develop relationships with people so that they may experience eternity.

For the financial disciple, this means that the most important goal is not to make money but to make friends, serve them, and influence people for the Lord.

As I look back on life, nothing has given me more joy or satisfaction than hearing from people, "Thank you so much for showing me how I can follow Jesus." I thank God that this happens regularly. This is the reason I can renounce some of the pleasures of the world. This is the reason I can learn to live on less so that I can invest more.

Jesus wants us to make friends with the help of the false mammon with an eye to the future - our eternal future. Jesus' life mission is recorded like this, "for also the Son of Man did not come to be served, but to serve and give his life as a ransom for many." (Mark 10:45) The ultimate goal is to invest whatever we can so that our friends to be 'taken up into the eternal dwellings' so that they can enjoy eternity with God.

The emphasis on friendship is crucial. Jesus uses the same language here as in the intimacy of the upper room the night before his crucifixion when he said, "There is no greater love than to give your life for your friends." (John 15:13) We are called to give up our lives, to renounce all that we possess, to use our ability to 'make friends' so that as many as respond may enjoy the fullness of eternal life with God. The material things that have been entrusted to us as stewards are primarily intended to be a blessing to others.

Jesus preceded us in 'making friends' with the financial entrepreneurs in the market. He was labelled 'friend of tax collectors'. He used all the material means at his disposal to show God's grace to mankind. The French professor of Sociology, the late Jacques Ellul, explains, "Grace must overcome the power of money because when mammon is destroyed by grace, money is no longer a significant power."[6]

Using money for eternity

Our parable describes a kind of born-again stewardship - using what you have been entrusted exactly as the Master would wish for His eternal goals!

"When the voice of the Master is calling
And the gates into heaven unfold
And the saints of all ages are gathering
and are thronging the city of gold
How my heart shall o'erflow with rapture
If a brother shall greet me and say
"You have pointed my footsteps to heaven,
You told me of Jesus the Way."[7]
One question to ask is, "What will be in heaven?" Obviously, there will be people in heaven; therefore, one way we lay up treasure in heaven is to invest in the lives of people. That kind of investment we will indeed take with us. Money invested in people is the best possible investment.

Suppose that a country decided to change over its entire currency to dollars and that the moment it did, all its previous currency would be worthless, but that we were not told when the monetary conversion would take place. In that situation, the wise course would be to turn our money into dollars, keeping only enough of our present currency to live day to day.

Now, this gives us something of the picture Jesus means to convey when he tells us to lay up treasure in heaven and to make friends with unrighteous mammon. The proper use of money is not for living high down here; that would be a very poor investment indeed. No, the proper use of money is to invest as much of it as possible in the lives of people so that we will have treasure in heaven. Of course, we need to keep a certain amount of money to carry on the day-to-day business of life, but we want to free up as much as we possibly can in order to place it where the return is eternal.

Just How Lasting Are Your Investments?

As an old man, Solomon agonised over the futility of his investments: "When I surveyed all that my hands had done and what I had toiled to achieve, everything was meaningless, a chasing after the wind; nothing was gained under the sun …so I hated life, because the work that is done under the sun was grievous to me …A chasing after the wind" (Ecclesiastes 2:11,17)

Do your investments parallel Solomon's? Or are you making the kind of investments that will outlive you, lasting for eternity?

A poignant statement to consider when answering our question is: "If you want one year return on your investment, plant grain. If you want a ten-year return on your investment, plant a tree. For an eternal return on your investment, plant people."

Can we, therefore, grasp the fact that only God, His Word, and people are eternal?

- Only God is eternal: Before the mountains were born or you brought forth the earth and the world, from everlasting to everlasting, you are God. (2 Pet. 3:8)
- Only His Word is eternal: Your word, O Lord, is eternal; it stands firm in the heavens. (Psalm 119:89)
- Only people are eternal: Multitudes who sleep in the dust of the earth will awake: some to everlasting life, others to shame and everlasting contempt. (Daniel 12:2)

The great missionary Charles Thomas Studd (1860-1931) lived and died by–this poem. [8]

"Only one life, 'twill soon be past;
only what's done for Christ will last."

However, few of us realise when he said those words. It was on his deathbed with his precious family gathered around him. He had already told each of his children that he wished he had something to give to them, but he had nothing left. Then he said, "… but I gave it all to Jesus long ago." [9]

Consequently, the only investments that will withstand time, with all that will be coming, will be those made in establishing Christ and His Word in the lives of people. Thus, God regularly places individuals in our path with whom He desires our investment.

As you encounter opportunities to invest in people, are you brushing past them to fulfil your agenda? Or are you viewing each one as a divine appointment? Are you responding to the prompting of the Spirit by graciously investing in their lives for the purpose of bringing Christ to them or building Christ in them?

I suppose the answers to these questions are determined by whether we are living for the temporal or investing in the eternal.

Investing in people

A biblical perspective on investing in people is rooted in the belief that every individual is created in the image of God and holds inherent value and worth. Here are some key principles to consider:

- Love and Compassion: The Bible encourages Christians to love and care for others (Mark 12:31, Galatians 6:10). Investing in people involves showing compassion, kindness, and support, helping meet their physical, emotional, and spiritual needs.
- Discipleship and Mentorship: Investing in people includes guiding and equipping them to grow in their relationship with God and develop their potential. Just as Jesus invested in His disciples, believers are called to disciple and mentor others, sharing wisdom and encouragement and helping them develop their gifts and talents (Matthew 28:19-20, 2 Timothy 2:2).
- Serving and Sacrifice: Following the example of Jesus, believers are called to serve others selflessly. Investing in people may require sacrificing time, resources, and personal ambitions to support and uplift those in need (Matthew 20:28, Philippians 2:3-4).
- Empowering and Encouraging: Investing in people involves empowering them to reach their full potential. Christians can offer guidance, resources, and opportunities to help individuals flourish and

make a positive impact in their communities (1 Thessalonians 5:11, Hebrews 10:24).

• Forgiveness and Restoration: Investing in people also includes extending forgiveness and offering opportunities for restoration. Christians are called to demonstrate grace and reconciliation and support individuals in their journey toward healing and transformation (Colossians 3:13, Galatians 6:1-2).

• Sharing the Gospel: The ultimate investment in people is sharing the good news of Jesus Christ. Christians are called to proclaim the message of salvation and invite others into a personal relationship with God. Investing in people's eternal well-being by sharing the gospel is of paramount importance. (Matthew 28:19-20, Romans 10:14-15)

A biblical perspective on investing in people emphasises love, compassion, discipleship, serving, empowerment, forgiveness, and sharing the gospel. By investing in people, believers can contribute to their well-being, growth, and spiritual development, fulfilling the call to love and serve others as Christ did.

Chapter 5. Warnings

The power of mammon

Managing money is not merely a technical exercise, but for the disciple, it is a spiritual discipline. Jesus warned us about the spiritual power behind money, which competes for our devotion and service. "No servant can serve two masters, for either he will hate the one and love the other, or he will be devoted to the one and despise the other. You cannot serve God, and (mammon) money." (Luke 16:13) Modern Bible translations use the word 'money' for the original Greek 'mammonas'.10 A Catholic translation even uses the word "money devil,' which is more in line with the original meaning.

Jesus could have said, more logically, you cannot serve both God and... Caesar ... or Baal ... or Moloch ... or Apollo ... or Athena .... all gods which were known and venerated at that time. However, he chose to warn us by unmasking a new god for us, mammon, which is a major competitor for our devotion, the power behind money!

The origin of the original word "*mammonas*" in Aramaic (the language Jesus spoke) comes from a word with the meaning of "permanent" or "that which one can rely on. It is said that Jesus used a play on words saying, '*m'aman*' or 'my trust,' using the word 'amen' or 'so be it'. American coins carry the words, 'In God we trust'. (If only it was like that! It reminds me of a sign I saw above the bar in an Irish pub. "In God we trust, all the rest pay cash!")

Mammon is not synonymous with money. God and mammon can never be integrated, but God and money should be! Mammon is the fallen spiritual power behind money, seeking to influence people in the spiritual realm to use money unwisely in the worldly or natural realm. "For our struggle is not against flesh and blood, but against the rulers, against the authorities, against the powers of this dark world and against the spiritual forces of evil in the heavenly realms." (Ephesians 6:12)

Mammon's power is something that acts by itself. It has spiritual meaning and direction. Power is never neutral. Money as power orients, moves, and controls. Power is also personal. We must not minimise the weight of the tension Jesus describes between God and mammon.
Mammon is completely opposed to God and wants to thwart God's plans with mankind. Money is his weapon to drive a wedge in relationships between people and between people and God. It is impossible, Jesus said, to serve both. He proposes us a choice: one or the other! There is no way between them. It is about hatred and love, about devotion and contempt, about clinging to one and despising the other. We are dealing with two masters who compete for our dedication and love.
Jesus consciously chose a word, a name to describe the power of money, with deep historical, religious, and commercial roots. He wanted to say that the power behind money has its roots in the fall of Lucifer and therefore has demonic characteristics directed squarely against God and aimed at winning people's hearts and minds. Mammon has conquered a bridgehead in the human soul and wants to extend this through our in-built propensity to desire and greed, a word that meant something like "more and more" in the daily Greek of that time.

Jesus described the spiritual status and properties of money when he unmasked mammon. This god, a driving force behind money, wants to give us direction, seduce us, whisper in our ears about important decisions, tell us that money is the most important motive for decisions, and persuade us to take sides with money instead of people and God.

The temptation to serve mammon is not the exclusive territory of the rich and prosperous. The long tentacles of mammon reach down to all levels of society and want to embrace the poor and failures with his temptations.

The emphasis of Jesus' words here falls on the power of mammon to claim not just our allegiance but our slave-like devotion and our worship. After all that Jesus has explained in the previous part of the chapter, it is obvious that any two-master pattern of living is impossible - 'No servant can ... You cannot .... ' We still try, but we still find it impossible.

The bottom line is - you cannot serve two masters. The American writer Logan Pearsall Smith echoed Jesus in his line: "Those who set out to serve both God and mammon soon discover there is no God."11

Money is a great servant but a terrible master.

The Christian is given the high calling of using mammon without serving mammon. We are using mammon when we allow God to determine our economic decisions. We are serving mammon when we allow mammon to determine our economic decisions. We must decide who is going to make our decisions - God or mammon. When we make a decision that is solely and completely money-focused, we are serving the wrong master. Other considerations must come first. If I know that God wants me to do something and I say, "I can't afford it", then I am neglecting the source of provision. God will pay for everything He orders!

Do we invest on the basis of the call of God or because of the availability of money? Do we buy stocks because we can afford them or because God instructed us to? If money determines what we do or do not do, then money is our boss. If God determines what we do or do not do, then God is our boss. My money might say to me, `You have enough to buy this or that,' but my God might say to me, `I don't want you to have it.' Now, who am I to obey? Most of us allow money to dictate our decisions: what kind of house we live in, what vacation we will take, what job we will hold. Money decides.

Throughout his career, Martin Luther fought against what he saw as the two-sided coin of what he called '*mammonism*," both the ascetic flight from money and the acquisitive drive for it. His foundation for this battle was the great reversal of the gospel that a person's worth is not determined by what he or she does or does not possess but rather by God's promise in Christ. Thus, money is not the lord of life but the gift of God to be used for worshipping Him, serving our neighbour, and building up our community.

He observed:[12] "Many a one thinks that he has God and everything in abundance when he has money and possessions; he trusts in them and boasts of them with such firmness and assurance as to care for no one. Lo, such a man also has a god, mammon by name, which is money and possessions, on which he sets all his heart, and which is also the most common idol on earth."

What Luther denounces here is actually not the possession of money or property but the human heart's misdirected trust in it, transforming possession into a divine entity and relying on it as if money could satisfy the most urgent need and provide security, protection and total care. Luther, however, warns that we should not become attached to our earthly possessions but use, administer, and possess them "as if we possessed not."

Mammon wants to tie us up in the world. C.S. Lewis observed, "Prosperity knits a man to the World. He feels that he is 'finding his place in it,' while really it is finding its place in him. His increasing reputation, his widening circle of acquaintances, his sense of importance, the growing pressure of absorbing and agreeable work, build up in him a sense of being really at home on earth."[13]

Investing under the power of mammon

Being under the power of mammon when investing refers to being driven by the love of money and involves a preoccupation with financial gain, a materialistic mindset, and a lack of consideration for ethical and spiritual values. It means putting financial gain above all else and making investment decisions solely based on personal wealth accumulation. This approach to investing can lead to excessive risk-taking, neglect of God's guidance, and a neglect of compassion and generosity towards others. As Christians, we are called to prioritise our relationship with God and love for others above the pursuit of wealth, ensuring that our investment decisions align with our faith and values.

Here are some symptoms of being under mammon's influence when investing:

Investing under mammon's influence might lead individuals to take excessive risks with their investments, solely aiming for high returns without adequately considering potential losses. This behaviour can lead to investing in highly speculative or risky ventures without conducting proper research or due diligence.

Another symptom of investing under mammon's influence may cause an individual to become obsessed with tracking market performance on a day-to-day basis. Constantly checking stock prices and becoming emotionally affected by short-term fluctuations may indicate a materialistic mindset focused solely on financial gains.

A person under mammon's influence might concentrate their investments in a single asset or industry to maximise potential returns. This lack of diversification can expose them to significant risks if the chosen asset class or industry faces adverse conditions.

Mammon's influence could cause us to invest in companies or industries that are morally questionable or harmful solely because of the potential for high returns. Ethical considerations, such as social and environmental impacts, may take a back seat to financial gain. When money becomes the primary motivation for investing, individuals may overlook the spiritual and human values that should guide their decisions. Compassion, empathy, and concern for the welfare of others may be overshadowed by the pursuit of financial success.

Investing under mammon's influence might involve neglecting God's guidance in financial matters. A person may prioritise financial advice from worldly sources without seeking wisdom from prayer, meditation on Scripture, or seeking counsel from fellow believers.

Lastly, an individual under mammon's influence may experience significant anxiety and stress levels, related to their investments. A preoccupation with financial success can lead to emotional distress and an inability to find contentment regardless of the investment outcomes.

Investing with borrowed money.

I would rather trust in the Lord, who can and will provide all we need, without putting myself into debt. I have never, ever borrowed for consumer items, which always depreciate in value. This is economically unsound. I prefer to save first and then buy. Borrowing to buy financial products should be prohibited!

The lure of greater gains, which can be gained by leveraging, can quickly turn into a financial nightmare. Investing with borrowed money is inherently risky due to the potential for losses that can exceed the initial investment. Market downturns, unexpected events, or poor investment decisions can lead to devastating consequences, resulting in debt that is difficult to repay.

Using borrowed funds involves interest payments, which can erode any potential gains. If the investments do not generate sufficient returns to cover the interest costs, the investor may face a negative cash flow situation, making it challenging to service the debt.

Additionally, leveraging increases the psychological pressure on investors, as they have not only their own money at stake but also borrowed funds. Emotions can influence decision-making, leading to impulsive choices that may not align with a wise, Biblical investment strategy.

The Bible is silent about borrowing money to invest in a business. Here is the rule of thumb I recommend:

Borrow as little as possible and pay it off as quickly as possible!

When you are launching a business or if it is not financially strong, lenders generally require you to personally guarantee its debt. When you personally endorse a debt, you pledge all of your assets as collateral. Many people personally guarantee business debts and don't realise that as long as the debt exists, everything they own is at risk. Proverbs 22:26-27 paints this word picture: "Do not be one who shakes hands in pledge or puts up security for debts; if you lack the means to pay, your very bed will be snatched from under you."

I would like to challenge you to work toward eliminating the need to personally guarantee business debts. When communicating with a lender, make certain the lender understands that the only security for the debt is the business and anything else you are pledging as collateral. You have the option of paying the debt in one of two ways: (1) in cash or (2) with the business assets you have pledged as collateral. The lender then has a decision to make. Do I feel good enough about the business and collateral to loan the money? This eliminates the need to risk all of your other assets. You are no longer a slave to the lender. (Proverbs 21:7) If the lender does not have such confidence in the business, that is a good sign that you shouldn't be borrowing at all!

Speculating

Mark Twain is famously quoted as saying, "There are two times in a man's life when he should not speculate: when he can't afford it and when he can."[14]

One of the world's most successful investors, Warren Buffet, said, "Speculation is most dangerous when it looks easiest."[15]

James 4:13-15 offers a balanced perspective on speculation: "Come now, you who say, 'Today or tomorrow we will go into such and such a town and spend a year there and trade and make a profit'—yet you do not know what tomorrow will bring."

This passage offers a balanced perspective on speculation and future planning by highlighting the importance of humility and acknowledging the uncertainties of life. In these verses, James addresses individuals who confidently make plans for the future without considering the unpredictability of tomorrow. Let's break down how this passage offers a balanced perspective on speculation:

1. Planning and Aspiration: The passage begins with individuals saying, "Today or tomorrow we will go into such and such a town and spend a year there and trade and make a profit." Here, we see people engaged in planning and aspiring to achieve financial success. This reflects the natural human inclination to set goals and work toward them, including financial and business goals.

2. Uncertainty of the Future: James introduces a note of caution by emphasising, "yet you do not know what tomorrow will bring." This statement serves as a reminder of life's inherent uncertainties. It encourages us to acknowledge that no matter how well we plan, we cannot control or foresee all future events. This recognition of uncertainty is a key aspect of the balanced perspective offered in this passage.

3. Humility and Dependency: The passage concludes with James stating, "What is your life? For you are a mist that appears for a little time and then vanishes." This statement encourages humility and a sense of perspective. It reminds us of our limited time on earth and our dependency on factors beyond our control. Recognising our own vulnerability and limitations can foster humility and a balanced approach to speculation and planning.

The Biblical view on speculation emphasises a balanced approach – one that combines diligence, wise planning, and humility. While the Bible does not prohibit speculation, it encourages individuals to assess their motivations and exercise caution against greed, envy, and arrogance. It underscores the importance of seeking God's guidance and aligning one's actions with principles of integrity and stewardship. The Proverb gives us wonderfully simple investment advice. "Steady plodding brings prosperity; hasty speculation brings poverty." (TLB)

We will discuss knowing your willingness and capacity to take risks in Chapter 9.

Developing a strategy to diversify will serve to mitigate the risks; more on this in Chapter 11.

Part 2: Starting on your journey

Let's use a car journey as a useful metaphor for investing, as both require careful planning, attention to detail, and a willingness to adapt to changing conditions in order to reach your destination.

It doesn't matter how large or small our car is; the principles will still apply. Likewise, how much money you have available to spend is irrelevant. The principles will still apply. By setting clear goals, developing a plan, and remaining flexible, investors can navigate the ups and downs of the market and achieve their financial goals.

When planning a car journey, it's important to start by setting a clear destination and determining the best route to get there. Similarly, in investing, it's important to set clear goals and develop a plan to achieve them. This may involve determining the right mix of investments to suit your risk tolerance and time horizon, as well as regularly monitoring your portfolio and adjusting as needed.

Just as a car journey can be affected by various factors such as traffic, weather, and road conditions, investing can also be affected by market conditions, economic trends, and other external factors. It's important to be aware of these factors and adjust your plan accordingly.

As you progress on your car journey, you may encounter unexpected obstacles or detours. Similarly, in investing, you may encounter unexpected events, such as a recession or a sudden change in interest rates. It's important to remain flexible and adapt to these changes rather than sticking rigidly to your original plan.

Just as a car journey is more enjoyable when you have the right companions, investing can also be more enjoyable when you have the right support. This may include working with a financial advisor or joining an investment club, where you can share ideas and strategies with other investors.

Finally, just as a car journey requires regular maintenance to keep it running smoothly, investing also requires regular monitoring and maintenance to ensure that it stays on track. This includes monitoring your portfolio, reviewing your goals, and adjusting as needed. It's also important to review your investment strategy periodically to ensure that it still aligns with your goals and risk tolerance.

Chapter 6: Whose car are we driving?

In the realm of Christian investing, the ownership of the car represents the fact that God owns the car and lends it to us to use. Just as a driver cares for and maintains their vehicle, Christians must responsibly manage the resources entrusted to them by God. Stewardship entails wise, ethical investment choices aligning with Christian values. It emphasises the importance of using financial resources for good and avoiding unethical or harmful investments. Just as a responsible car owner ensures their vehicle's longevity, Christian investors seek to preserve and grow their assets while honouring their faith. Ownership in this context underscores the accountability Christians have in managing their financial "vehicle" with integrity and purpose.

When starting out on our journey of investing the money we have available, we must remember that the money actually is not ours. It belongs to God, and He has an opinion on how it should be invested!

The Bible provides five compelling reasons why God is the rightful owner of everything:

1. He is Creator and Sustainer: The Bible declares that God is the creator of all things (Genesis 1:1) and that through Him, all things were made and continue to exist (Colossians 1:16-17). As the

ultimate source of life and existence, God's ownership is inherent in His role as the Creator and Sustainer of the universe.

2. Ownership by Design: The Scriptures affirm that everything in the world belongs to God by design. Psalm 24:1 says, "The earth is the Lord's, and everything in it, the world, and all who live in it." This verse highlights God's rightful ownership over all creation, emphasising that He is the ultimate authority and possesses complete sovereignty.

3. Stewardship Principle: The Bible teaches the principle of stewardship, whereby human beings are entrusted with managing and caring for God's resources. In the Parable of the Talents (Matthew 25:14-30), Jesus illustrates the concept of stewardship, emphasising that we are given resources by God to use wisely and for His purposes. This principle highlights God's ownership and our responsibility to manage His possessions faithfully.

4. God's Sovereignty: Scripture repeatedly emphasises God's sovereignty and His control over all things. Psalm 115:3 declares, "Our God is in the heavens; he does all that he pleases." This verse and others like it affirm that God has complete authority and ownership over everything, including the material and spiritual realms.

5. Redemption through Christ: The New Testament reveals that God's ownership is affirmed and demonstrated through the redemptive work of Jesus Christ. Believers are reminded that they have been "bought with a price" (1 Corinthians 6:20) and are now called to glorify God with their bodies. This acknowledgement of God's ownership reinforces the idea that everything, including our very lives, belongs to Him.

When Christians acknowledge that everything they have ultimately belongs to God, it greatly impacts how they handle their financial resources.

For instance, a Christian who recognises God's ownership may prioritise giving a portion of their income to support charitable causes and meet the needs of others. They view their financial resources as a means to advance God's kingdom and bless others rather than solely for personal accumulation or consumption. They may faithfully tithe, which involves giving a percentage of their income to the church or other charitable organisations. This act of giving reflects their understanding that God has entrusted them with resources to be used for His purposes.

Living by the principle of God's ownership also influences their financial decision-making. They seek wisdom and guidance from God in managing their money, considering ethical considerations, and seeking to align their investments and financial activities with biblical principles. They may prioritise investments that have a positive impact on society and the environment, avoiding those that contradict their Christian values.

They understand that their financial well-being is not solely a result of their efforts but also a blessing from God. This perspective guards against greed, materialism, and an overemphasis on wealth, allowing them to find contentment in God's provision rather than pursuing an insatiable desire for more.

The Maker's Manual

Following a car's manufacturer's manual is important for several reasons.

Firstly, the manual contains important safety information. It provides details on how to properly operate the car and alerts the driver to any potential hazards. Failure to follow these safety guidelines can result in accidents or injury.

Secondly, the manual provides information on how to properly maintain the car. Regular maintenance is necessary to keep the car running smoothly and to prevent costly repairs down the road. The manual contains information on recommended maintenance schedules, such as when to change the oil or rotate the tires, as well as how to troubleshoot common problems.

Thirdly, following the manual can help to preserve the car's warranty. Many manufacturers' warranties are void if the car is not properly maintained or if non-approved parts are used. By following the manual, you can ensure that you are taking the necessary steps to protect your warranty.

Lastly, a car that has been properly cared for is more likely to be reliable and last longer, providing more value to the owner.

In our case of investing, our Makers Manual is the Bible. There, we read that "All Scripture is inspired by God and is useful to teach us what is true and to make us realise what is wrong in our lives. It corrects us when we are wrong and teaches us to do what is right. God uses it to prepare and equip his people to do every good work." (2 Timothy 3:16,17 NLT)

We cannot get specific investment advice from the Bible, but as we are known and loved by God, He will lead us and guide us into 'good works - good investing.'

Global developments, consistent change and the rise of individualism and relativism reveal that our need for Biblical truth is greater than ever. We ignore God's wisdom at our peril.

Why is it important for a Christian investor to acknowledge God's ownership?

For Christian investors, acknowledging God's ownership of all they have is a foundational principle that shapes their perspective on wealth, stewardship, and decision-making. Here are several reasons why this acknowledgement holds great significance:

Acknowledging God's ownership brings about a sense of accountability in how one manages their investments. Christian investors are motivated to make ethical choices, considering the impact of their investments on society, the environment, and individuals. They prioritise principles such as justice, fairness, and compassion in their investment decisions.

Recognising God's ownership encourages responsible financial management. Christian investors understand the importance of being diligent, wise, and prudent stewards of the resources entrusted to them. They prioritise long-term sustainability and seek to avoid excessive greed or materialism, striving for a balanced approach to wealth accumulation and distribution.

God's ownership reminds Christian investors that their wealth is temporary and earthly. They understand that true riches lie in heavenly treasures and the eternal impact of their investments. This perspective helps them avoid placing undue emphasis on material possessions and instead focus on using their resources to advance God's kingdom and bless others.

A Christian investor who acknowledges God's ownership is more inclined to practice generosity and cheerful giving. They recognise that their wealth is not solely for personal gain but also a means to bless others and meet the needs of the less fortunate. They actively seek opportunities to share their blessings and make a positive difference in the lives of others.

Investing from a distance

Acknowledging that we are not the owners of any money we have under our control but simply managers of God's resources helps us to manage our money more objectively and look at investment decisions from a distance.

By embracing objectivity, investors can navigate the complex world of finance with clarity, discipline, and a higher probability of achieving their financial objectives.

I saw this wonderfully at work in our very successful project to help people out of debt. We were helping all people, regardless of their faith. At the beginning of our relationship with people in debt, we could not talk openly about God's ownership. However, we taught them to consider their position as treasurer of a football club, managing money that did not belong to them. This gave them a different perspective on managing their money and helped them be objective in their decisions, avoiding the emotions of indebtedness. They started to make wiser, more informed decisions.

One of the major problems in managing money, I have found, is the emotional attachment we have to money. In fact, most buying decisions are highly influenced by our emotions. My friend Andrew Panasiuk says, "You have to cut the umbilical cord, which still ties you to money.".

Objectivity is of utmost importance in managing money for several key reasons:

Objectivity helps investors make rational and informed decisions. By setting aside personal biases, emotions, and subjective opinions, individuals can evaluate financial opportunities based on objective criteria such as risk, return, and market analysis. This rational approach enhances the likelihood of making sound financial choices.

Objectivity enables a realistic assessment of risks associated with investments. Emotion-driven decision-making can lead to impulsive actions and overlooking potential risks. By maintaining objectivity, investors can conduct thorough risk assessments, diversify their portfolios, and implement appropriate risk management strategies, thereby safeguarding their financial well-being.

Objectivity plays a crucial role in long-term financial planning. It helps investors focus on their goals and maintain a disciplined approach. Objectivity encourages the consideration of various factors, such as investment horizon, financial objectives, and market conditions, to develop a well-thought-out plan that aligns with their aspirations.

Markets and economic conditions are ever-changing. Objectivity allows investors to adapt to fluctuations and adjust their strategies accordingly. By objectively analysing market trends and evaluating the performance of investments, individuals can make timely adjustments, seize opportunities, and avoid undue attachment to failing ventures.

Human beings are prone to behavioural biases that can adversely affect financial decisions. These biases include confirmation bias, herd mentality, overconfidence, and loss aversion, among others. Objectivity helps mitigate these biases, allowing investors to take a step back, consider all relevant information, and make decisions based on facts rather than emotional impulses.

Objectivity is crucial when seeking professional financial advice or engaging with financial institutions. Investors place their trust in experts who can provide objective guidance, free from conflicts of interest. Objectivity ensures that the advice received is in the best interest of the investor, promoting transparency, accountability, and professionalism in the financial industry.

Chapter 7: Who is driving?

Investing is like driving a car, and self-awareness is the steering wheel. Without knowing yourself, it's like driving blindfolded. Just as a driver's awareness of their speed, destination, and road conditions is vital for a safe journey, an investor must be self-aware to navigate the financial markets. Ignoring your values, temperament, and objectives can lead to reckless decisions, much like driving recklessly without regard for traffic signals. Self-knowledge helps you stay in control, make informed choices, and steer your investments towards a successful financial journey.

It is important to know yourself when investing money because your personal characteristics, such as your risk tolerance, time horizon, and investment goals, will greatly influence the types of investments that are suitable for you.

Risk tolerance refers to how comfortable you are with the potential for loss in your investments. Some individuals may be more comfortable with a higher level of risk, while others may prefer a more conservative approach. Knowing your risk tolerance will help you to select investments that align with your comfort level.

There are no safe investments (at the most, those with more or less risk). The Bible recommends a completely different way of risk management, namely the way of diversification. Within diversification, the investor can live out his risk tolerance. More on diversification later. The investment must fit the objectives and the risk-bearing capacity of the investor but not the subjective risk tolerance of the investor.

Time horizon refers to the amount of time that you plan to invest your money. If you have a long-term investment horizon, you may be more willing to accept a higher level of risk in exchange for the potential for higher returns. If you have a shorter time horizon, you may prefer investments that are more stable and less risky.

Investment goals refer to what you hope to achieve with your investments. For example, are you saving for retirement, a down payment on a house, or a child's education? Knowing your investment goals will help you to select investments that align with your objectives.

Additionally, knowing yourself also means being aware of your own biases, emotions, and limitations. For example, if you tend to be impulsive or emotional, you may need to develop strategies to avoid making hasty investment decisions or to help you manage your emotions during market downturns.

Being aware of your own biases, emotions, and limitations can help you make better investment decisions and avoid costly mistakes.

Money personalities

Different money personalities can significantly influence an individual's approach to investing. These personalities are shaped by various factors, including upbringing, personal experiences, and attitudes towards money. Here are a few common money personalities that can impact investing:

Here are some popular "money types", highlighting how they can influence investing:

1. Adventurous Allan: This money type is an intrepid risk-taker, constantly seeking out high-reward investment opportunities. Adventurous Allan is willing to dive into uncharted territories and invest in speculative ventures, aiming for significant gains. However, he must exercise caution to ensure their pursuit of adventure doesn't lead to reckless decision-making or excessive exposure to risk.

2. Cindy Custodian: This investor is meticulous and vigilant, placing utmost importance on capital preservation. She favours conservative investments, prioritising stability and security. She tends to choose safer options or low-risk assets, ensuring the protection of their principal. While her approach offers peace of mind, it may limit potential growth and returns.

3. Impulsive Iris: She is known for their spontaneous and impulsive investment decisions. This type thrives on excitement and is easily enticed by the allure of quick gains. However, their impulsive nature can lead to hasty choices, overlooking thorough analysis and long-term consequences. The challenge for the Iris Impulse is to exercise restraint and avoid being swayed by fleeting market trends.

4. Strategic Simon: He possesses a keen intellect and employs meticulous planning in his investment approach. The type delves into comprehensive research, analyses market trends, and makes decisions based on solid data. His focus is on long-term strategies, seeking opportunities that align with his well-thought-out plans. While his analytical nature is an asset, he must guard against overanalysing or becoming paralysed by excessive caution.

5. Emotional Edward: This type allows their feelings and instincts to guide their investment decisions. They may be easily influenced by market volatility or swayed by emotional biases. The emotional investor should strive to balance feelings with rationality, avoiding impulsive choices driven by fear or greed. Developing a disciplined and objective approach to investing can help harness their strengths while mitigating emotional pitfalls.

6. Patient Patricia: She embodies a long-term perspective and possesses great patience. The type understands the power of compounding and the benefits of time in investment growth. She is not easily swayed by short-term fluctuations, maintaining a steadfast commitment to their investment strategy. Her ability to stay focused on long-term goals enables her to weather market storms and reap the rewards of gradual and sustainable growth.

Remember, these are simply metaphors to describe common tendencies in investing. Each investor is unique and may exhibit a combination of these traits. Recognising one's money type can help individuals better understand their inclinations and biases, enabling them to make informed investment decisions aligned with their goals and risk tolerance.

It is important to note that these money personalities are not mutually exclusive, and individuals can exhibit a combination of traits. Understanding one's money personality can help investors recognise their strengths, weaknesses, and biases, enabling them to make more informed and balanced investment decisions. Seeking professional financial advice can provide guidance tailored to an individual's specific money personality and investment goals.

Which season of life are you in?

The season of life that you are in can be an important consideration when investing money, as it can influence your investment goals, risk tolerance, and time horizon.

For example, if you are in the accumulation phase of life, you may have a longer time horizon and a higher risk tolerance, allowing you to invest in higher-growth, higher-risk assets such as stocks. This is because you have more time to ride out market fluctuations and recover from potential losses.

On the other hand, if you are in the distribution phase of life, you may have a shorter time horizon and a lower risk tolerance, as you may need to start withdrawing money from your investments to support your lifestyle. In this case, it may be more appropriate to invest in lower-risk, income-producing assets such as cash deposits, annuities, or treasury securities.

Additionally, if you are nearing retirement age, you may want to consider factors such as how much you will need to support yourself in retirement and how much risk you can tolerate in order to achieve that goal.

Furthermore, the stage of life you are in also affects your financial priorities and goals. For example, if you are starting out in your career, you may want to focus on saving for a down payment on a house, starting a family, or paying off student loans. If you are nearing retirement age, you may want to focus on preserving your savings and generating a steady income stream.

The season of life that you are in can influence your investment goals, risk tolerance, and time horizon. Factors such as your age, career stage, financial priorities and goals are all important to consider when making investment decisions. Additionally, as life progresses, it's important to regularly review your investment strategy, goals, and risk tolerance to make sure they align with your current stage of life.

Your family circumstances.

Investment considerations for singles and families can be quite different, and it's important for both groups to take into account their own personal situations and goals when making investment decisions.

First, singles typically have fewer financial obligations than families. For example, they may not have dependents to support or a mortgage to pay. As a result, they may have more disposable income to invest and may be able to take on more risk in their investments.

Second, families typically have a longer time horizon for their investments than singles. They may be saving for their children's education or for their own retirement, which can be decades away. As a result, they may be more willing to invest in long-term, higher-growth assets such as stocks, which can provide higher returns over the long term.

Third, families may have different investment goals than singles. For example, they may be saving for a down payment on a house, while singles may be focused on saving for retirement. This can influence the types of investments they choose, as well as their risk tolerance.

Fourth, families may also need to consider their insurance needs, such as life and health insurance, to ensure that they are protected in case of unexpected events. Singles may not have the same level of need for insurance.

Fifth, families may also need to consider estate planning to make sure that their assets are passed on to their loved ones in the most tax-efficient way possible. This is not something that single people typically have to worry about.

Chapter 8: Fuel for the journey

In the world of investing, having enough fuel is akin to having sufficient capital. Just as a car can't move without fuel, investments can't grow without adequate funds. Without enough capital, investors may struggle to seize opportunities or withstand market downturns. Like a car running on fumes, undercapitalised investments can stall or lead to forced liquidation, incurring losses. Adequate capital ensures stability, provides room for diversification, and allows for long-term growth. It's the essential fuel that powers the investment engine, propelling it towards financial goals and weathering the unpredictable twists and turns of the market journey.

The money we have available is, of course, the fuel for our journey.

There are essentially six uses of money. When money enters our income cycle (e.g. in the form of a salary, a profit distribution from your company or from returns on your investments), we can only spend it on one of six possible uses in the short term. No matter how much or how little money we take in each month, roughly speaking, there are only these six possible uses:

1. Giving
2. Paying taxes.
3. Paying off debts.
4. Financing our lifestyle

5. Risk management through insurance
6. Saving or investing surplus for long-term uses.

Each euro can only be spent once: The more money we spend on one of the six areas, the less is available for the other five uses. If, for example, we cultivate a sprawling consumption style, there is less or no room for financial investment. Of course, we could also reduce our lifestyle or our donations to a minimum in order to maximise saving and investing, but whether that would be particularly wise is another question. Paying off debts is one of the best investments possible and will liberate funds to invest.

Ultimately, any financial planning is about bringing these six uses of money into a healthy balance according to your life plan in consultation with God.

The Bible has a lot to say about giving, saving, taxes, debt, lifestyle, risk protection, and investing. Compass - finances God's way has numerous helpful books and studies for you to discover Biblical principles on handling money.

Generating money to invest

To ensure full for the journey, we need to make sure we have surplus money to invest.

There are basically only two ways to generate money to invest from your income. Either by decreasing expenses or by increasing income. Generally, it is much easier to increase your available cash for investing by decreasing your expenses.

Make it a priority to set aside a portion of your income to save and invest. A rule of thumb that I have always tried to follow is to pay God first, then taxes, then myself (savings), and then live off the rest.

Prioritising personal savings and investments before allocating funds to other expenses helps you create a solid foundation for future financial security and growth. This approach cultivates discipline and ensures that your long-term goals remain a priority. Whether it's building an emergency fund, saving for a major purchase, or investing for retirement, this strategy encourages consistent and intentional saving. Automating this process through direct deposits or automated transfers further enforces the habit. This not only fosters financial stability but also reduces the temptation to overspend. It's a proactive step towards achieving your aspirations and building wealth over time, providing you with a stronger footing to navigate life's uncertainties and opportunities.

Look to decrease spending by making a spending plan, creating a budget, and prioritising saving a portion of your income with which you could invest. Can you reduce unnecessary expenses such as subscriptions, dining out, and entertainment in order to release more to finance your long-term plans?

There are several ways you can increase your income, depending on your skills, interests, and availability. Here are some ideas to consider:

- Ask for a raise or promotion: If you have been with your current employer for a while and have been performing well, it might be time to ask for a raise or promotion. Make sure to prepare a strong case for why you deserve it and be willing to negotiate.
- Freelance or start a side business: If you have a particular skill or talent, you can offer your services as a freelancer or start your own side business. This can include anything from graphic design and writing to tutoring and pet-sitting.
- Take on additional work: If you have the time and energy, you can take on additional work in the form of a part-time job or gig work. This can include anything from driving for a ride-sharing service to delivering groceries.
- Invest in yourself: Consider taking courses or training to improve your skills and knowledge, which can lead to higher-paying job opportunities or enable you to start your own business.
- Rent out your property: If you have a spare room or property, you can rent it out or use online platforms like Airbnb or HomeAway.
- Sell unused or unloved items online: You can sell items you no longer need or want on online marketplaces like eBay or Amazon.

Remember that increasing your income may take time and effort, so it's important to find a strategy that works for you and that you enjoy. Be careful not to overwork or take on too many responsibilities, which may lead to family or health issues.

Plug the leaks!

Unsecured debt like personal loans and credit card balances are the major fuel leaks for your investment journey. These are dangerous, and we should consumer credit lines as soon as we can. It's important to come up with a debt repayment plan and stick to it. This will help you to stay motivated and on track to achieving your goal of becoming debt-free.

Getting out of debt is important for several reasons:

1.	Debt can be a major source of stress and anxiety, and it can be difficult to think about anything else when you're constantly worrying about how to make your next payment. Getting out of debt can help to reduce this stress and provide a sense of financial freedom.

2.	High levels of debt can negatively impact your credit score, which can make it difficult to get approval for loans in the future. Paying off debt can help to improve your credit score and give you more options for any necessary borrowing in the future.

3.	The interest you pay on top of your debt can add up quickly. The longer you carry debt, the more interest you will pay, which can make it even more difficult to get out of debt. Paying off debt can help you to save money on interest in the long run.

4.	Carrying high levels of debt can make it difficult to save for other financial goals, such as buying a house, starting a business, or saving for retirement. Paying off debt can free up more money to put towards these goals.

5.	Debt can make it difficult to make important financial decisions, such as buying a home, starting a business, or starting a family. Getting out of debt can give you the freedom and flexibility to make these decisions without creditors pressuring you for the first call on your money.

6.	High levels of debt can also have a negative impact on emotional well-being. It can cause feelings of guilt, shame, and hopelessness. Paying off debt can improve emotional well-being by reducing these negative emotions and providing a sense of accomplishment.

Don't forget the tithe!

When generating more money to invest, don't forget to tithe. Giving the tithe, which is one-tenth of your income, as a priority to the Lord, acknowledges that God is the Owner and Provider of all you control.

He is the source of our funds to use, and we return the tenth part to Him because of His provision and care for us. Jacob realised this and promised the tenth for God. "Then Jacob made a vow, saying, 'If God will be with me and will keep me in this way that I go, and will give me bread to eat and clothing to wear so that I come again to my father's house in peace, then the LORD shall be my God, and this stone, which I have set up for a pillar, shall be God's house. And of all that you give me I will give a full tenth to you.'" (Genesis 28:20-22)."

Returning the first tenth part to the Lord breaks the power of mammon in our financial life. When we bring the tithe into the Lord's storehouse, he promises to multiply the gift and pour out His blessings. In addition, He promises to Protect the giver from 'the devourer.' Mammon, the fallen spirit behind the power of money, is out to speed banana skins across our path and tempt us to fall and destroy our financial lives. "Bring the full tithe into the storehouse, that there may be food in my house. And thereby put me to the test, says the LORD of hosts, if I will not open the windows of heaven for you and pour down for you a blessing until there is no more need. I will rebuke the devourer for you so that it will not destroy the fruits of your soil, and your vine in the field shall not fail to bear, says the LORD of hosts." (Malachi 3:10-11)

Chapter 9: Be protected

Investing is akin to driving a car, and protection is like wearing a seatbelt. Both provide a safety net when things go awry; just as a seatbelt safeguards against accidents, protective measures like diversification, risk management, and asset allocation shield investments from unexpected market turbulence. Without these safeguards, investors risk financial collisions. The protection ensures resilience against market volatility and potential losses. Just as responsible drivers prioritise safety, prudent investors prioritise strategies that shield their financial well-being. In both cases, protection is the key to a smoother and more secure journey, reducing the impact of unforeseen obstacles and paving the way to financial success.

Driving a car is a risky business due to human factors, such as becoming distracted, fatigued, or driving poorly. You could experience mechanical failures, such as tire blowouts or brake failures. Weather conditions such as rain, snow, or ice can make driving hazardous. Road conditions like potholes on the road, construction works, or poor visibility can hamper your driving.

Likewise, investing comes with risks, and it is important to know the risks involved with particular investments. Your personal risk capacity also affects your investing decisions.   Risk capacity is your ability to endure potential losses or volatility in pursuit of higher returns.

A person with a high-risk capacity is comfortable with taking bigger investment risks for the potential of greater returns, while someone with a low-risk capacity prefers to minimise potential losses and is more risk-averse. It can be influenced by factors such as age, financial situation, and personal values.

Biblical perspective

What is the role of taking financial risks in the life of a disciple? When does stepping out in faith turn to foolishness? The key lies in faithful risk-taking. This means submission to the Lord's will, prayerful consideration of the risks involved and getting professional, godly advice.

The Bible offers guidance and principles that can inform a disciple's approach to risk-taking.

- James 4:13-17: "Come now, you who say, "Today or tomorrow we will go into such and such a town and spend a year there and trade and make a profit"— yet you do not know what tomorrow will bring. What is your life? For you are a mist that appears for a little time and then vanishes. Instead, you ought to say, "If the Lord wills, we will live and do this or that." As it is, you boast in your arrogance. All such boasting is evil. So whoever knows the right thing to do and fails to do it, for him it is sin." Here, we are warned about the uncertainty of life and the necessity to seek the Lord's will and be obedient to His guidance.
- Proverbs 3:5-6: "Trust in the Lord with all your heart and lean not on your own understanding; in all your ways submit to him, and he will make your paths straight." This verse encourages believers to put their trust in God and seek His guidance in decision-making.
- Ecclesiastes 11:4: "He who watches the wind will not plant, and he who looks at the clouds will not reap." This verse can be interpreted as a warning against being overly cautious and avoiding taking necessary risks.

- Luke 14:28-30: "For which of you, intending to build a tower, does not sit down first and count the cost, whether he has enough to finish it— lest, after he has laid the foundation, and is not able to finish, all who see it begin to mock him." This verse highlights the importance of careful planning and consideration before taking risks.

The Christian attitude towards taking risks can vary and is often influenced by personal interpretation of Biblical teachings. However, some common beliefs include:

- Trusting in God's plan: Believers may feel that taking risks is part of following God's will and trusting in His plan for their lives.
- Pursuing wisdom: Christians may believe in seeking wisdom and making informed decisions rather than taking reckless risks.
- Balancing faith and caution: Taking risks can be seen as a form of obedience to God's call, but it also requires caution and wise decision-making.
- Helping others: Taking calculated risks can also be seen as a way to use resources and opportunities to help others and further God's kingdom.

Ultimately, each person's attitude towards taking risks is influenced by their individual circumstances and their relationship with God.

In Part 3, we will consider the risks involved in choosing a particular investment type.

Insurance

Insurance is important to protect against financial loss, provide peace of mind, comply with laws and regulations, and protect assets and businesses. Additionally, having insurance can also be a way to mitigate risks and help plan for the future; it's important to choose the right type and amount of coverage based on your needs and budget.

- Protection against financial loss: Insurance provides a safety net in case of unexpected events such as accidents, illnesses, or natural disasters. It can help to protect you and your family from the financial burden of unexpected costs such as medical expenses, property damage, or liability claims.
- Peace of mind: Having insurance can provide peace of mind, knowing that you and your loved ones are protected in case of unexpected events. Knowing that you have a plan in place to manage potential financial losses can also help to reduce stress and anxiety.
- Compliance with laws and regulations: Some types of insurance, such as auto insurance, are legally required to operate a vehicle. Additionally, some lenders may require you to have certain types of insurance, such as homeowners insurance, in order to qualify for a loan.
- Protection of assets: Insurance can help to protect your assets, such as your home and car, from damage or loss. It can also help to protect your income in case of disability or loss of life.
- Protection of business: For businesses, insurance is important to protect against potential losses and liability claims that could threaten the financial stability of the company.

Insurance is nothing other than a risk-sharing community, as we can learn in Deuteronomy 14:28-29 for the widows, orphans, and foreigners in Israel. The early church in Jerusalem, from the Acts of the Apostles, was also such a risk-sharing community in which costs that would overburden individuals are redistributed to all. In this way, small or large risks of individuals are borne by the community. In this way, the early church formed a kind of forerunner of the modern foundation-insured community.

Nowadays, the community is most often organised by commercial insurance companies as risk carriers.

These types of insurance are primarily used to protect against various risks that could put one's financial security at risk:

1. Liability and damages protection: If someone carelessly, negligently, or intentionally causes harm to others, they are legally obligated to pay for the damages. This legal responsibility is recognised in most countries and applies to more than just minor

incidents like staining a friend's clothes or denting a neighbour's car. It can involve substantial obligations, reaching millions, for which the responsible person must bear the full financial burden. Personal liability insurance is a way for individuals to transfer this risk to an insurance company. Many policies even cover damages caused by gross negligence, but intentional harm is naturally excluded from coverage.

2.   Safeguarding work capacity: Our ability to work, a gift from God, allows us to convert the time we have into money by providing skills and time to employers or customers in exchange for income. If there is a restriction or loss of work capacity due to health reasons, the foundation for generating income in our economic system crumbles. This risk, along with its financial consequences, can be transferred to an insurance company through options like occupational disability insurance or insurance against serious illness.

3.   Life insurance: In families where one person is the main earner or when there are dependent children, it's essential to consider term life insurance. This helps cushion the loss of income in case the breadwinner passes away. With these insurances, the policyholder receives a predetermined benefit if the insured event occurs, such as occupational disability or death. If the event does not occur, there is no payout, and the premiums paid support the insured community in the form of surpluses.

4.   Health insurance: In many countries, health and long-term care insurance is mandatory. While it doesn't cover all health-related expenses, it does help with a portion of the costs in case of illness or extended care needs.

In light of these four risks that can threaten a family's financial stability, insurance coverage is sensible and particularly recommended for parents with dependent children. However, not every risk requires insurance coverage, despite the insurance industry's offerings for almost every imaginable risk.

Chapter 10: Know where you are going

In the world of investing, knowing where you are going is akin to having a clear destination in mind before embarking on a car journey. Understanding your destination enables you to make informed decisions, such as choosing the right investment vehicles and adjusting your risk tolerance along the way. Without a clear vision of where you want to be, you risk wandering aimlessly, making hasty investment choices based on short-term trends or hearsay. Knowing your destination gives you purpose and direction, keeping you motivated and focused during times of market turbulence. It also allows you to measure progress and make necessary course corrections as you move closer to achieving your financial objectives. So, before you rev up your investment engine, ensure you have a clear destination in mind, for it will be the guiding light throughout your journey toward financial success.

Without goals, our financial decisions are dictated by other people, unchecked emotions, and perceived urgency, all of which obstruct wise decision-making. Most of us are satisfied with simply accumulating as much as we can, which is the world's way of thinking.

Since the longing for more is insatiable, we never experience financial freedom. When we choose to set financial objectives, our choices become purposeful, and we stay focused on what is most important. But just developing goals is not enough.

I have three convictions:
1. Goal setting is the beginning of meaningful life planning.
2. A goal is not a goal until it is measurable; it is, at best, a good intention.
3. Only a Christian has the ability to set faith goals and ask, "God, what do you want me to achieve?" This is a way to experience the hand of God in my financial situation.

Before we start off on our investing journey, we should sit down with the Lord and, if applicable, our partner and determine our God-given goals.

A good investment as a disciple seeks to glorify God by simultaneously ensuring the companies invested in align with God's values while also earning respectable returns.

Setting goals

Setting goals is an extremely important aspect of personal and professional development. It helps to provide clarity, direction, and motivation and helps to measure progress, prioritise activities and increase self-awareness.
1. Clarity and direction: Setting goals provides clarity and direction for your actions and decisions. When you have specific goals in mind, you can focus your efforts and resources on achieving them rather than wasting time and energy on irrelevant activities.
2. Motivation: Setting goals can help to increase motivation and drive. Having a clear objective to work towards gives you a sense of purpose and a reason to take action.
3. Measurable progress: Setting goals allows you to measure your progress and track your success. You can set measurable and specific goals, such as increasing your savings by a certain percentage, which allows you to track your progress and adjust your actions if necessary.

4. Prioritisation: Setting goals helps you to prioritise your time and resources. When you have a clear understanding of your goals, you can make better decisions about how to allocate your time and resources to achieve them.

5. Self-awareness: Setting goals can help to increase self-awareness. Reflecting on your goals and the actions you take to achieve them can help you to better understand your strengths, weaknesses, and areas for improvement.

Faith Goals

So, what do we understand by "Faith goals"?

A faith goal is a statement: "I believe that God would have me to… whatever it is." I need to believe in my whole heart that I need to take this and internalise it.

I need to believe …
1. that they give direction and purpose.
2. passionately that goals help crystallise thinking.
3. goals provide personal motivation, and
4. that God will direct my steps.

God's Word has a lot to say about goal setting and the process. "The heart of man plans his way, but the Lord establishes his steps" (Proverbs 16:9).

Setting goals gets me moving, and God can direct my steps. "Now to Him who is able to do far more abundantly than all that we ask or think, according to the power at work within us…" (Ephesians 3:20).

This is all part of the faith process. My goal-setting comes from God; I seek His will and His wisdom, I start to move, and He can direct my steps. "The plans of the heart belong to man, but the answer of the tongue is from the Lord. All the ways of a man are pure in his own eyes, but the Lord weighs the spirit. Commit your work to the Lord, and your plans will be established" (Proverbs 16:1-3).

Seven major areas in which to set goals.

1. Homeownership

Investing in home ownership can be a great way to build wealth and create a sense of stability and security. Here are a few more ways that investing in home ownership can benefit you:

1. Appreciation: The value of a property can appreciate over time, which can result in a significant return on investment.
2. Tax benefits: Mortgage interest may be tax-deductible (depending on national conditions), which can help reduce your overall tax bill.
3. Forced savings: A mortgage payment can serve as a form of forced savings, as you are required to make regular payments towards the eventual ownership of your home.
4. Equity: As you make mortgage payments, you are building equity in your home, which can be used as collateral for loans or as a source of cash in the future.
5. Stable housing costs: Renting a property can result in unpredictable housing costs, whereas a fixed-rate mortgage can provide more stability and predictability in terms of housing expenses.
6. Sense of community: Owning a home can provide a sense of community and belonging and can be a good way to establish roots in a neighbourhood.

However, it's important to keep in mind that buying a home also comes with risks. The value of a property can also depreciate, and the housing market can be affected by factors such as interest rates and economic conditions. It's also important to consider whether you can afford the costs associated with home ownership, such as mortgage payments, property taxes, and maintenance expenses.

2. Financial independence

Financial independence refers to the state in which an individual has enough wealth to support their lifestyle without having to rely on regular employment or government benefits. Financial independence is often associated with the concept of retirement, but it can also refer to the ability to leave a job or take time off to pursue other interests.

As believers, we work from the principle of being financially dependent on the Lord as our Provider. There is also no such thing as retirement for the believer, as we are commanded to continue to work as a calling from God and an essential part of our life as disciples. However, we may be in a position to live off the income from investments and work while being dependent on paid employment!

Financial independence can be achieved through a combination of saving, investing, and building a diverse portfolio of assets. The goal is to accumulate enough wealth to cover one's living expenses through investments and passive income streams, such as rental properties, dividends, and interest.

Some key characteristics of financial independence include:

1. Passive income: Financial independence requires having a reliable source of passive income, such as rental properties, dividends, or interest.

2. Low living expenses: Financial independence is easier to achieve if you can keep your living expenses low.

3. Investment in diversified assets: A diversified portfolio of assets, including stocks, bonds, and real estate, can provide a steady stream of income.

4. Savings and budgeting: Financial independence requires having enough savings to support your lifestyle without relying on regular employment.

5. Minimal debt: Financial independence is easier to achieve if you have minimal debt and can avoid taking on new debt.

Reaching financial independence can take many years, and it is a journey that requires discipline, patience, and a long-term perspective. It is also important to note that financial independence is not the same as being rich; it's about having enough money to support yourself without relying on regular employment.

3. Education

Saving for college fees is important because a college education can be expensive and can put a significant financial burden on families. The cost of tuition, room and board, books and supplies, and other expenses can add up quickly and may be difficult to afford without proper planning and saving. Here are some reasons why saving for college fees is important:

1. Financial stability: Saving for college can help alleviate the financial burden of paying for college and allow families to plan for the cost in advance.

2. Access to better opportunities: A college education can open up better job opportunities and lead to higher earning potential in the long run.

3. Avoiding student debt: Saving for college can help reduce or avoid the need for student loans, which can have a long-term impact on an individual's financial stability.

4. Tax benefits: Many college savings plans, such as 529 plans, offer tax advantages that can help families save more for college.

5. Preparing for the future: Saving for college can help prepare for the future and set children up for success in their education and careers.

It's never too early or too late to start saving for college. The earlier you start, the more time you have for your savings to grow. Saving for college can involve a combination of personal savings and financial aid. It's important to start planning early and explore different savings options, such as savings accounts, college savings plans, and scholarships.

4. Retirement

Building a retirement fund is important because it provides a financial safety net for when an individual is no longer able to work and earn an income. Without a retirement fund, individuals may have to rely on Social Security or other government benefits, which may not be enough to maintain their standard of living. A retirement fund can also help to ensure that an individual has enough money to pay for healthcare expenses, which tend to increase as people age.

Here are some reasons why building a retirement fund is important:

1. Financial peace: A retirement fund can provide a sense of financial peace, knowing that you have capital to fall back on when you retire. Your retirement age comes quicker than you realise!

2. Maintaining standard of living: A retirement fund can help you maintain your standard of living after you retire and avoid having to make drastic changes to your lifestyle.

3. Meeting healthcare expenses: As people age, healthcare expenses tend to increase, and a retirement fund can help you meet these expenses.

4. Avoiding dependence on government benefits: A retirement fund can help you avoid having to rely on government benefits such as Social Security, which may not be enough to maintain your standard of living.

5. Tax benefits: Many retirement savings plans offer tax advantages that can help you save more for retirement.

It's important to start building a retirement fund as early as possible so that your money has more time to grow and compound. Building a retirement fund requires a consistent effort over time, and it's important to have a plan and stick to it.

5. Generosity

Saving for a large donation can be a great way to support a cause or organisation that you are passionate about.

Setting a specific savings goal and creating a plan to reach it can help you stay motivated and on track to reach your donation target.

It's important to remember that the process of saving for a large donation may take time and discipline, but the satisfaction of making a significant contribution to a cause you care about can be very rewarding. It's also important to research the organisation and ensure that the donation aligns with your values and that the organisation is using the funds effectively.

6. Legacy

Leaving a financial legacy refers to the act of passing on wealth and assets to future generations, and it can be an important aspect of financial planning. A financial legacy can provide a sense of security and stability for loved ones and can help to ensure that they have the resources they need to achieve their goals and dreams.

Here are some reasons why leaving a financial legacy is important:

1. Providing for future generations: A financial legacy can ensure that future generations have the resources they need to achieve their goals and dreams, such as buying a house, starting a business, or pursuing higher education.

2. Maintaining family values and traditions: A financial legacy can help to preserve family values and traditions by providing the resources needed to support them.

3. Passing on wisdom and knowledge: A financial legacy can also be an opportunity to pass on wisdom and knowledge about money management, investing, and financial planning to future generations.

4. Charitable giving: A financial legacy can also be used for charitable giving and philanthropy, which can have a positive impact on the community and society.

5. Estate planning: A financial legacy also involves estate planning, which can help to ensure that assets are distributed according to an individual's wishes and to minimise taxes and other expenses.

It's important to keep in mind that leaving a financial legacy is not just about passing on money and assets but also about passing on values, traditions, and life lessons. Building a financial legacy often requires careful planning and a long-term perspective. It's important to work with a financial advisor and legal professional to ensure that your assets are protected and distributed according to your wishes.

7. Business

Investing in someone's business can be a way to help them start and grow their own company. It can be a great way to provide financial support, as well as mentorship and guidance.

There are several ways to invest in a business, including:

1. Equity investment: This involves buying shares of the company, which gives the investor ownership of the company and a percentage of the profits.

2. Debt investment: This involves lending money to the business and receiving interest and principal payments in return.

3. Angel investment: This is a type of equity investment, often in a riskier business, where an individual investor, known as an angel, provides capital to a start-up in exchange for ownership equity.

4. Crowd-investing: This is a method of raising money by appealing to a large number of people, typically via the Internet. Crowd-investing platforms allow individuals to invest small amounts of money in a business in exchange for rewards or equity.

Investing in a business can be a great way to help someone start and grow their own company, but it's important to keep in mind that it also comes with risks. It's important to conduct thorough research and due diligence to understand the business model, the industry, and the management team before making an investment. It's also important to set clear expectations and agreements with the business owner to ensure that the investment aligns with your goals and investment strategy.

Chapter 11: Make your plan

Embarking on an investing journey without a well-thought-out plan is like setting off on a road trip without a map or GPS. A plan serves as your reliable navigation system, guiding you through the winding financial roads and helping you stay on course toward your investment goals. It outlines your destination, the routes to take (different investment options), and the estimated travel time (investment timeline). Just as you consider factors like distance, road conditions, and fuel stops before hitting the road, a thoughtful investment plan considers your risk tolerance, financial goals, time horizon, and diversification strategies. Having a plan not only instils confidence in your decisions but also allows you to stay focused and composed when faced with unexpected roadblocks or market turbulence. A well-crafted investment plan sets you up for a smoother and more enjoyable journey, increasing the likelihood of reaching your desired financial endpoint.

The purpose of a financial plan is to set you on a path to achieving your financial goals. There are no independent financial decisions, and there is a greater ability to make wise choices when we are able to see with a long-term perspective. A well-crafted, integrated plan is a road map showing an efficient way to get to your desired destination.

It starts with God at the centre and my relationship with Him. Our challenge is to maintain balance in the various areas of life. Often, we get out of balance in our vocation and our work as we strive to produce more wealth at the cost of our relationship with God, family, and other meaningful relationships. Then, the process of financial planning helps us to step back and assess our God-given goals and priorities, managing our finances in a way that relieves financial pressure and provides peace of mind. By balancing our lives through financial planning, we are able to focus on Life Impact to develop social and spiritual capital in our lives and those around us.

An exclusive focus on money can so easily bring us off-balance. Remember, Jesus unmasked a power behind money, which He called mammon, and this power uses money to disturb our lives and take us away from God.

Build wealth, not riches!

It is important that, in our financial planning, we are seeking to build wealth, not riches – there is a difference!

Riches, in a Biblical sense, represent money accumulated, and Solomon said that this would never satisfy. "He who loves money will not be satisfied with money, nor he who loves wealth with his income; this also is vanity. When goods increase, they increase who eats them, and what advantage has their owner but to see them with his eyes?" (Ecclesiastes 5:10,11).

Wealth, on the other hand, is money put to use for a purpose. "You shall remember the Lord your God, for it is He who gives you power to get wealth, that He may confirm his covenant that He swore to your fathers, as it is this day" (Deuteronomy 8:18). The purpose for which God gives us the ability to create wealth is to establish Gods covenant.

This covenant establishes the relationship between God and man, interpersonal relationships, and the covenant with the resources which the earth provides.

Therefore, the goal of life planning is to build wealth in all areas of life.

- Physical wealth to enjoy work, strength, and good health.

- Emotional wealth to enjoy inner mental strength to cope with tough situations.
- Relational wealth to enjoy friendships and mutual assistance.
- Material wealth to enjoy beauty and material things.
- Spiritual wealth to enjoy God's presence and activity.

From experience, I know just how much the pursuit of financial capital can come at the expense of one or more of the above life capitals. The art is to keep life in balance with God at the centre directing each area of my life.

Financial planning

Financial planning is the process of setting financial goals and creating a plan to achieve them. It involves assessing an individual's current financial situation, identifying their financial goals, and developing a strategy to reach those goals. A financial plan typically includes budgeting, saving, investing, and managing debt. It can also include planning for retirement, college education for children, and insurance needs.

The first step in financial planning is to assess your current financial situation. This includes looking at your income, expenses, assets, and liabilities. This will give you an idea of your current net worth and help you determine where you need to focus your efforts in order to reach your financial goals.

Next, you will need to identify your financial goals. These can be short-term goals, such as saving for a down payment on a house or paying off credit card debt, or long-term goals, such as saving for retirement or college education for children. It's important to set realistic and specific goals that are based on your current financial situation and your time horizon.

Once you have identified your goals, you can develop a strategy to achieve them. This may include creating a budget, increasing your income, reducing your expenses, paying off debt, and saving and investing. A financial plan should include a mix of different types of investments to help you achieve your goals and minimise risk.

It's also important to regularly review and update your financial plan as your situation and goals change over time. For example, if you get a raise or a promotion, you may want to adjust your savings and investment strategy. Or, if you have a child, you may want to adjust your plan to account for the additional expenses.

In summary, financial planning is simply the process of setting financial goals and creating a plan to achieve them. It involves assessing your current financial situation, identifying your goals, and developing a strategy to reach them. It includes budgeting, saving, investing, and managing debt. It can also include planning for retirement, college education for children, and insurance needs. Regularly reviewing and updating your plan as your situation and goals change is an important part of the process.

Four levels of planning

Follow these four levels of planning for sound money management.

Level 1: Become debt-free.

Becoming debt-free allows individuals to save and invest more effectively. When people are burdened with debt, a considerable portion of their income goes towards interest payments, leaving them with less money to save and invest for the future. By eliminating debt, individuals can redirect those funds towards savings and investments, leading to greater financial security and the potential for long-term wealth accumulation. Being debt-free also puts individuals in a better position to take advantage of investment opportunities and respond to unexpected financial challenges.

Furthermore, being debt-free improves one's financial standing and creditworthiness. It enhances the ability to access credit when necessary and often results in better interest rates on future loans, saving money in the long run. Overall, becoming debt-free is a crucial step towards achieving financial independence and enjoying the freedom to make financial choices that align with one's goals and values. "The rich rules over the poor, and the borrower is the slave of the lender." (Proverbs 22:7)

Level 2: Invest in a freedom account.

I call this a freedom account so that you can be free to meet emergencies and make larger purchases without having to borrow. It helps individuals avoid falling into the trap of excessive debt. When major purchases, such as a car, home, or expensive item, are financed through loans or credit cards, it can lead to a cycle of debt and interest payments that can be difficult to escape. Saving up for these purchases in advance allows individuals to make the purchase with cash or a more manageable down payment, reducing the need for costly debt.

It also promotes financial discipline and responsible money management. When individuals set aside money regularly and work towards a specific goal, they develop good financial habits. This process involves budgeting, prioritising expenses, and delaying immediate gratification to achieve a more substantial long-term reward.

By cultivating the habit of saving, individuals can create a solid foundation for their financial journey, making it easier to achieve their goals and navigate life's financial challenges.

I try to maintain at least one month's expenses in an emergency account so that I can cope with changing circumstances or unexpected bills. Then, invest money in a savings account so I can take cash and buy what I need, like house improvements, maintenance, appliances, and savings for a car.

"There are four things on earth that are small but unusually wise: Ants—they aren't strong, but they store up food all summer." (Proverbs 30:24,25)

Level 3: Investing your surplus.

Investing only your surplus funds is crucial for financial stability and security. When you invest your surplus, you ensure that your basic needs and essential expenses are adequately covered, and you are not putting your financial well-being at risk.

Investing your surplus allows you to take advantage of potential opportunities in the financial markets without jeopardising your ability to meet essential financial obligations.

Investing your surplus funds allows you to be more patient and take a long-term perspective in your investment approach. If you invest money that you can afford to leave untouched for an extended period, you can weather short-term market fluctuations and benefit from compounding returns over time. Rushing to liquidate investments during market downturns to meet immediate financial needs can lead to significant losses and undermine the potential growth of your investment portfolio. By investing your surplus, you can align your investment strategy with your long-term financial goals and be better positioned to navigate the ups and downs of the market.

Only when you have paid back consumer debt and managed your family's financial needs over and above the previous level should you progress to level three because here, the risk of loss becomes a determining factor.

Level 4: Diversify your investments to reduce risk.

Diversifying your investments is a fundamental principle of sound portfolio management. And it is crucial because it helps manage risk and enhance the overall stability of an investment portfolio. By spreading investments across various asset classes, industries, and geographic regions, an investor reduces the impact of any single investment's poor performance on the entire portfolio. Different asset classes, such as stocks, bonds, real estate, and commodities, have unique risk and return characteristics. When one asset class underperforms, another may perform well, helping to offset potential losses. Diversification also reduces exposure to the risk of individual companies or sectors facing financial difficulties, providing a safety net against significant losses due to the failure of a single investment.

Furthermore, diversification can lead to improved risk-adjusted returns. While diversification may not eliminate risk entirely, it can improve the risk-to-reward ratio. A well-diversified portfolio seeks to optimise returns for a given level of risk, ensuring that investors are not overly exposed to excessive risk without the potential for proportionate rewards. This can result in a smoother and more predictable investment experience over the long term. Diversification also provides the flexibility to adapt to changing economic conditions and market cycles, allowing investors to maintain a more balanced and resilient portfolio regardless of market conditions.

Look back at previous chapters to consider your investment personality, the season of life you are in, your risk tolerance level, and the goals which you are aspiring to achieve. Don't forget to align your investments with your faith goals and Biblical values.

Diversification strategy

"But divide your investments among many places, for you do not know what risks might lie ahead." (Ecclesiastes 11:3 NLT)

A diversification strategy in investing refers to the process of spreading your investments across different asset classes, sectors, and geographies, in order to reduce overall portfolio risk. Diversification can be achieved through several methods:

- Asset allocation: This involves spreading your investments across different asset classes, such as stocks, bonds, real estate, and cash. By allocating your investments across different asset classes, you can reduce the overall risk of your portfolio and increase the potential for returns.
- Sector diversification: This involves investing in different sectors such as technology, healthcare, energy, and finance. By diversifying across sectors, you can reduce the impact of any negative events or conditions in one particular sector on your portfolio.
- Geographic diversification: This involves investing in different geographic regions such as the US, Europe, Asia, and emerging markets. By diversifying across different regions, you can reduce the impact of any negative events or conditions in one particular region on your portfolio.
- Active and passive diversification: Active diversification is where an investor actively chooses different securities, sectors, or regions to invest in based on their own research and market analysis. Passive diversification is where an investor invests in a

broad market index fund or ETF (Exchange Traded Fund) that tracks a market index. Time diversification: This involves investing over different time periods, such as short-term, medium-term, and long-term. By diversifying across different time periods, you can reduce the impact of any negative events or conditions in one particular time period on your portfolio.

Process of setting investment goals

Here's a step-by-step checklist to help you when sitting down to set your financial goals.

1. **Identify Your Objectives**: Start by determining your financial objectives. These could include saving for retirement, buying a house, funding your children's education, or achieving a specific amount of wealth. Make sure your goals are specific, measurable, achievable, relevant, and time-bound (SMART).

2. **Quantify Your Goals**: Assign a specific dollar amount to each of your financial goals. For example, if you want to save for retirement, estimate how much money you would need to have in your retirement fund by a certain age.

3. **Determine Time Horizons**: Establish the time frame within which you want to achieve each goal. Some goals may have short-term horizons (1-3 years), while others may be medium-term (3-10 years) or long-term (10+ years).

4. **Consider Risk Capacity**: Assess your risk capacity level for each goal. Short-term goals may require more conservative investments, whereas long-term goals may allow for a higher level of risk and potential return.

5. **Create a Financial Plan**: Develop a comprehensive financial plan that outlines how you will achieve each of your goals. This plan should include how much you need to save and invest regularly to reach each target.

6. **Choose Investment Vehicles**: Select appropriate investment vehicles that align with your goals and risk tolerance. Diversification is essential to manage risk, so consider a mix of asset classes, such as stocks, bonds, real estate, and cash equivalents.

7.   **Regularly Review and Adjust**: Revisit your financial plan periodically to track your progress and make adjustments as needed. Life circumstances and market conditions can change, so it's essential to stay flexible and adapt your plan accordingly.

8.   **Seek Professional Advice**: If you're unsure about creating a financial plan or choosing investments, consider consulting with a financial advisor. A professional can help you develop a personalised investment strategy based on your goals and risk profile.

9.   **Stay Disciplined**: Achieving your financial finish line requires discipline and consistency in saving and investing. Stick to your plan and avoid making impulsive decisions based on short-term market fluctuations.

10. **Celebrate Milestones**: As you make progress toward your financial goals, take time to celebrate your achievements. Celebrating milestones can help keep you motivated and focused on reaching the ultimate financial finish line.

Chapter 12: Which roads to navigate

Investing is akin to driving a car through a complex network of roads. Knowing which roads to navigate is crucial. Just as a driver relies on GPS or maps to choose the best routes, investors need knowledge and research to select the right investment paths. Without this understanding, they risk getting lost or taking the wrong turns, leading to financial setbacks. Knowing which markets, industries, and assets to navigate is essential for a successful investment journey. It ensures that investors make informed choices, avoiding the pitfalls of blind speculation and enhancing the prospects of reaching their financial destinations.

There are two major roads to take along your investment journey - lending and owning, also known as debt investing and equity investing.

Selecting between debt and equity investing is comparable to deciding on the type of fuel that powers your car for a journey. Debt investing is like filling your tank with stable and predictable fuel, offering a fixed return over time, much like a smooth ride on a well-paved highway. It suits cautious investors seeking steady income and lower risk. On the other hand, equity investing resembles a high-octane fuel that might fluctuate in price and performance but has the potential for higher returns, similar to taking on an adventurous off-road route with greater uncertainty but exciting prospects. It caters to those willing to accept volatility and aim for long-term growth. Understanding the nature of each fuel (investment) is vital, as it impacts your entire journey—going with debt for stability or embracing equity for potential growth.

The key is finding the right balance, knowing your risk appetite, and blending the fuels judiciously to optimise your investment journey towards financial success.

Debt investing and equity investing are two different forms of investing that have distinct characteristics.

Debt investing, also known as lending, involves lending money to an individual or organisation with the expectation of receiving interest and the return of the principal at a later date. Examples of debt investments include bonds, loans, and mortgages. Debt investors are considered creditors and have a higher priority in the event of a company's bankruptcy or liquidation. This means that they are more likely to receive their money back, but the returns are generally lower than equity investments.

Equity investing, also known as owning, involves purchasing a stake in an asset, such as a stock or a real estate property, with the expectation of earning a return through appreciation of the asset or through the distribution of dividends or rental income. Equity investors are considered owners and have a claim on the assets and profits of the company or property. The returns on equity investments can be higher than debt investments, but they also come with a higher level of risk as the value of the asset can decrease.

In summary, debt investing is considered lower risk but with lower potential returns, while equity investing has higher potential returns but also comes with a higher level of risk.

Debt investing

- Debt investing, also known as fixed-income investing, is the process of lending money to a borrower, such as a corporation or government, in exchange for regular interest payments and the return of the principal amount at maturity. Some of the key characteristics of debt investing include:

- Regular income: Debt investing provides a regular stream of income in the form of interest payments. The interest rate and payment schedule are typically fixed and agreed upon at the time of investment.
- Low volatility: The value of debt investments is generally less volatile than that of equity investments. This is because the value of debt investments is based on the ability of the borrower to make interest payments and repay the principal at maturity rather than the performance of the borrower's underlying business.
- Credit risk: The risk that a borrower will default on its debt obligations is known as credit risk. This can lead to a loss of principal and interest for the lender.
- Interest rate risk: Interest rate risk is the risk that an investment's value will change due to a change in interest rates. When interest rates rise, the value of existing debt investments can decrease as new investments offer higher returns.
- Maturity: Debt investments typically have a maturity date, which is the date on which the principal amount is repaid to the lender. Short-term debt investments have shorter maturities and are considered less risky than long-term debt investments, as the likelihood of default increases with the length of time that the debt is outstanding.
- Tax Benefits: Interest earned on debt investments is generally taxed at a lower rate than other types of income.
- Credit rating: Debt investments are often rated by credit rating agencies, which provide an assessment of the borrower's creditworthiness. A higher credit rating indicates a lower risk of default.
- Diversification: Debt investments can be diversified by investing in different types of debt securities, such as bonds, Treasury bills, and municipal bonds, and by investing in debt securities issued by different borrowers, such as companies and governments.

Dent investing provides a regular stream of income with low volatility but also carries credit and interest rate risks. It has maturity, tax benefits, and credit rating and can be diversified. Debt investments are considered less risky than equity investments, but they also tend to offer lower returns.

Debt investing, also known as fixed-income investing, carries several risks. Some of the key risks associated with debt investing include:

- Credit risk: The risk that a borrower will default on its debt obligations is known as credit risk. This can lead to a loss of principal and interest for the lender.
- Interest rate risk: Interest rate risk is the risk that an investment's value will change due to a change in interest rates. When interest rates rise, the value of existing debt investments can decrease as new investments offer higher returns.
- Reinvestment risk: Reinvestment risk is the risk that an investor will not be able to reinvest interest and principal payments from a debt investment at the same or higher interest rate.
- Inflation risk: Inflation risk is the risk that an investment's returns will not keep pace with inflation, which can erode the purchasing power of an investment's returns.
- Currency risk: Currency risk is the risk that an investment's value will change due to changes in currency exchange rates. If the value of a currency falls relative to other currencies, it can decrease the value of an investment denominated in that currency.
- Liquidity risk: The risk that an investor will not be able to buy or sell a debt security when they want to because there are no buyers or sellers at the current market price.
- Default risk: Default risk is the risk that a borrower will fail to make the interest or principal payments on a debt security.
- Call risk: The risk that a bond issuer will redeem a bond before its maturity date, which can reduce the value of the bond for the holder.

It's important to keep in mind that debt investing can also be a high-risk, low-return endeavour, and investors should carefully consider the risks before investing and should diversify their investments.

Biblical perspective on debt investing.

It's important to recognise that individual perspectives on debt investing can vary among Christians based on personal beliefs, interpretation of biblical teachings, and cultural factors. Some Christians may be comfortable with responsible debt investing that adheres to ethical principles and seeks to help others, while others may choose to avoid debt investments altogether to align with their faith and values. As with any financial decision, seeking guidance through prayer, studying scripture, and seeking wise counsel can help Christians navigate these considerations thoughtfully.

While it's important to note that not all Christians may object to debt investing, here are some common reasons some Christians may have reservations about it:

- Biblical Warnings about Debt: The Bible cautions against being in debt. Proverbs 22:7 states, "The rich rule over the poor, and the borrower is slave to the lender." Christians may interpret this verse as a warning against helping people to become financially obligated to others.
- Avoiding Usury: The Bible prohibits charging excessive interest on loans, known as usury. Charging high interest rates that burden borrowers is seen as exploitative and contrary to the principles of fairness and compassion.
- Risk of Enslavement to Debt: Debt investing involves lending money to others in exchange for interest payments. Some Christians may be concerned that this practice can lead to financial dependence and potential hardship for those who may struggle to repay the debt.
- Supporting Unbiblical Practices: Debt investments may involve funding businesses or ventures that engage in activities contrary to Christian values. Investing in such businesses can be seen as indirectly supporting actions that go against one's faith.
- Putting Money before God: Some Christians may be wary of debt investing if they believe it places too much focus on financial

gain and diverts attention from a deeper relationship with God and reliance on His providence.

- Risk of Unintended Consequences: Debt investing carries inherent risks, such as default or bankruptcy of the borrower, which could lead to financial loss for the lender. Christians may be cautious about the unintended consequences of lending money that may exacerbate financial challenges for others.

Equity investing

Equity investing, also known as stock investing, is the process of purchasing shares of ownership in a publicly traded company. Some of the key characteristics of equity investing include:

- Potential for high returns: Equity investing has the potential for high returns, particularly over the long term. The value of a company's stock can rise significantly if the company performs well and its earnings and revenue increase.
- Risk: Equity investing also carries a higher level of risk than other forms of investing, such as bonds, as the value of a company's stock can decrease significantly if the company performs poorly or the overall market conditions change.
- Volatility: The value of a company's stock can fluctuate widely, particularly in the short term. This volatility can be influenced by a variety of factors, such as market conditions, economic conditions, and company-specific events.
- Liquidity: Stocks are highly liquid, meaning that they can be easily bought and sold on stock exchanges. This allows investors to move in quickly and easily and out of positions, depending on market conditions.
- Active management: Equity investing often requires active management, meaning that investors need to constantly monitor and research the companies in which they are investing. This can involve keeping track of financial statements, attending earnings calls, and monitoring news and market conditions.
- Diversification: Equity investing can be diversified by investing in different sectors, industries, and companies to spread

the risk across different investments.

Equity investing has the potential for high returns but also carries a higher level of risk. It is characterised by volatility, liquidity, active management, and diversification.

Some of the key risks associated with equity investing include:

- Market risk: The value of a company's stock is closely tied to the overall performance of the stock market. When the market falls, the value of a company's stock can fall as well, even if the company itself is performing well.
- Company-specific risk: The value of a company's stock can be affected by events specific to the company, such as poor financial performance, management changes, or lawsuits.
- Interest rate risk: Interest rate risk is the risk that an investment's value will change due to a change in interest rates. Higher interest rates can lead to lower stock prices, as they increase the cost of borrowing for companies and make bonds more attractive to investors.
- Inflation risk: Inflation risk is the risk that an investment's value will decrease due to inflation. Inflation can erode the purchasing power of an investment's returns, making it less valuable in real terms.
- Political and economic risks: Political and economic risks are the risks that the value of a company's stock will be affected by political or economic events such as war, natural disasters, or changes in government policies.
- Liquidity risk: The risk that an investor will not be able to buy or sell a stock when they want to because there are no buyers or sellers at the current market price.
- Credit risk: This refers to the risk that a company will default on its debt obligations. If a company is unable to pay its debts, its stock price can fall, which can lead to losses for equity investors.
- Currency risk: Currency risk is the risk that an investment's value will change due to changes in currency exchange rates. If the value of a currency falls relative to other currencies, it can decrease the value of an investment denominated in that currency.

Chapter 13: Your decision making

Investing, much like embarking on a car journey, requires constant decision-making as you navigate towards your financial destination. At the outset, you meticulously plan your route, setting clear goals and identifying potential obstacles. As you start driving, you encounter various road signs and detours, representing the ever-changing market conditions and investment opportunities.

Each decision you make is akin to choosing a turn at a crossroads – you may need to adjust your strategy based on traffic conditions or weather (market fluctuations) and sometimes even reroute to avoid unforeseen roadblocks (financial crises). Staying focused and attentive, you must assess risks and potential rewards, much like adjusting your speed to maintain a steady pace. The journey demands prudence, as reckless driving (risky investments) can lead to accidents (losses), while overly cautious driving (playing it too safe) might impede progress. Ultimately, reaching your financial destination depends on making informed decisions, continuously adapting to the road ahead, and having a clear understanding of your long-term objectives.

Inside- out investing

Many times, investments are evaluated by their economic performance, but for the financial disciple, this is certainly not the major criterion against which we manage performance!

Jesus often criticised the Pharisees for having the outward appearance of holiness and obedience to God while inside, they were actually dead, rotten, and sinful: "Woe to you, scribes and Pharisees, hypocrites! For you clean the outside of the cup and the plate, but inside, they are full of greed and self-indulgence. You blind Pharisee! First, clean the inside of the cup and the plate, so that the outside also may be clean. "Woe to you, scribes and Pharisees, hypocrites! For you are like whitewashed tombs, which outwardly appear beautiful, but within are full of dead people's bones and all uncleanness. So you also outwardly appear righteous to others, but within you are full of hypocrisy and lawlessness." (Matthew 23:25-28)

Christian investors can fall into the same trap if we only look at the outward appearance of our portfolios, how well they are performing, the diversification and risk management statistics, the income yield they are producing, and so forth. These are the outside of the cup and the outer walls of the tomb. But Jesus is more concerned with what is inside the cup.

What are the companies inside your portfolio, and what products and services are they selling? Are there abortion drugs, pornographic video streaming, labour exploitation, or immoral activities contaminating the inside of your portfolio?

To be good stewards, we must invest in activities that glorify God, avoiding investments in immoral businesses. Then, we can move on to consider the outside of the cup, shrewdly managing our portfolio for optimal financial returns. A good investment steward seeks to glorify God by simultaneously ensuring the companies invested in aligning with God's values while also earning respectable returns. Between the two objectives of holiness and profit, the Bible tells us that we should give priority to holiness, "Better is a little with righteousness than great revenues with injustice," (Prov.16:9)

This is certainly a higher calling, a harder job, and a greater responsibility than what the secular investor is faced with. More on this in the next chapter.

Don't forget yourself.

I must confess that I invested a large sum in what I thought would bring a great return, only to discover later that the high return was partly affected by ethical misrepresentation. A question Jesus posed determined my thinking afterwards. "For what does it profit a man to gain the whole world and forfeit his soul?" (Mark 8:36). I was guided by outward considerations and neglected my inward convictions.

One of our ministry friends is Austin Pryor of Sound Mind Investing. He said,

"Where do investment decisions originate for many investors? The starting point is found in the impersonal 'outside' world of current events, magazine articles, and brokers' recommendations. *Their decisions are guided primarily by outside considerations.* As they respond to the data thrown at them — sometimes buying, sometimes selling — their personal 'inside' financial world takes shape. Their thinking is 'outside-in.' They need a continual stream of outside information to stimulate their thinking and provoke them to action. Decision-making would be impossible without it." [16]

Austin advises that the starting point for good decision-making is 'inside' information. The focus is on their own values, financial needs and a personalised long-term strategy designed to meet those needs. Their decisions are made based on what's required to make sure their financial holdings are in accord with their values and their plan. The 'outside' world of investment professionals comes into the picture only because assistance is needed to execute decisions already made.

'Inside-out' thinking occurs where decisions are primarily shaped by inside considerations. Thus, current market fads, trends and so-called expert opinions are largely irrelevant to inside-out investors.

In other words, make your investing decisions as you would other consumer purchasing decisions. For example, if your family has grown to the point where you need a larger car or a van to take your kids around, you wouldn't buy a sporty new car because you like the look of it, or a magazine has sold its charms to you.

You won't let irrelevant external influences (outside-in thinking) steer you into making such inappropriate purchases. Instead, you make your decisions based on your needs at the time, irrespective of what the marketplace would like to sell you. This is obvious, you say. Yet, many people have a difficult time applying this consumer mindset to their investing decisions.

Here's a checklist an inside-out investor might use in deciding on an investment opportunity.

1.   Do I have a clear vision of what God's values are when investing, and am I committed to upholding these no matter how lucrative the opportunity is?

2.   Do I have a solid financial foundation? Am I getting out of debt, and is my emergency fund sufficient? If not, I should free some cash to repair any cracks in my foundation.

3.   Are my calculations, assumptions and expectations about my earnings, retirement and lifestyle goals, health needs, life expectancy and emotional tolerance of risk still valid? If in doubt, re-visit these and make the necessary changes.

4.   Am I meeting my giving goals? If not, perhaps I should make lifestyle adjustments or sell some of my investments in order to fund my giving.

The focus is on my personal needs and circumstances and not on the headlines of the day, which almost never tell you anything that will enhance the quality of your decision-making. While current events may provoke you to run through your personal list of review questions, they should not dictate the answers.

Another important aspect of 'inside-out investing' is to check my motives. God looks at the motives of the heart for evidence of righteousness in our hearts. Our motives reveal who we are living for and the things we care about. When God searches the heart, He can see the "why" behind our thoughts and choices. The Bible tells us that God judges the intents of the hearts. (Psalm 139:23-24) Search me, God, and know my heart; test me and know my anxious thoughts. See if there is any offensive way in me and lead me in the way everlasting."

As a Christian, decision-making is guided by a set of principles that are rooted in biblical teachings and the example of Jesus Christ. These principles are intended to align our choices with God's will and reflect the values and character of Christ. Here are eight key decision-making principles for a Christian:

1.   Seek God's Guidance: Christians believe in the importance of seeking God's guidance through prayer and studying His Word, the Bible. By seeking His will and wisdom, we invite God to lead us in making decisions that honour Him. "if any of you lacks wisdom, let him ask God, who gives generously to all without reproach, and it will be given him. 6 But let him ask in faith, with no doubting, for the one who doubts is like a wave of the sea that is driven and tossed by the wind." (James 1:5)

2.   Apply Biblical Principles: The Bible provides a wealth of principles and wisdom that can be applied to decision-making. For example, the principles of honesty, integrity, forgiveness, and seeking the welfare of others can help Christians make ethical and righteous decisions. "All Scripture is breathed out by God and profitable for teaching, for reproof, for correction, and for training in righteousness, that the man of God may be complete, equipped for every good work." (2 Timothy 3:16)

3.   Obedience to Jesus' teaching: The life and teachings of Jesus serve as a model for decision-making. His emphasis on love, compassion, humility, and justice can guide Christians in making choices that reflect these values. "Not everyone who says to me, 'Lord, Lord,' will enter the kingdom of heaven, but the one who does the will of my Father who is in heaven." (Matthew 7:21)

4.   Consider the Consequences: Christians are encouraged to consider the potential consequences of their decisions. Will the choice bring glory to God, promote peace, and benefit others? Evaluating the

potential impact on oneself and others can help Christians make decisions that are aligned with their values. "Do not be deceived: God is not mocked, for whatever one sows, that will he also reap." (Galatians 6:7)

5. Seek Wise Counsel: Christians are encouraged to seek counsel from wise and godly individuals, such as pastors, mentors, or trusted friends, who can provide biblical perspectives and help navigate complex decisions. Proverbs 15:22 states, "Plans fail for lack of counsel, but with many advisers, they succeed."

6. Trust in God's Sovereignty: Recognising God's sovereignty and trusting in His ultimate control over all things can bring comfort and confidence in decision-making. Even when faced with uncertainty, Christians can trust that God will work all things together for their good (Romans 8:28).

7. Embrace Humility and Surrender: Decision-making requires humility and surrender to God's will. Christians are called to submit their plans and desires to God, recognising that His ways are higher than ours (Isaiah 55:9).

8. Don't make quick decisions - take time to think and pray. (Psalm 37:7) Stop and consider what you are doing. Once again, you are God's steward, and you need to handle His money appropriately and prayerfully.

By applying these principles, Christians can approach decision-making with a Christ-centred perspective, seeking to honour God, love others, and make choices that reflect their faith. Ultimately, the goal is to live a life that is pleasing to God and brings glory to His name in all decisions, big or small.

Take along your financial advisor.

It is important to find an advisor who shares your biblical perspective on investing.

Of course, you need an advisor who is competent, does good work, has humility and integrity, and primarily seeks to advance your interests above any other. Many advisors, Christian or secular, could meet these requirements. But what is the difference with a qualified Christian advisor?

I believe that a Christian financial advisor should

1. Fear the Lord: "The fear of the Lord is the beginning of wisdom" (Psalm 111:10),

2. Be sensitive to God's leadership. "The mind of man plans his way but the Lord directs his steps." (Proverbs 16:3).

3. Give financial advice which is consistent with and informed by God's Word.

4. Have a Biblical perspective on the power of money, with its inherent temptations and how God wants to use money.

5. Have a focus on generosity to further God's Kingdom, as opposed to an accumulation focus.

6. Demonstrate integrity, maintaining confidentiality and commitment to legal and ethical practices.

7. Be professionally competent, with the training and experience to perform a wide range of financial services.

8. Have a good reputation. Proverbs tells us that "a good name is more desirable than great riches" and "to be esteemed is better than silver or gold." S/he should be held in regard by industry peers and church circles and have good references from clients.

When looking for a financial advisor, there are several key factors to consider, ensuring that you find someone who can help you meet your financial goals. Here are a few things to look for:

1. Professional designations and credentials: Look for an advisor who holds professional qualifications and is a member of a professional financial planning organisation.

2. Experience and track record: Look for an advisor who has several years of experience and a proven track record of helping clients achieve their financial goals.

3. Investment philosophy and strategy: Look for an advisor who has a clear investment philosophy and strategy that aligns with your own investment goals and risk tolerance.

4.   Compliance and registration: Make sure that the advisor is registered with relevant regulatory authorities and that they have a clean compliance record.

5.   Communication style: Look for an advisor who communicates clearly and effectively and who is willing to answer all of your questions.

6.   Fee structure: Look for an advisor who is upfront about their fees and charges and whose fee structure aligns with your needs.

7.   Availability: Consider how available the advisor is to meet with you and how responsive they are to your needs.

8.   Confidence and Trust: It is important to feel confident and trust in your advisor. Look for someone who listens to your needs, understands your goals, and makes you feel comfortable discussing your financial situation.

It's also important to meet with a few different advisors before deciding and to ask them questions about their experience, qualifications, and investment philosophy. It is also important to check their background wherever possible. Remember that choosing a financial advisor is a personal decision and that the right advisor for you will depend on your specific needs and goals.

The Rise of the 'Finluencer.'

A Finluencer is an influencer specialising in promoting financial products and advising on specific investment strategies using a social media platform; they are popping up like mushrooms, and we are listening to them!

On social media, anyone can pose as a financial expert, with all the potential risks and consequences that that entails. They mix charismatic personalities with entertainment and education to promote financial products. NBC Uni reports that "more than a third of GenZ goes to TikTok and YouTube for financial advice." 17 The report says that top 'finfluencers' can earn between $275,000 and $750,000 each year by posting two sponsored posts a week.

It goes on to say that "At its worst, however, Finance TikTok perpetuates financial myths, scams, and dangerously misleading information. What users end up seeing is often not good advice from trusted sources; it's just one random person's experience."

Nannerl Kok, a researcher at the Dutch Tilburg University, writes, "The growth of 'finfluencers' on online platforms is hugely risky. People who have little to no knowledge about investing can present themselves as financial experts on social media. Rapper Boef is one such example. He offers courses and provides young people with financial recommendations so they—like him—can become financially independent.

'Young people see him as a role model and are more likely to follow his recommendations as a result. That such a person could potentially encourage non-professional investors—people like you and me —and young people to make the wrong financial choices, I find worrisome.'[18]

Just this week, Dutch media reported that hundreds of Dutch investors lost at least € 5 million to an investment platform that was promoted by several 'finfluencers.'

Listening to 'finfluencers' comes with lots of risks. They often show a conflict of interests, collaborating with products and receiving compensation, prioritising financial gain over their audience's best interests. They are not experts, trusting more in personality and style than good knowledge and expertise. They often portray unrealistic expectations.

Who are you listening to?

Listening to influencers comes with inherent risks that individuals should be aware of. While influencers can be entertaining and charismatic, it is crucial to approach their content with a critical mindset. Here are some risks associated with blindly following influencers' advice or opinions:

1. Lack of expertise: Influencers often gain popularity for their personality or style rather than their knowledge or expertise in a specific field. It is important to differentiate between influencers who provide credible information backed by research or qualifications

and those who merely offer personal opinions or anecdotal experiences.

2. Conflicts of interest: Many influencers collaborate with brands or receive compensation for promoting products or services. This can lead to biased recommendations or endorsements that prioritise financial gains over the audience's best interests. It is essential to consider the potential underlying motivations behind their recommendations.

3. Misinformation and pseudoscience: Influencers are not always bound by the same rigorous standards as journalists or experts. Some may spread misinformation, pseudoscience, or unfounded conspiracy theories, leading to the dissemination of inaccurate or harmful information. It is crucial to fact-check and seek evidence-based sources before accepting their claims.

4. Unrealistic expectations: Influencers often portray idealised versions of themselves, showcasing a glamorous and curated lifestyle. This can create unrealistic expectations, leading individuals to feel inadequate or dissatisfied with their own lives. It is important to remember that influencers' lives are often selectively presented, and reality may differ significantly.

5. Mental health impact: Constant exposure to influencers' content, particularly when it revolves around appearances, success, or material possessions, can contribute to feelings of inadequacy, comparison, and low self-esteem. It is essential to prioritise mental well-being and limit exposure to content that negatively affects mental health.

To mitigate these risks, individuals should engage in critical thinking, fact-checking, and diversifying their sources of information. Relying on experts, peer-reviewed research, and credible news outlets can provide a more balanced and reliable perspective. Additionally, cultivating a healthy understanding of personal values, self-worth, and individual goals can help individuals navigate the influencer culture while maintaining a sense of authenticity and well-being.

Ultimately, our approach to investing as a disciple should be guided by a desire to honour God, make responsible choices, and use financial resources in ways that reflect biblical values. By seeking wisdom, practising discernment, and considering the impact of investments on both personal and societal levels, disciples can strive to invest in a manner that aligns with their faith. "Don't copy the behaviour and customs of this world, but let God transform you into a new person by changing the way you think. Then you will learn to know God's will for you, which is good and pleasing and perfect." (Romans 12:2)

Join a Compass group and discuss your investment plans with other believers, pray together and seek God's wisdom.

Seek to understand.

Understanding an investment opportunity is essential for making well-informed decisions, managing risk, optimising returns, and aligning your investments with your financial goals. It empowers you to navigate the complexities of the financial markets and ensures that you are in control of your financial future.

Understanding an investment is paramount because it empowers investors to make informed decisions and manage risks effectively. By comprehending the investment's underlying asset, market dynamics, and potential risks and returns, investors can align their choices with their financial goals and risk tolerance. A deep understanding allows investors to differentiate between short-term market fluctuations and long-term trends, helping them stay focused on their investment objectives rather than being swayed by emotional reactions to market noise.

Moreover, understanding an investment ensures that investors are aware of the associated costs and fees. Every investment carries transaction costs, management fees, and, in some cases, taxes that can erode returns over time. An informed investor can make cost-effective choices and select investments that offer competitive fees while delivering the expected returns. Being aware of the costs involved allows investors to calculate their net returns more accurately and make more precise projections for their future financial needs.

Furthermore, understanding an investment fosters accountability and financial responsibility. When investors grasp the intricacies of their investments, they are more likely to take ownership of their financial decisions and be actively involved in managing their portfolios. It encourages continuous learning and engagement with the financial markets. Additionally, investors who understand their investments are better equipped to communicate with financial advisors and make well-informed adjustments to their portfolios as needed, ensuring they remain on track to achieve their financial goals.

Don't invest in anything you don't understand. Behind every stock, there is a company. Find out what it does, its strengths and weaknesses and the industry in which it operates. What are its competitive advantages, its markets and supply chains?

Select stocks as if you were searching for business partners. Buy into well-managed companies with businesses you can understand.

Be sure you understand the investment you are considering. "A house is built by wisdom and becomes strong through good sense. Through knowledge its rooms are filled with all sorts of precious riches and valuables. The wise are mightier than the strong, and those with knowledge grow stronger and stronger." (Proverbs 24:3-4) You are God's steward, and you need to understand how it will be used. If you don't understand, then don't invest.

Your chief advisor, if married

If married, your chief advisor should be your partner. I believe that in marriage, God speaks to each partner separately and differently, and together, this is the whole of God's wisdom for each partner.

Marriage is a God-ordained partnership: It is a sacred union instituted by God, where a husband and wife become one flesh. This concept of unity emphasises the idea that both spouses are equal partners in the marriage, and they complement each other in various aspects of life.

1. **Respect and Love:** Scripture emphasises the importance of mutual respect, love, and honour between spouses. This means valuing and appreciating each other's opinions, insights, and wisdom.

2. **Wisdom and Discernment:** The Bible speaks highly of wisdom and encourages seeking counsel from wise individuals.

Proverbs 15:22 says, "Without counsel, plans fail, but with many advisers, they succeed." If your wife exhibits wisdom and discernment, it is natural to seek her advice and perspective.

3. **Intimacy and Communication:** Marriage is a relationship built on intimacy and deep communication. Sharing concerns, thoughts, and decisions with your spouse fosters a strong emotional bond and can lead to making better, well-informed choices.

4. **Biblical Roles:** In Ephesians 5:22-23, the Bible instructs wives to submit to their husbands, but it is essential to understand this submission in its proper context. The following verse, Ephesians 5:25, also instructs husbands to love their wives sacrificially, just as Christ loved the church. This implies that the husband's leadership should be characterised by love, humility, and selflessness, while the wife's role involves supporting and respecting her husband.

5. **Shared Goals and Visions:** In a Christian marriage, spouses often share common goals and values, including spiritual growth and serving God together. In making important decisions, seeking input from your wife aligns with the shared vision of the family.

However, it's essential to remember that every marriage is unique, and roles and dynamics can vary from one couple to another. What matters most is the mutual love, respect, and support between spouses, striving to honour God in their relationship and seeking His guidance in all aspects of life. Ultimately, the husband and wife should work together as a team, recognising each other's strengths and relying on each other's advice and support to navigate life's challenges.

Chapter 14: Keep your focus

In the world of investing, keeping your focus is akin to being an attentive driver on a long car journey. Just as a driver must keep their eyes on the road, hands on the wheel, and minds on the task at hand, an investor must remain vigilant and disciplined in monitoring their investments. Distractions, much like unexpected potholes or detours, can arise in the form of market noise, short-term fluctuations, or emotional impulses. By staying focused on your long-term investment goals and adhering to a well-crafted financial plan, you can navigate through the ups and downs of the market with confidence and composure.

Avoiding reckless decisions driven by fear or excitement and instead maintaining a steady course based on thorough analysis and rational judgment allows you to weather storms and overcome challenges, ultimately reaching your desired financial destination. Like a safe and skilful driver, a focused investor stays in control, steers clear of hazards, and maximises the potential for a successful and rewarding investment journey.

During our journey of investing, we need to stay focused on our primary goal, which is to glorify God.

Practically glorifying God means living in a way that reflects His character and values in all aspects of life. It involves aligning our thoughts, actions, and intentions with the teachings and principles found in sacred texts, such as the Bible. Glorifying God requires developing a deep and personal relationship with Him through prayer, worship, and a commitment to following His guidance. This entails living a life of integrity, honesty, compassion, and love, treating others with respect and kindness, and seeking justice and righteousness.

Furthermore, glorifying God involves using our gifts, talents, and resources to serve others and contribute positively to the world. It means recognising that all that we have comes from God and using these blessings to benefit others and make a difference in their lives. This can be through acts of charity, volunteering, or supporting causes that promote social justice and improve the well-being of others. By being good stewards of our time, talents, and treasures, we demonstrate our gratitude to God and glorify Him through acts of love and service.

Lastly, glorifying God means sharing the message of His love and salvation with others. This involves being a light in the world, spreading hope, and pointing others to the transformative power of faith. Through our words and actions, we can be witnesses to God's grace and redemption, helping others find purpose and meaning in their lives. Glorifying God practically means living as a reflection of His love and grace, continually growing in faith and becoming more Christ-like in character, and positively impacting the lives of those around us through our deeds and interactions.

Investing as a Disciple ... From Conscience to Impact

One of the best-known expressions of faith-based investing has been investing for a clean conscience, which sought to avoid investing in morally bad companies by screening them out for involvement with things like tobacco, gambling, alcohol, or abortion - things they were trying to avoid. However, by avoiding investing in certain bad companies, Christians can lose their voice in influencing corporate decisions.

A more positive approach would be seeking to impact investing for good, not just trying to avoid what is wrong.

Three strategies for positive investing
Investing can be redeemed in three ways.

1.   Values-Driven Integration: This approach involves investment managers using ethical criteria to guide their analysis and selection of companies for investment. Instead of merely excluding problematic companies, they actively seek out businesses that contribute positively to society, such as those addressing basic human needs, supporting medical research, or promoting sustainable practices. While this approach does not guarantee superior financial returns or immediate social change, it aims to promote companies with higher moral standards and work towards making the world a better place.

2.   Impactful Investing: Another strategy involves investing in funds explicitly aiming to make measurable impacts on social or environmental issues. Some faith-based funds pursue this approach by investing in projects like affordable housing, supporting medical clinics through micro-finance, developing renewable energy sources, and providing loans to improve education. While less common in public markets, a few faith-based mutual funds have started embracing this intentional impact approach.

3.   Corporate Engagement: The third strategy involves actively engaging with corporations to address practices that conflict with moral values. This can manifest in various ways, such as sustained dialogues about issues like forced child labour in the chocolate industry or unfair drug pricing. Other methods include utilising proxy voting and making official statements at investor meetings. Engaging with companies acknowledges that no corporation is perfect, providing Christian investors with a means to influence corporate behaviour from within, expressing their values in the business world, and potentially fostering positive changes within the corporate landscape.

Responsible Investing

Biblically Responsible Investing (BRI) is a movement embraced by Christian financial advisors and investors, focusing on investing in a way that brings glory to God. BRI seeks to align investments with biblical principles, which means avoiding companies involved in morally or ethically questionable activities like gambling, pornography, or abortion. Instead, BRI aims to invest in companies that uphold positive social and environmental practices and align with biblical values like fairness, honesty, and integrity. The goal is to ensure that investors' money is not supporting activities contrary to their religious beliefs.

When considering companies to invest in, BRI encourages investors to assess their products, services, and business practices, asking if they contribute to human flourishing. Value creation is seen as serving others, while value extraction is viewed as exploiting. BRI seeks companies that serve stakeholders well, including customers, employees, suppliers, the environment, and society as a whole, as these firms are believed to have more sustainable business models for long-term success.

On the other hand, Socially Responsible Investing (SRI) is a similar strategy that considers financial returns alongside social impact. SRI focuses on avoiding companies involved in harmful practices like weapons manufacturing, tobacco, or environmental pollution while also investing in companies that promote positive social and environmental practices. The key difference between BRI and SRI lies in the guiding principles: BRI is based on biblical teachings, while SRI is shaped by personal value systems.

Both BRI and SRI share some ethical filters, such as avoiding investments in gambling, tobacco, pornography, and alcohol. While SRI tends to be more secular, BRI is specifically rooted in religious beliefs and values found in the Bible. Both approaches aim to align investments with investors' values and ethical principles.

ESG criteria

ESG criteria, standing for Environmental, Social, and Governance, are essential factors used by investors to assess the sustainability and ethical impact of potential investments. In the context of investing, ESG criteria have become increasingly significant in evaluating companies and businesses for their long-term performance and potential to generate positive social and environmental outcomes.

The Environmental component of ESG focuses on a company's impact on the environment and its efforts to address climate change and resource conservation. Investors examine a company's carbon footprint, energy efficiency, waste management, and adoption of renewable energy sources. Companies committed to reducing greenhouse gas emissions, minimising waste generation, and implementing environmentally responsible practices are favoured by ESG-conscious investors.

The Social aspect of ESG evaluates how a company interacts with its employees, communities, customers, and other stakeholders. Companies promoting diversity and inclusion in their workforce, maintaining labour rights, ensuring fair wages, and fostering a safe work environment are viewed positively. Additionally, social criteria also assess a company's contributions to the well-being of local communities, its approach to human rights issues, and its engagement in philanthropic efforts or social initiatives.

The Governance component of ESG concentrates on a company's internal policies, leadership structure, and overall management practices. Investors analyse board independence, executive compensation, and transparency in financial reporting. Companies with strong governance practices, independent boards, and clear accountability are considered more reliable and less prone to risks related to corruption or unethical conduct. ESG criteria thus empower investors to identify sustainable and socially responsible companies, allowing them to make informed investment decisions that align with their values and contribute to a more sustainable and equitable future.

From a Biblical view, there are certain limitations to consider when using Environmental, Social, and Governance (ESG) criteria for evaluating investments:

1. **Potential Moral Conflicts:** While ESG criteria may align with some biblical principles, they do not encompass all moral aspects that are important to Christians. ESG assessments may prioritise certain issues over others, leading to potential conflicts with biblical values and priorities.

2. **Relativism and Worldviews:** ESG criteria are often influenced by various worldviews and ethical frameworks, which may not necessarily align with biblical teachings. As a result, investments based solely on ESG assessments might not fully reflect a Christian perspective.

3. **Secular Nature:** ESG criteria are primarily driven by secular considerations, and they may not account for spiritual dimensions or

the eternal perspective emphasised in biblical teachings. As Christians, the focus on eternal values and God's Kingdom might not be fully addressed through ESG evaluations.

4. **Lack of Scriptural Basis:** ESG criteria are not explicitly derived from biblical teachings. While they may align with some general ethical principles found in the Bible, they lack direct scriptural guidance, which could limit their application in specific investment decisions for devout Christians.

5. **Changing Standards:** ESG criteria are subject to ongoing developments and can vary across different organisations and rating agencies. As standards change, it may become challenging to maintain consistent alignment with biblical principles over time.

6. **Neglect of Individual Spiritual Discernment:** Relying solely on ESG assessments might overlook the importance of personal spiritual discernment and prayer in investment decisions. Individual Christians may feel called to support specific causes or missions that are not adequately captured by ESG evaluations.

7. **Focus on Earthly Impact:** ESG criteria tend to emphasise the impact of investments on this earthly life, but they may not fully account for the eternal significance of investments that contribute to the spread of the Gospel or support Christian ministries.

While ESG criteria can offer valuable insights and considerations for ethical investing, disciples should approach investment decisions with a broader understanding of biblical teachings, prayerful discernment, and a focus on eternal values, seeking to align their investments with their faith and God's Kingdom principles.

Can I delegate my responsibility?

"Is a Christian shareholder morally responsible for the actions of a corporation?

As a Christian shareholder, your moral responsibility for the activities of the organisation in which you invest depends on your individual beliefs, values, and the specific activities of the organisation.

From a Christian perspective, investing in companies or organisations that engage in morally questionable activities or unethical practices raises ethical dilemmas. Some Christians may feel a sense of moral responsibility and wrestle with the idea of indirectly supporting actions that go against their faith principles.

If we build our investment on the basis that God owns everything, including all capital, then we need to make sure we are representing his interests. Of course, Scripture does not give any specific guidance on such ethical dilemmas. Responding requires wisdom and judgment based on knowledge, prayer, and counsel. Coming to a conclusion is not easy.

Investing in public companies can be complex, and it may not always be possible to completely avoid exposure to businesses that have activities that conflict with your values. In such cases, investors may choose to engage with the companies they invest in, advocating for positive change and responsible business practices through shareholder activism or proxy voting.

By investing in alignment with their moral beliefs, Christian shareholders should aim to be responsible stewards of God's resources while seeking financial returns that reflect their values.

However, ultimately, the decision of whether to invest in a particular organisation and the level of moral responsibility a Christian shareholder feels can be deeply personal and may require prayer, reflection, and guidance from spiritual advisors. Each individual's approach to investing and their moral responsibility for the activities of the organisations they invest in will vary based on their faith convictions and convictions regarding ethical investing.

Your Values

Your personal values play a significant role in investing as they shape your investment philosophy. Your values can determine the types of companies and industries you are willing to invest in and can influence your decision-making, such as avoiding companies that are involved in practices that go against their values. Personal values also impact an investor's overall financial goals and investment time horizon. By considering their values and aligning them with their investment strategy, an individual can feel more confident and satisfied with their investment decisions.

2 Peter 1:3-7 says, "His divine power has given us everything we need for a godly life through our knowledge of him who called us by his own glory and goodness. Through these he has given us his very great and precious promises, so that through them you may participate in the divine nature, having escaped the corruption in the world caused by evil desires. For this very reason, make every effort to add to your faith goodness; and to goodness, knowledge; and to knowledge, self-control; and to self-control, perseverance; and to perseverance, godliness; and to godliness, mutual affection; and to mutual affection, love."

Although this passage does not directly mention investing money, it provides a valuable framework for making wise financial decisions. The passage emphasises the importance of developing qualities such as faith, goodness, knowledge, self-control, perseverance, godliness, mutual affection, and love. These qualities can also be applied to financial decision-making.

Faith: Investing requires a certain amount of faith that the money invested will yield a return. However, faith in the stock market alone is not enough. It's important to also have faith in God and trust that he will guide your financial decisions.

Goodness: It's important to consider the ethical implications of your investments. Invest in companies that align with your values and do not contribute to harm.

Knowledge: Before investing, take the time to educate yourself on the market and various investment options. Make informed decisions based on research rather than speculation.

Self-control: Don't let emotions drive your investment decisions. Avoid making impulsive decisions based on fear or greed. Stay disciplined and stick to your investment strategy.

Perseverance: Investing is a long-term game. It's important to persevere through market fluctuations and stay committed to your investment strategy.

Godliness: Consider how your financial decisions align with your faith. Are you using your money in a way that honours God and benefits others?

Mutual affection and love: Consider how your investments can benefit not only yourself but also others. Look for ways to invest in companies that are making a positive impact in the world.

Screening investments

The first verses of Ephesians 5 exhort us, as 'imitators of God and His children', to shun the things of this world and, in verse 11, to "Take no part in the unfruitful works of darkness, but instead expose them."

When confronted with investment opportunities, it is helpful to make a checklist of sinful practices in which you would want to avoid investing.

My top 5 for a checklist, based on Christian values, would be:

1.   Life - abortion - research, drugs, institutions, tobacco, alcohol.

2.   Stewardship - gambling, online, casinos, racetracks, software.

3.   Purity - porno, promiscuity… where the marriage covenant is under threat.

4.   Family - media, games, entertainment (through violence, language, sex, and drugs).

5.   Freedom - trafficking, slave labour, terrorism, persecution.

In conclusion, Biblically Responsible Investing accomplishes this in three ways:

* Avoid – investments that don't align with Biblical values (such as pornography, abortion, etc.)
* Advocate – use influence to encourage positive change in companies they invest in
* Affirm – invest in companies that are doing good.

Criteria

Dr. Paul Mills, an economist at the UK finance ministry, provides some helpful criteria for evaluating investment opportunities. [19]

1.   Personal stewardship - I am responsible for the money entrusted to me. Can I delegate this responsibility?

We have relinquished the stewardship of our savings to intermediaries, such as fund managers and banks. In most cases, we have no idea of the activities and methods used to derive a return on our money. The financial disciple ought to be positively engaged in investing, ensuring godly values are held high.

2.   Relationship potential - God's desire is to build redemptive relationships.

Does my investment promote loving and redemptive relationships? The Bible teaches the subjugation of wealth to the cultivation of loving relationships. Jesus specifically urges the use of this world's wealth to develop friendships since the good done to others will be the only return on investment that will ultimately last (Luke 16:9).

3.   Knowledge of use - am I aware of how God's money is being utilised?

By being aware of where your investments are directed, you can ensure that your money is not supporting activities that contradict your faith or contribute to harm in society. Transparency in investment allows you to make intentional choices that positively impact the world and align with your Christian values, promoting a sense of accountability and integrity in your financial decisions.

4.   Non-hoarding? Loving riches (The Rich Fool)

Hoarding can range from stuffing banknotes in a mattress to amassing valuables in a bank vault. Although the practicalities of life require some degree of storage, hoarding to protect one's wealth is quickly dismissed by biblical writers. (Luke 12:16-21; James 5:3; see also Psalm 39:6; Ecclesiastes 5:13; Zechariah 9:3.) Hoarding is an anti-social act in that it deprives the economy of the employment-generating consequences of the resources being spent, donated, lent, or invested.

5.   Non-speculation (gambling, presuming on future?

Investment decisions primarily revolve around expectations for the future. While it is not contradictory to trust in God's providence while planning for financial needs, wisdom lies in maintaining a humble attitude towards the unknown future. To claim certainty about the future and make financial commitments based on such assumptions is akin to assuming a divine attribute for oneself. (James 4:13-16)

Dr. Mills made this matrix as an overview of his five criteria and which type of investment meets these criteria.

	Personal steward-ship	Under-standing	Equity vs interest	Non-hoarding	Non-speculation
Business investment	√√	√√	√√	√√	√
Owner-occupied housing	√√	√√	√√	√	–
Personal shares	√	√	√√	√	?
Ethical unit trust/fund	√	√	√	√	–
Building society deposit	√	√	X	√	–
Pension fund/ unit trust	X	X	√	√	–
Govt debt / National Savings	X	–	X	√	–
Bank deposit	X	X	X	√	–
Cash	–	–	–	XX	–

Should we be concerned about a diminished return?

This movement seeking to avoid profiting from companies involved in immoral practices like abortion, drug manufacturing, adult entertainment distribution, alcohol, and human trafficking could cause concern about being less profitable, and questions about investment performance often arise. Investors wonder if they might have to sacrifice returns by adopting Biblical principles.

These concerns stem from the perception that doing the right thing may lead to unfavourable outcomes or the fear of venturing outside the conventional investment approach. Yet, various research data challenge the notion that good values and good returns are mutually exclusive.

Jesus called people to follow Him simply and authoritatively, without elaborate explanations or coercion. When Jesus called His first disciples, like Simon Peter and Andrew, they immediately left their livelihood as fishermen and followed Him. In contrast, the rich young ruler, seeking eternal life, was asked by Jesus to sell all his possessions and follow Him. The rich man's sadness and refusal revealed the cost of following Jesus.

The point is that sometimes Jesus calls individuals to make earthly sacrifices to follow Him faithfully. Not everyone is called to abandon their business or wealth, but for those who are, there should be no deliberation, only counting the cost and immediate obedience. When God asks you to invest with biblical values, it becomes a call to pursue investing for His glory.

While concerns about hypothetical performance sacrifices may arise, the relevance of such concerns is trivial compared to obeying God's calling. Even if investing as a disciple led to lower returns, Christians should not reject God's call because of potential performance losses. The primary concern should be immediate obedience and following Him wholeheartedly.

The question of performance should not hinder one's decision to pursue investing as a disciple, as immediate obedience to God's call and the pursuit of His glory outweigh any potential sacrifices in return.

Chapter 15: Know when you have arrived

Knowing when you have arrived on an investment journey means recognising the moment you reach your desired destination during a car trip. Just as a traveller looks for specific landmarks or signs to confirm they have reached their target, an investor must regularly assess their progress and measure it against their financial objectives.

Without acknowledging that you have arrived, you risk missing opportunities to enjoy the fruits of your investments or make informed decisions about the next leg of your financial journey. It's crucial to define clear milestones and have a well-defined exit strategy so that when you achieve your intended financial goals, you can celebrate your success and make thoughtful choices about reinvestment, risk management, or adjusting your course. Knowing you have arrived allows you to savour the sense of accomplishment and take stock of how far you've come, providing motivation and confidence for future financial expeditions.

The finish line

Setting a finish line helps to determine when we have finished the race. I encourage you to set a finish line for your income and wealth accumulation and cap your spending accumulation at a pre-determined point. As your wealth increases, the endless ways to spend it also increases.

Our consumer culture promotes one overarching goal: The accumulation of more and more. We are endlessly told that we need a bigger house, a newer car, a nicer vacation, more money in savings, and so on.

A small but growing number of Christians are declaring that they don't need more. They have stated what is enough and drawn a 'financial finish line.' Could I be content with food and clothing that are enough for just today, as Paul admonishes Timothy? "But if we have food and clothing, with these we will be content." (1 Timothy 6:8)

How much is enough? How much do I need to accumulate to reach my long-term goals, such as retirement, education, inheritance, and business goals? Could I be content with food and clothing that are enough for just today? Could I go on a spending freeze instead of a spending frenzy? How much is enough for long-term goals, retirement, education, inheritance, business, etc.?

If we know the finish line, we can pace ourselves, knowing when to speed up and when to slow down. When we reach the line, we can stop and take stock.

A financial finish line is that stage of your financial growth at which you don't have to accumulate any more. Your financial finish line is the answer to an all-important question: "How much is enough?" Here are some reasons why it is prudent to set a financial finish line.

Without a finish line, you won't know how much you need to accumulate, how much to invest, and when you reach your goal. If you have a clear view of your destination, and the goals you want to achieve, then setting out a strategy to reach that destination is much easier. If you aim at nothing, you will hit that every time.

You will be able to periodically evaluate if you are on track or lagging behind.

The best part of racing is crossing the finishing line. It gives us a sense of satisfaction and achievement. We can then sit back a while and ponder.

- To run a race successfully, it is necessary to keep our eyes on the finish line and not get distracted. Without a finish line, we will never know when we have arrived. Financially, we could never realise what 'enough' is. Without a finish line, we don't really know where we are heading.

- A financial finish line serves as a benchmark for measuring your progress toward your goals. Regularly tracking your investment performance against your goals enables you to identify if you're on track, falling behind, or exceeding expectations.

- Having a tangible financial finish line can be highly motivating. It gives you a sense of purpose and helps you stay disciplined in your investment approach, as you are more likely to remain committed to achieving the target you have set.

- Your financial finish line helps determine your investment time horizon and risk tolerance. Short-term goals may require more conservative investments, while long-term goals may allow for a more aggressive approach.

- Without a clear financial finish line, investors may be tempted to make emotional decisions based on short-term market fluctuations. Having a defined goal can help reduce emotional reactions and keep you focused on the bigger picture.

- A financial finish line is especially crucial in retirement planning. It helps you estimate how much you need to accumulate for a comfortable retirement and how much you need to save and invest regularly to reach that goal.

- A finishing line will help us to commit to a lifestyle of becoming content with what we have and spending less so that we can save more for future goals.

If we set our financial faith goals in prayer, agreeing with God what these should be, then we can rest knowing that the Lord will guide us and keep us content and thankful, no matter what the outcome. We can keep the finish line in view but remain flexible and open to the Lord's guidance.

Contentment doesn't come from accumulating more but from desiring less. When you set a financial finish line, you have answered the question of how much is enough.

Setting and achieving the finish line is not the same as finishing well: it's a precursor. The finish line is a milestone within your plan to finish well. Setting a finish line positions you to finish well and helps you to stay on track. Jesus warns us to be careful not to allow a spirit of greed to invade our wealth growth but to be 'rich toward God,' employing our wealth to practically love God and our neighbour. That is the standard by which we shall be judged.

Jesus' parable of the rich fool causes us to consider exactly how much we will really need to save in order to achieve our God-given goals. He teaches us about the danger of crossing a line of enough into greed at the expense of generosity.

To avoid blindly saving with no limits and building bigger barns, I set financial finish lines for each strategic goal and make a financial plan to know how much I will need to reach specific goals. This protects me from striving for false security and leaves more room for giving.

The Rich Investor

The great painter Rembrandt knew what it was like to be rich and live a lavish lifestyle. He also knew what it was like to go bankrupt and lose it all. One of my favourite paintings hangs in a Berlin museum, in which Rembrandt describes the parable of the rich fool. (I once heard a preacher lament, "It is curious how the popularity of this passage is inversely related to how much money the hearer has, being very much enjoyed by the poor but leaving the rich shifting uncomfortably in their seats!")

Let's take a look at the painting.

We see an elderly man who has 'pince-nez' spectacles perched on his nose, sitting at a table which is overloaded with books and papers, some written in Hebrew. He is looking carefully at one of his gold coins.

On the desk, we can see scales to weigh the gold. A large book of accounts is opened as he tallies his treasure. The table is covered with many large books, which, as Rembrandt painted in the 17th century, symbolises pride.

He is clothed in expensive attire, reflecting his wealth.

But there are also details that indicate the fragility of this man. While there are magnifying glasses around him, which is another symbol of how wealthy he is, it also indicates that his eyesight is going. His eyes seem misted up, and his glasses show that his vision is deteriorating. His whole face seems to reflect old age.

Despite his wealth, his whole body is failing him.

I think that if Rembrandt were to paint this in our times, he would choose a wealthy investor in a sharp suit watching the Dow Jones index on one screen, his spreadsheet on the other, thinking about how to expand his wealth. There would be tablets strewn on his desk and a glass of whisky at hand. His face would show anguished stress lines as he ponders his portfolio. This proud man is totally focused on his money.

Jesus told his listeners about a man who grew a bumper crop of grain. Too much of a good thing meant he had nowhere to store it. Instead of helping other people, he decided to build bigger barns. Then, he could have years' worth of grain to sell. He could retire. In this story, there are 11 references (use of the words "I" or "my") to how this rich fool focused on himself. Count them!

The rich fool thought, "What shall I do, for I have nowhere to store my crops? . . . I will do this: I will tear down my barns and build larger ones, and there I will store all my grain and my goods. And I will say to my soul, 'Soul, you have ample goods laid up for many years; relax, eat, drink, be merry.' But God said to him, 'Fool! This night, your soul is required of you, and the things you have prepared, whose will they be?'"

Jesus concluded, "So is the one who lays up treasure for himself and is not rich toward God." (Read Luke 12:13-21.)

So, what does it mean to be rich toward God? The Bible commands them to do good, to be rich in good deeds, and to be generous and willing to share. It's no wonder that Augustine said, "The rich fool didn't realise the bellies of the poor were much safer storerooms than his barns."

Then Paul writes to Timothy, "As for the rich in this present age, charge them not to be haughty, nor to set their hopes on the uncertainty of riches, but on God, who richly provides us with everything to enjoy. They are to do good, to be rich in good works, to be generous and ready to share, thus storing up treasure for themselves as a good foundation for the future, so that they may take hold of that which is truly life" (1 Timothy 6:17-19).

Bigger barns?

The parable of the Rich Fool (Luke 12:16-21) gives us an example of someone who ignored his finish line and continued accumulating. The farmer tore down his barns and built bigger ones. Jesus warns through this parable that those who never stop accumulating are greedy and foolish as they "lay treasures up for themselves" and are not "rich towards God."

The other element in the story relates to the potential implications of retirement and God's view of multiplication as a journey rather than a destination. In the story, part of the issue Jesus had with the rich fool could have been that he simply stopped. His idea of a finish line was a simple thought: 'My work is done; it's time to relax and enjoy life to the full.'

Judging by his outcome, we can clearly conclude that God desires something better for us and expects something better from us as financial disciples rather than rich fools. *"But God said to him, 'Fool! This night your soul is required of you, and the things you have prepared, whose will they be?'"* (Luke 12:20).

Be sure not to confuse earthly concepts like retirement with eternal concepts like fulfilling the Great Commission. That work never stops! The expectation Jesus has for us is to make disciples right up to the day we meet Him.

The parable of the rich fool tells us that the farmer was already rich when a season of abundance came. God called him a fool when he "thought to himself" that he would tear down his existing barns and build newer, bigger ones. God was not angry that the farmer was rich. He called the farmer a fool because of his attitude. He said to himself, "Soul, you have ample goods laid up for many years; relax, eat, drink, be merry." (verse 19)

God does not want us to store up things for ourselves; rather, He expects us to be rich toward Him, to experience true wealth. " So is the one who lays up treasure for himself and is not rich toward God" (verse 21). The rich fool had a distorted view of financial independence. To be financially independent for the farmer was to be dependent on money and independent from God. True financial independence means to be fully and completely dependent on the Lord!

He was oblivious to the fact that wealth is a blessing from God. "The blessing of the LORD makes rich, and he adds no sorrow with it." (Proverbs 10:22) He did not realise that wealth should be shared to meet the needs of those around him. He was engrossed with himself. Five times he says, "I …"

He did not realise that he would be held accountable to the One who had given him life.

My very good friend, Albert Diepeveen, says, "When I die, I don't want to leave behind a large sum of money in the bank. My ultimate goal is to use as much wealth as possible to advance the cause of God's kingdom during my lifetime."

So, what exactly constitutes your "barn" in financial terms? A barn is a fixed structure. It is planned for and built to exact specifications once; then, it doesn't change. It holds a certain amount of grain based on those specifications. It can hold less, but it can't hold more. It has a clear purpose – to store grain, usually for the short term when the grain is then moved to create value in other ways (e.g., to make cereal or tortillas).

Barn building means accumulating wealth. Without any specific God-given goals for investing surplus cash to build wealth, it can quickly become a kind of idol in which we trust for the provision of what we need.

We need to plan intentionally to meet our needs and remain vigilant that accumulating does not become hoarding.

According to a definition in Wikipedia, hoarding is a mental disorder characterised by the accumulation of possessions due to excessive acquisition of or difficulty discarding them, regardless of their actual value, leading to clinically significant distress or impairment in personal, family, social, educational, occupational, or other important areas of functioning. [10]

The farmer in Jesus' parable demonstrated this mental disorder, as it was clearly diagnosed by God.   Having proudly talked to his soul about his achievement, God called him a fool.

Building barns is fine for saving wealth for future goals that have been planned together with God in prayer.

Part 3: Investment vehicles

Just as choosing the right vehicle is essential for a successful road trip, selecting the most appropriate "investment vehicles" is paramount when setting off on the path to financial growth and well-being.

Imagine embarking on a cross-country road trip, the open road stretching out before you, and an array of vehicles to choose from. The car you pick will not only determine your comfort and speed but also influence your entire journey experience. Similarly, the financial vehicles you select for your investment journey will significantly impact your ability to reach your destination, whether it's retirement provision, wealth accumulation for your life goals, or funding a lifelong dream.

In this segment of our book on investing, "Different Investment Vehicles," we invite you to join us on a journey through the diverse options available to investors. These investment vehicles come in all shapes and sizes, each with its unique set of features, advantages, and risks. As we explore the financial landscape, we'll draw parallels between the world of investing and the choices one faces when deciding which car to take on a cross-country adventure.

Just as a sports car offers exhilarating speed but limited cargo space, stocks provide the potential for high returns but come with high risks. Bonds, on the other hand, resemble a reliable sedan, offering steady income, while real estate can be compared to a spacious SUV, providing both shelter and growth potential. Meanwhile, alternative investments such as hedge funds and private equity are like the off-road vehicles of the investment world, capable of navigating challenging terrain but requiring specialised skills.

Navigating your financial journey can be as thrilling and rewarding as any epic road trip. However, without a clear understanding of the various investment vehicles at your disposal, you may find yourself on an aimless drive, missing out on opportunities, or worse, facing unexpected financial detours. Our goal in this segment is to provide you with some knowledge and insights needed to navigate your chosen investment vehicles, discuss the risks involved, and give a Biblical perspective on each vehicle.

Whether you're an inexperienced investor looking to start your journey or a seasoned financial traveller seeking to diversify your portfolio, this section will serve as your roadmap, guiding you through the twists and turns of the investment landscape. Together, we will unlock the keys to successful investing, enabling you to steer your financial journey toward choosing your investments wisely.

Chapter 16: Your investment vehicle

An asset refers to any resource that has economic value and can be owned or controlled by an individual, organisation, or entity. Assets play a crucial role in personal and business finance, as they contribute to an individual's or organisation's performance and net worth and can generate income or provide future benefits. It's important to note that assets carry risks and liabilities, and their value can fluctuate over time due to changing circumstances.

Assets can come in various forms and can be tangible or intangible. Here are a few examples:

- Tangible assets: These are physical assets that can be seen and touched. Examples include real estate properties, vehicles, machinery, equipment, inventory, and cash.
- Intangible assets: These are assets that lack physical substance but still hold value. Examples include intellectual property such as patents, copyrights, trademarks, and brand names. Other intangible assets can include goodwill, customer relationships, software, and licenses.
- Financial assets: These are assets that derive their value from a contractual claim or ownership rights. Examples include stocks,

bonds, mutual funds, certificates of deposit (CDs), and cash equivalents like savings accounts or money market funds.

• Natural resources: These are assets that exist in nature and can be exploited for economic purposes. Examples include oil, gas, minerals, timber, and water rights.

• Investments: Equity investments or ownership stakes in companies or other ventures.

Asset Classes

An asset class refers to a group of financial instruments or assets that share similar characteristics and behave similarly in the financial markets. Investors often categorise their portfolios based on asset classes to diversify their investments and manage risk effectively. Each asset class typically has distinct risk and return characteristics, making it important for investors to understand them to create a well-balanced investment strategy.

1.   **The Different Lanes of the Investment Highway (Asset Classes):**
Imagine the investment world as a vast highway with various lanes, each representing a different asset class. Just like cars on the road, investors have the option to choose which lane to travel in based on their investment goals. One lane is the stock lane, where you can experience the thrill of potential high-speed growth as you become a partial owner of companies. Another lane is the bond lane, generally offering a smoother ride with regular interest payments and stability. The real estate lane takes you to properties, providing rental income and potential appreciation. The precious metals lane offers a touch of luxury and safety with assets like gold. And the cash lane is like a rest stop, providing liquidity and a safe haven. As a skilled driver, a well-diversified portfolio combines different asset classes, smoothly navigating through the investment highway and ensuring a balanced and successful journey toward your financial destinations.

2.   The All-Weather Tires of Diversification   (Diversified Portfolio):

A smart investor equips their investment vehicle with all-weather tires, known as diversification. Just like how all-weather tires provide stability and grip on various road conditions, a diversified portfolio ensures stability and resilience in different market environments. By spreading investments across multiple asset classes, you reduce the impact of bumps and potholes in the financial markets. When one lane faces challenges, the others can still keep your journey on track. Diversification allows you to manage risk effectively and avoid putting all your eggs in one basket. With the right combination of asset classes, your investment vehicle can confidently handle both smooth highways and bumpy terrains, ensuring a steady and secure drive towards your long-term financial goals.

By diversifying across multiple asset classes, investors can potentially reduce overall risk and enhance the chances of achieving their financial goals.

Asset allocation, the process of distributing investments across different asset classes, is a critical element in portfolio management. It involves determining the right mix of asset classes that align with an investor's financial goals, time horizon, and risk tolerance.

Keep in mind that investing involves risk, and the performance of each asset class can vary over time. The investment triangle

In our car journey of investing, the three critical factors of liquidity, time horizon, and risk tolerance form the foundation for mapping out your route and ensuring a smooth and successful trip:

1. **Liquidity - Filling Up Your Financial Tank:** Liquidity is like the fuel that keeps your investment vehicle running. Just as you need enough fuel to cover the distance on your journey, having sufficient liquidity ensures you can meet your short-term financial needs. Having accessible cash or liquid assets allows you to handle unexpected expenses and emergencies or to take advantage of immediate opportunities without derailing your long-term investment plans. Like stopping at gas stations along the way, maintaining liquidity helps you avoid running out of financial resources during your investment journey.

2. **Time Horizon - Planning Your Journey Length:** Every car journey has a specific destination and a planned duration, and your investment journey is no different. Your time horizon represents the length of your investment journey, whether it's short-term, medium-term, or long-term. Just as you would choose a different route and travel strategy for a weekend getaway versus a cross-country road trip, your investment decisions should align with your time horizon. A longer time horizon allows you to weather short-term market fluctuations and capitalise on the power of compounding. On the other hand, a shorter time horizon requires a more cautious approach with a focus on preserving capital and ensuring that your financial goals cannot be endangered within the set timeframe.

3. **Risk Tolerance - Adapting to the Road Conditions:** Just like driving on different roads with varying conditions, the investment journey presents different levels of risk. Risk tolerance is like your adaptability to changing road conditions during your investment trip. It represents your comfort level with potential fluctuations in the value of your investments. Some investors prefer the scenic route with moderate risks, while others may opt for the fast lane with higher risks for the chance of greater returns. Understanding your willingness and capacity for risk allows you to choose the appropriate asset allocation and investment strategy that matches your comfort level and financial objectives. Just as a cautious driver adjusts their speed based on road conditions, a prudent investor aligns their risk exposure to their risk tolerance for a smooth and enjoyable investment journey.

By considering the interplay of liquidity, time horizon, and risk tolerance, you can chart a well-planned investment route that takes you closer to your financial goals with confidence and peace of mind.

The relationship between these three components forms a triangle, where any adjustment to one factor affects the others:

- High returns often come with higher risk and lower liquidity. Investments with the potential for significant returns, such as stocks or high-yield bonds, typically involve a higher level of risk and may have limited liquidity.

- Low-risk investments, such as government bonds or savings accounts, offer lower returns but higher liquidity. These investments provide a higher degree of stability and easier access to funds but may not generate substantial returns over time.
- Investments with high liquidity and low risk, such as cash or money market funds, offer safety and flexibility but tend to have lower returns compared to riskier assets.

The investment triangle can help investors understand the trade-offs they need to consider when constructing their portfolios. Balancing risk, return, and liquidity is essential to meet individual financial goals while managing exposure to potential losses and ensuring access to funds when needed. It is crucial for investors to evaluate their risk tolerance, investment horizon, and liquidity needs before making investment decisions.

Considering risk tolerance, investment horizon, and liquidity needs before making investment decisions is crucial for disciples, just as it is for any other investor. These factors play a vital role in ensuring that investment choices align with individual financial goals, values, and responsibilities as stewards of God's resources. Here's why each of these considerations is significant:

- Risk tolerance refers to an individual's willingness and ability to handle the ups and downs of the financial markets. As disciples, we are called to be responsible stewards of the resources God has entrusted to us (1 Peter 4:10). Understanding our risk tolerance helps us avoid making emotional decisions based on fear or greed; both may lead to impulsive or unwise investment choices. By assessing risk tolerance, we can strike a balance between potential returns and the level of risk we are comfortable taking, ensuring a more disciplined and rational approach to investing.
- Investment horizon refers to the length of time an investor plans to hold their investments before needing access to the funds. As disciples, we are called to have a long-term perspective in our lives and decision-making (Philippians 3:13-14). Aligning our investment horizon with our financial goals and life plans allows us to select appropriate investment vehicles that match our timeframes. Long-term investments, like stocks, have historically provided higher

returns, but they may involve more short-term volatility. Short-term needs, such as upcoming expenses or emergencies, may be better served by more liquid and stable investments like cash or short-term bonds.

- Liquidity refers to the ability to access funds quickly without significant loss of value. As disciples, we should be prepared to respond to unexpected needs or opportunities for generosity (Proverbs 3:27-28, Luke 6:38). Evaluating liquidity needs helps us ensure that we have adequate funds available for emergencies or to fulfil our financial obligations. Balancing liquidity requirements with long-term investment goals helps create a financial safety net and provides peace of mind during uncertain times.

By being intentional and thoughtful in our investments, we can honour God with our financial choices and use our resources wisely to support our families, serve others, and advance God's kingdom on Earth.

It's important to note that no investment strategy can guarantee complete economic security, as all investments carry some degree of risk. However, implementing these scenarios can help individuals strengthen the overall security and resilience of their investment portfolios.

Remember that economic security is ultimately found in God and not in financial resources (Psalm 62:5-7). Trusting in God's provision and adhering to biblical principles can help Christians navigate economically turbulent times with wisdom and confidence. By seeking economic security in a manner consistent with Christian values, we can honour God and be responsible stewards of the resources He has entrusted to us.

Rely on prayer and trust in God's guidance during uncertain times. Seek wisdom and discernment in your investment decisions, knowing that God is in control of all circumstances (Proverbs 3:5-6).

Stay informed about economic developments but avoid excessive exposure to media or news that may induce fear or anxiety. Balance information with a focus on God's sovereignty and providence.

Impact investments

Investments geared towards helping people live and flourish are often referred to as "impact investments" or "socially responsible investments." These investment approaches go beyond solely seeking financial returns and also aim to create positive social and environmental impacts.

For example, here are just ten types of investments that fall under this category:

1. **Social Impact Bonds**: Social Impact Bonds are a form of performance-based contracting where private investors provide upfront funding for social programs. If the program achieves predefined outcomes that benefit society, the investors receive a return on their investment. SIBs are often used to address social issues like homelessness, recidivism, and education.

2. **Micro-finance**: Micro-finance involves providing financial services, such as small loans and savings accounts, to low-income individuals and underserved communities. These investments help empower individuals to start or expand small businesses, improve their living conditions, and build a pathway out of poverty.

3. **Renewable Energy**: Investing in renewable energy projects, such as solar, wind, or hydroelectric power, contributes to sustainable energy sources and reduces reliance on fossil fuels. These investments address climate change concerns while promoting environmental stewardship.

4. **Community Development:** Community development investments focus on projects that revitalise or uplift disadvantaged communities. This may include affordable housing initiatives, community infrastructure development, or supporting local businesses.

5. **Education:** Investments in education can range from funding schools and educational programs to supporting start-ups that aim to enhance access to quality education for all.

6. **Healthcare:** Investments in healthcare may involve funding medical facilities, research, or companies developing innovative healthcare solutions to improve people's access to quality healthcare services.

7. **Clean Water and Sanitation**: Investing in clean water and sanitation projects can significantly impact public health, especially in developing regions where access to clean water is limited.

8. **Socially Responsible Funds**: These are investment funds that incorporate environmental, social, and governance (ESG) criteria into their investment strategies. They aim to support companies that adhere to sustainable and ethical practices while avoiding those with negative social or environmental impacts.

9. **Fair Trade Enterprises**: Investing in fair trade businesses ensures that workers and producers are compensated fairly and work in humane conditions, promoting social justice and economic development.

10. **Agriculture:** Agriculture can be a powerful impact investment, as it directly addresses several critical social, economic, and environmental challenges while promoting sustainable development and positive change through food sustainability and alleviation of poverty.

Impact investments allow individuals and institutions to align their financial goals with their values, fostering positive change while seeking reasonable returns. It's essential to conduct thorough research and due diligence to ensure that the investments chosen truly align with the intended positive impact.

Types of investments available

In the next chapters, we will look at the most common types of financial investments available to us. Financial investments play a crucial role in building wealth and securing a prosperous future. They offer individuals an opportunity to grow their money over time through various asset classes and investment vehicles. Understanding the different types of financial investments is essential for making informed decisions and achieving financial goals.

After a brief description of the investment types, we will look at the specific risks involved, give a Biblical perspective on each type, and offer some suggestions for impact investing.

Chapter 17. Bank products

Investing in bank products, using our analogy of the car journey of investing is akin to making a strategic pit stop at a reliable service station along the way. Just as you stop at a trusted gas station to refuel and ensure your vehicle's smooth performance, investing in a bank provides you with a secure and convenient place to park your funds and earn potential returns.

When you invest in a bank, you become a depositor, entrusting your money to the institution for safekeeping and growth. It's like handing over your keys to the attendants at the gas station, knowing that they will take care of your vehicle. Similarly, the bank offers various deposit products, such as savings accounts, certificates of deposit (CDs), or money market accounts, each with its own features, risks and benefits.

A savings account can be likened to a regular gas refill, providing easy access to your money whenever you need it while also earning some interest. It offers liquidity, allowing you to withdraw funds quickly, just as you can pull into a gas station whenever your fuel gauge is running low. A deposit account, on the other hand, resembles a pre-paid card, where you agree to leave your money parked for a fixed period, and in return, the bank offers you a higher interest rate. Just as a prepaid card gives you a discounted rate for purchasing fuel in advance, a cash deposit rewards you with better returns for committing your money for a specified term.

Investing in bank products is a conservative option that provides stability and security during your investment journey. Like a reliable service station, the bank acts as a trusted partner, safeguarding your funds and offering various options to suit your financial needs. While it may not offer the same exhilarating returns as some other investment vehicles, it serves as an essential stop on your financial trip, ensuring your money is protected and growing while you continue on your journey to achieve your long-term financial goals. Care must be given to investing in extremely high-return deposit accounts offered by banks that do not offer any deposit guarantees or have poor ratings.

By depositing funds in a bank, we not only ensure their safety and liquidity but also participate in the banking system that supports economic growth and stability. As we navigate the world of banking and investments, it is essential to be mindful of ethical considerations, avoiding participation in practices or services that go against our Christian values.

Investing in bank products

There are several options for investing in bank products, including:

1. Certificates of deposit (CDs): CDs are low-risk investments that pay a fixed rate of interest over a specified period. They can be purchased from banks and credit unions, and the term can range from a few months to several years. CDs typically have higher interest rates than savings accounts and are insured.

2. Savings accounts: Savings accounts are low-risk investments that pay a low rate of interest. They can be opened at banks and credit unions, and they typically require a low minimum balance. They are insured, and they provide easy access to your money.

3. Money market accounts: Money market accounts are similar to savings accounts, but they typically pay a higher rate of interest. They can be opened at banks and credit unions and may require a higher minimum balance than savings accounts. They also provide easy access to your money and are insured.

4. Treasury bills: These are government-issued debt securities that have a maturity of one year or less. They are considered to be among the safest investments and are issued by the national Treasury Department.

5. Bank-issued bonds: Banks may issue bonds to raise capital; these bonds pay a fixed rate of interest and return the face value of the bond at maturity. The credit rating of the bank should be taken into consideration when evaluating the risk of these bonds.

6. Deposit accounts: Banks offer other deposit accounts, like current or checking accounts, which can be used for transactions and to store cash; these accounts usually do not pay interest or pay a very low interest rate.

It's important to consider the bank's credit rating, interest rate, maturity, minimum deposit, and fees before investing in bank products. Also, it's important to consider the government insurance guarantee available and the access to the money when evaluating the risk. It's also important to consult with a financial advisor or a bank representative to understand the options, the costs and the risks involved. Additionally, it's important to have a well-diversified portfolio that includes different types of bank products to mitigate the risk.

Credit Unions

Saving in a credit union involves depositing money into a savings account offered by the organisation, which is a cooperative financial institution owned and operated by its members. Saving with a credit union offers unique advantages for disciples, as these financial institutions prioritise ethical values, member ownership, personalised service, lower fees, competitive rates, financial education, and support for local communities.

Saving with a credit union offers several specific advantages for Christians compared to a traditional bank. These advantages are rooted in the credit union's unique structure and mission, which align closely with Christian values. Choosing to save with a credit union can be a tangible expression of living out Christian values in financial decisions and aligning our resources with principles of stewardship and community support.

Here's an overview of the process and benefits of saving in a credit union:

- Membership: To save in a credit union, you typically need to become a member by meeting specific eligibility criteria, such as residing in a particular geographic area, belonging to a certain organisation, or meeting other requirements outlined by the credit union.
- Savings Account Options: Credit unions typically offer various savings account options, including regular savings accounts, share accounts, or certificates of deposit (CDs). These accounts serve as secure places to deposit and grow your savings.
- Competitive Interest Rates: Credit unions often offer competitive interest rates on savings accounts. The rates may be higher than those offered by traditional banks due to the not-for-profit nature of credit unions, which allows them to pass on earnings to their members.
- Dividends: Credit unions may distribute dividends to their members based on the profits earned by the credit union. Dividends are typically paid on share accounts or other types of savings accounts, providing an additional way to grow your savings.
- Cooperative Structure: Credit unions are owned and operated by their members, distinguishing them from banks. This cooperative structure often translates into a member-focused approach, with a commitment to providing personalised service and meeting the financial needs of their members.
- Financial Services: In addition to savings accounts, credit unions may offer various financial services, including checking accounts, loans, credit cards, and investment products. By saving in a credit union, you may have access to a range of financial products and services to help manage your finances effectively.
- Community Involvement: Credit unions often have a strong emphasis on community involvement and may support local initiatives and charitable causes or sponsor events within their

membership communities. Saving in a credit union can contribute to supporting these community-focused efforts.

• Democratic Voting Rights: As a member of a credit union, you typically have the right to vote in the credit union's decision-making processes, including the election of board members who oversee the credit union's operations. This democratic structure allows members to have a say in how the credit union is run.

Risk chat

Investing in bank products can provide a steady stream of income and can help diversify an investment portfolio, but it also comes with certain risks. Some of the risks associated with investing in bank products include:

1.   Interest rate risk: Interest rate risk is the risk that changes in interest rates will affect the value of a bank product. When interest rates rise, the value of existing bank products decreases, resulting in a loss for investors. This is particularly true for long-term investments like CDs, where the investor may not be able to reinvest at a higher rate when the CD matures.

2.   Credit risk: Credit risk refers to the risk that the bank may default on its debt obligations. This can happen if a bank is unable to make its interest or principal payments. Credit risk is higher for banks with lower credit ratings and for banks in countries with weaker economies.

3.   Inflation risk: Inflation can erode the value of bank products and other fixed-income investments. As the cost of goods and services increases, the value of a bank product's fixed interest payments decreases, resulting in a decrease in the value of the bank product.

4.   Liquidity risk: Some bank products can be difficult to sell in times of market stress, resulting in lower prices and losses for investors. This can be especially problematic for those who need to liquidate their investments quickly.

5.   Political and economic instability: Political and economic instability can affect the bank product market and the performance

of individual bank products. Wars, natural disasters, and other events can lead to market downturns and decreased bank product values.

6.   Deposit insurance: Deposit insurance is a type of insurance that protects depositors in case a bank or credit union fails. In the European Union, the Central Bank guarantees deposits up to € 100.000 per person. In the United States, the Federal Deposit Insurance Corporation (FDIC) insures deposits of up to $250,000 per depositor per institution. In the European Union, deposits are guaranteed up to € 100.000. However, there is a risk that the deposit insurance scheme may not be able to cover all depositors in case of a bank failure.

7.   Cybersecurity risks: Cybersecurity risks are a significant concern for banks and investors alike. Hackers can target bank accounts, steal personal information, and use it for fraudulent activities. This can lead to financial losses and can cause a lack of trust in online platforms.

8.   Tax implications: Investing in bank products may have tax implications depending on the country and the bank product. It's important to consult with a tax professional to understand the tax implications of investing in bank products.

It's important to note that these risks can vary depending on the specific bank product and the overall market conditions. To minimise the risks, it's important to do your due diligence before investing.

Biblical perspective

Should we invest in a bank at all? Jesus did not object to putting money in a bank - but only as a last resort, as described in His parable of the Talents. "So you ought to have deposited my money with the bankers, and at my coming, I would have received back my own with interest." (Matthew 25; 27). This was one of the options to invest, but certainly not preferred not excluded. The original Greek words used for 'deposited' mean to 'throw money on the banker's table. The word for bankers is 'τραπεζίτης', ('*trapezitēs*'), which is used as a money-broker or banker - one who exchanges money for a fee and pays interest on a deposit. These money changers or bankers were quite common in Palestine and wherever the Jewish community was established. They received deposits at interest and engaged in transactions such as are usual in modern times.

Some Christian objections to debt lending when investing are rooted in biblical principles and ethical considerations. While not all forms of debt lending are inherently problematic, certain practices and scenarios may raise concerns for Christians. Here are some objections:

- Usury and Exploitation: The Bible warns against usury, which refers to the charging of excessive interest on loans (Exodus 22:25, Leviticus 25:36-37). Christians may object to investing in businesses or institutions that engage in exploitative lending practices, taking advantage of vulnerable borrowers and perpetuating cycles of debt.
- Encouraging Consumerism: Some forms of debt lending, particularly those targeting consumer purchases, may encourage materialism and consumerism. As Christians, we are called to avoid being driven by the desire for wealth and possessions and instead seek contentment in God (1 Timothy 6:10, Philippians 4:11-12).
- Enabling Unwise Financial Decisions: Investing in debt lending platforms that cater to individuals with poor credit or limited financial literacy may raise ethical concerns. Christians may question whether supporting such practices aligns with the biblical principles of wisdom and stewardship (Proverbs 3:13, Proverbs 22:7).
- Social Impact: Christians may be concerned about the social impact of debt lending, especially in cases where loans contribute to poverty, financial distress, or economic inequality. Investing in institutions that prioritise profit over the well-being of borrowers may contradict the call to love and care for others (Proverbs 14:31, Proverbs 22:22).
- Ethical Considerations: Some Christians may object to debt lending investments due to the nature of the borrowers or the use of funds. For instance, investing in payday lending companies that charge exorbitant interest rates could be viewed as exploiting the financially vulnerable (Proverbs 22:16, James 5:4).

- Risk of Default: Debt lending investments carry inherent risks of borrower default, which can lead to financial losses for investors. Christians may be cautious about investing in ventures that may cause financial harm to others if they are unable to repay their debts.

It is essential to note that not all debt lending practices are inherently unethical, and some forms of lending can be beneficial when used responsibly and ethically. As with any investment decision, Christians are encouraged to seek wisdom, discernment, and guidance from God through prayer and study of the Scriptures. Understanding the implications of debt lending investments and considering the potential impact on borrowers and society can help Christians make informed decisions that align with their faith and values.

Christian Banks

Christian banks, also known as faith-based or values-based banks, are financial institutions that operate with a distinct Christian mission and align their operations with biblical principles. While each Christian bank may have its unique characteristics, some common features differentiate them from traditional banks. Here are some key aspects that make Christian banks different:

- Faith-Based Mission: The primary differentiator of Christian banks is their faith-based mission. These institutions are founded on Christian values, guided by biblical principles, and seek to integrate their faith into all aspects of their business operations.
- Ethical and Responsible Banking: Christian banks prioritise ethical and responsible banking practices. They avoid investing in or financing activities that go against Christian values, such as gambling, alcohol, tobacco, or industries that harm people or the environment.
- Stewardship and Community Focus: Christian banks often emphasise stewardship principles and prioritise the well-being of their customers and communities. They may offer financial literacy

programmes and community development initiatives and support local charities and ministries.

- Personalised Service: Christian banks typically offer personalised and relational customer service. They focus on building long-term relationships with their customers, understanding their unique financial needs, and providing tailored solutions.
- Tithing and Giving: Some Christian banks may have programs or options that allow customers to allocate a portion of their profits or interest towards charitable causes or their church. This reinforces the concept of tithing and encourages giving back to the community.
- Transparency and Accountability: Christian banks aim to operate with transparency and accountability, ensuring that their actions align with their stated values and that they are held to high ethical standards.
- Socially Responsible Investments: Christian banks may offer socially responsible investment options that allow customers to invest in businesses and projects that align with their Christian values and have a positive social and environmental impact.
- Non-Profit Status: Some Christian banks operate as non-profit institutions, reinvesting their earnings back into their operations and the communities they serve rather than maximising profits for shareholders.

It is important to note that while Christian banks emphasise their faith-based mission, they are subject to the same regulatory requirements as other financial institutions and offer similar banking services and products. Individuals considering banking with a Christian bank should research their specific offerings, values, and mission to ensure alignment with their own beliefs and financial needs.

Examples of Christian banks include:

Kingdom Bank - UK. The bank states; [20]

"We give your money a mission. Customers depositing with us can be assured that their money is being used with gospel priorities. Money deposited with us is used to support Kingdom work across the country through churches, Christian charities, and ministry workers. By receiving a slightly lower rate than they might find elsewhere, they have the reward of seeing their money put to work for the gospel in eternally valuable ways, as it is used to support churches, Christian charities, and ministry workers."

The American AdfeFi Bank makes sure its investments reflect biblical values. They write, [21]

"Across the globe, AdelFi members partner with fellow believers to steward God-given financial resources and substantially affect the world for Christ through purposeful investing and giving. Our promise is that we give at least 10% of profits each year to organisations that help spread Christian values. We can impact the world through every account, loan, and dollar our members entrust to us. For nearly 60 years, we have collaborated with those of shared faith to create positive change and be the salt and light of the earth. In 2022 alone, we've contributed over $3.5 million through grants, tithes, and donations and volunteered 670+ staff hours to non-profits, ministries, and missionaries committed to serving the Lord and spreading His word.

Unlike traditional big banks, which may invest their customers' money in causes that may not be aligned with Christian values or financial institutions that are beholden to Wall Street investors, AdelFi is owned and controlled by its members who share the same faith. Supporting individuals, families, ministries, businesses, and those wanting their banks to be aligned with their same values is what separates AdelFi from others in the industry."

Impact investing

Christian impact investing in banks combines the principles of impact investing with a biblical worldview, aiming to align financial decisions with Christian values and contribute to positive social and environmental outcomes. It involves directing capital towards financial institutions that actively support projects and businesses aligned with biblical principles of justice, compassion, and stewardship.

Christian impact investing seeks to address various societal challenges through investments that promote human flourishing and sustainable development. These investments may focus on areas such as poverty alleviation, affordable housing, clean energy, healthcare, education, and ethical business practices. By choosing to invest in banks that prioritise social responsibility and environmental stewardship, Christians can actively participate in advancing God's Kingdom values in the world of finance.

A key aspect of Christian impact investing is a thorough evaluation of the social and environmental impact of investment opportunities. Banks engaging in this approach conduct rigorous assessments to ensure that the projects they finance contribute to the well-being of individuals and communities while respecting human dignity and promoting justice and fairness.

Moreover, Christian impact investing emphasises the concept of stewardship, recognising that all resources, including financial assets, belong to God. As stewards of God's resources, Christians are called to use them responsibly and for the greater good, seeking to be faithful in making a positive impact on society and the environment.

Christian impact investing in banks goes beyond seeking financial returns; it also aims to achieve measurable and lasting positive outcomes in alignment with biblical teachings. By investing in projects that promote human dignity, care for the vulnerable, and respect for God's creation, Christians can be actively involved in fulfilling their calling to be agents of positive change in the world.

Through intentional and principled investment choices, Christian impact investing in banks provides an opportunity for individuals and institutions to integrate their faith with their financial decisions, making a meaningful difference and contributing to a more just, compassionate, and sustainable world. This approach exemplifies the belief that financial resources can be a powerful tool for advancing God's Kingdom and bringing about transformational change in society.

Chapter 18: Bonds market

A bond is a type of investment in which an investor loans money to an organisation (such as a government or enterprise) in exchange for regular interest payments and the return on the original investment at the end of the agreed period.

Investing in bonds in the car journey of investing is akin to choosing a reliable and comfortable passenger car for a smooth and steady ride. Bonds are debt securities issued by governments or corporations, and they represent loans that investors provide to these entities in exchange for regular interest payments and the return of the principal amount at maturity.

Just like a passenger car that offers a secure and predictable travel experience, investing in bonds provides a level of safety and stability in your investment journey. Bonds are considered less volatile compared to other asset classes like stocks, making them a suitable choice for conservative investors seeking steady income and capital preservation.

The interest payments received from bonds are like the well-maintained engine of the passenger car, providing a consistent source of income throughout the investment period. These interest payments, also known as coupon payments, are typically paid at fixed intervals, such as annually or semi-annually. The predetermined interest rate of the bond is like the fuel efficiency of the car, providing a clear understanding of the returns you can expect.

Furthermore, the maturity date of the bond is like the planned arrival time for your investment. Just as a passenger car ensures you reach your destination on schedule, bonds offer a predetermined date when your initial investment will be returned in full. This aspect of bonds allows investors to match their investment time horizon with their financial goals, whether short-term or long-term.

However, just as passengers might encounter some traffic along the way, investing in bonds is not entirely risk-free. The main risk associated with bonds is interest rate risk. If interest rates rise after you purchase a bond, its value may decrease in the secondary market. Yet, by holding the bond to maturity, investors can avoid this risk and receive the promised returns as agreed.

In conclusion, investing in bonds is like choosing a reliable passenger car for your investment journey. Bonds offer stability, consistent income, and a predetermined timeline for the return of your initial investment. As an integral part of a diversified portfolio, bonds provide a balanced and secure ride, complementing other asset classes in your quest to achieve your financial goals.

Investing in bonds

Investing in bonds can provide a steady stream of income and can help to diversify an investment portfolio. Some of the ways to invest in the bond market include:

1. Corporate bonds: Corporate bonds are issued by companies as a way to raise capital. They pay a fixed rate of interest and return the face value of the bond at maturity. Corporate bonds can provide a higher rate of return than government bonds, but they also come with a higher level of risk.

2. Government bonds: Government bonds, also known as Treasury bonds, are issued by national governments as a way to raise capital. They pay a fixed rate of interest and return the face value of the bond at maturity. Government bonds are considered to be among the safest investments, but they also come with lower returns compared to other types of bonds.

3. Municipal bonds: Municipal bonds, also known as munis, are issued by state and local governments as a way to raise capital for public projects. They pay a fixed rate of interest and return the face value of the bond at maturity. Municipal bonds are tax-free at the federal level and may also be tax-free at the state and local levels, making them an attractive investment for those in high tax brackets.

4. Treasury inflation-protected securities (TIPS): TIPS are a type of government bond that is designed to protect against inflation. The interest rate and the face value of the bond are adjusted for inflation, providing a hedge against rising prices.

5. Floating rate bonds: Floating rate bonds are a type of bond that pays a variable rate of interest that is tied to a benchmark interest rate, such as the London Interbank Offered Rate (LIBOR). This can provide a higher rate of return in a rising interest rate environment but also comes with the risk of lower returns in a falling interest rate environment.

6. High-yield bonds: High-yield bonds, also known as junk bonds, are issued by companies with lower credit ratings. They pay a higher rate of interest than investment-grade bonds but also come with a higher level of risk.

7. Bond funds: Bond funds are a way to invest in a diversified portfolio of bonds. They provide the benefits of diversification and can be a good option for those who want to invest in bonds but do not want to buy individual bonds.

8. Bond ETFs: Bond ETFs are similar to bond funds, but they trade on stock exchanges like individual stocks. They provide a way to invest in a basket of bonds or a specific sector or index with the convenience of buying and selling shares like stocks.

9. Bond laddering: Bond laddering is a strategy that involves buying bonds with different maturity dates. This can provide a steady stream of income and can also help to mitigate the risk of interest rate fluctuations.

10. Zero-Coupon Bonds: Bonds that do not pay regular interest but are sold at a discount to face value and mature at face value.

Risks chat

It's important to note that investing in bonds comes with different levels of risk and reward. It's important to consult with a financial advisor or investment professional to understand the options, the costs, and the risks involved and also to evaluate which one would best fit your individual needs and goals. It's also important to do your own research and stay informed about current market conditions and trends in the bond market. Additionally, it's important to have a well-diversified portfolio that includes bonds with different credit ratings, maturities, and sectors to mitigate the risks involved.

Bonds cannot be described as safe or unsafe per se. As we have already seen, the risk of a bond stands and falls with the solvency of the borrower. Therefore, the biggest risk with bonds is the so-called issuer risk: If the issuer of a bond gets into financial difficulties and, in the worst case, becomes insolvent, he can only repay the borrowed money with delay, proportionally or, in the worst case, not at all. In this case, there is a risk of total loss of the invested or lent money.

Investing in bonds can provide a steady stream of income and diversify an investment portfolio, but it also comes with certain risks. Some of the risks associated with investing in the bond market include:

1. Interest rate risk: Interest rates and bond prices have an inverse relationship, meaning when interest rates rise, bond prices fall, and vice versa. This can result in losses for bondholders, particularly for those holding long-term bonds.

2. Credit risk: Credit risk refers to the risk that a bond issuer will default on its debt and fail to make interest or principal payments. This risk is higher for bonds issued by companies with lower credit ratings.

3. Inflation risk: Inflation can erode the value of fixed-income investments, such as bonds, over time. As the cost of goods and services increases, the purchasing power of the income generated by bonds decreases, which can result in a loss of purchasing power for bondholders.

4. Liquidity risk: Bonds can be difficult to sell in times of market stress, resulting in lower prices and losses for investors. This can be especially problematic for those who need to liquidate their investments quickly.

5. Reinvestment risk: When a bond matures, the bondholder must reinvest the proceeds at prevailing interest rates, which may be lower than the bond's coupon rate. This can result in a lower income stream for the investor.

6. Political and economic instability: Political and economic instability can affect the bond market and the performance of individual bonds. Wars, natural disasters, and other events can lead to market downturns and decreased bond values.

7. Currency risk: If the bond is denominated in foreign currency, the bond price and the interest payments will be affected by the currency exchange rate. This can result in a loss of value for the bondholder if the currency depreciates.

8. Call risk: Some bonds can be called by the issuer before maturity, which means the issuer can redeem the bond at a set price before the maturity date. This can result in a loss of income for the bondholder and can also limit the bondholder's ability to reinvest the proceeds at a higher rate.

9. Duration risk: Bonds with longer maturities have a longer duration, which means they're more sensitive to interest rate changes. This can result in a greater loss of value for long-term bonds if interest rates rise.

10. Market risk: The bond market can be affected by changes in the overall economic conditions; this can lead to market downturns and decreased bond values.

It's important to note that these risks can vary depending on the specific bond and the overall market conditions. To minimise the risks, it's important to do your due diligence before investing in any bond and also to consult with a financial advisor or investment professional to understand the options, the costs and the risks involved. Additionally, it's important to have a well-diversified portfolio that includes bonds with different credit ratings, maturities, and sectors to mitigate the risk.

Biblical perspective

From a Christian perspective, investing in bonds can be subject to critique and consideration. While not inherently wrong, there are certain aspects to be mindful of:

• Stewardship of Resources: Christians are called to be good stewards of the resources entrusted to them by God. Investing in bonds can be seen as responsible stewardship, as it allows for the preservation and growth of wealth, which can be used to support one's family, contribute to the community, and further God's kingdom. However, the motivation behind investing should be examined. If the desire for financial gain becomes excessive or supersedes priorities such as helping the needy or supporting charitable causes, it can be a cause for concern.

• Ethical Considerations: Bonds may involve supporting entities whose activities are inconsistent with Christian values. Some bonds may be issued by companies involved in practices that go against biblical principles, such as gambling, tobacco, or pornography. Christians should carefully research the issuer and consider whether investing in such bonds aligns with their ethical beliefs.

• Trust in God vs. Reliance on Financial Security: Investing in bonds can become a means of seeking security and control over one's financial future. While wise financial planning is important, Christians are reminded to trust in God's provision and not place their ultimate trust in worldly wealth. It is crucial to maintain a balance between financial prudence and reliance on God's guidance and provision.

Ultimately, the decision to invest in bonds should be based on individual discernment, guided by biblical principles, and seeking the wisdom of the Holy Spirit. Christians should prayerfully consider the potential impact of their investments, ensuring that their financial choices align with their faith and contribute to the greater good in a manner consistent with their values.

The whole gamut of government spending, from overseas aid to defence spending, is financed by government borrowing since it makes up the shortfall in taxation that would otherwise be needed. Essentially, public borrowing takes current savings and uses them to finance the present and past unwillingness of governments to impose upon their taxpayers the full costs of their spending decisions. As such, buying government debt serves little productive purpose.

There is not even the risk of default to justify this return, and future generations of taxpayers are burdened to finance current expenditures.

Impact investing in the bonds market

By engaging in Christian impact investing with bonds, Christians can integrate their faith with their financial decisions, using their resources to support projects and initiatives that reflect God's love and concern for the well-being of all individuals. It represents a purpose-driven approach to investing that seeks to make a positive difference in the world while achieving both financial and ethical objectives.

Impact investing in the bonds market involves making investment decisions in fixed-income securities, such as bonds, with the intention of generating positive social or environmental impact alongside financial returns. Impact investors seek out bonds issued by organisations, municipalities, or governments that are actively addressing pressing societal and environmental challenges.

Here's how impact investing in the bonds market typically works:

- Identifying Impact Objectives: Impact investors begin by defining their specific social or environmental objectives. These could include supporting clean energy projects, funding affordable housing initiatives, financing education programs, promoting sustainable agriculture, or addressing healthcare disparities.

- Research and Analysis: Once the impact objectives are set, investors research and analyse different bonds to find issuers whose projects align with their goals. They consider the issuer's mission, sustainability practices, and the intended use of the bond proceeds.

- Impact Measurement: Measuring the impact of bond investments is essential. Impact investors often work with organisations that provide impact measurement metrics to assess the social and environmental outcomes of their investments.
- Green and Social Bonds: In recent years, green bonds and social bonds have gained popularity in the bonds market. Green bonds finance environmentally beneficial projects, such as renewable energy installations or climate change adaptation efforts. Social bonds, on the other hand, fund projects with specific social objectives, like affordable housing, healthcare, or education initiatives.
- Engagement and Advocacy: Impact investors may engage with bond issuers to encourage further commitment to sustainability or social progress. They may also advocate for greater transparency and disclosure of impact data.
- Integration with Fixed-Income Portfolio: Impact bonds can be integrated into a broader fixed-income portfolio to diversify risk while maintaining a focus on impact goals.
- Financial Returns: Impact investors recognise that while generating positive social and environmental impact is essential, financial returns are also a crucial aspect. They aim to achieve competitive returns while contributing to positive change.

Impact investing in the bonds market enables investors to leverage their capital to support projects and initiatives that align with their values and contribute to a more sustainable and equitable world. By investing in bonds that drive positive change, impact investors play an active role in addressing global challenges and influencing organisations and governments to prioritise social and environmental responsibility.

Chapter 19: Shares - stock market

Investing in the stock market in the car journey of investing is like embarking on an exciting and adventurous road trip. The stock market represents a dynamic highway filled with various companies, each offering a unique opportunity for investors to become partial owners and share in their successes and challenges.

Just as a road trip offers a range of destinations to explore, the stock market presents a diverse array of companies from different industries and sectors. Each company is like a distinct vehicle on the road, with its own performance history, growth potential, and risk profile. Investing in the stock market allows you to select the companies you believe will thrive and benefit from their success.

Similar to how a road trip can have some twists and turns, the stock market can experience ups and downs. Share prices can fluctuate due to market conditions, economic factors, or company-specific news. Just as travellers adjust their driving speed according to road conditions, investors must assess their risk tolerance and make informed decisions on when to accelerate, slow down, or even take a detour.

The stock market journey provides the potential for high-speed growth and exhilarating returns. Like a thrilling ride on a highway, investing in the stock market can offer the opportunity to build wealth and achieve significant long-term gains. However, it is important to exercise caution and prudence, as stock market investing also involves risks. Just as a responsible driver follows traffic rules and wears a seatbelt, a prudent investor diversifies their portfolio and research to make well-informed investment choices.

Moreover, investing in the stock market requires a long-term perspective. Like a well-planned road trip, successful stock market investing involves setting clear financial goals, developing a strategy, and staying focused on the destination despite occasional detours. By taking a patient and disciplined approach, investors can weather market volatility and benefit from the power of compounding over time.

As we delve into stock investments, it's not necessary to perceive the stock market solely as a competitive arena driven by individual pursuits of profit. Instead, we can regard it as a chance to channel our financial resources into productive and life-enriching ventures that contribute to the flourishing of the world.

Investing in the stock market

Investing in the stock market can be a great way to build wealth and create a diversified investment portfolio. Some of the ways to invest in the stock market include:

1. Direct stock purchase: This method of investing involves buying shares of a specific company directly from the company or through a direct stock purchase plan (DSPP). DSPPs are investment plans offered by companies that allow investors to purchase shares directly from the company, usually at a discounted price.

2. Stockbrokers: Another way to invest in the stock market is through a stockbroker. Stockbrokers are licensed professionals who buy and sell stocks on behalf of their clients. They can provide advice and recommendations on which stocks to buy and sell and can also assist with the buying and selling process.

3. Online trading platforms: Online trading platforms, also known as online brokers, are a popular way for individuals to invest in the stock market. These platforms allow investors to research, buy, and sell stocks online with little or no human intervention. They tend

to have lower fees than traditional stockbrokers but also come with the risk of a lack of human expertise and guidance.

4. Mutual funds: Mutual funds are investment vehicles that allow investors to pool their money together to buy a diversified portfolio of stocks. This can help to mitigate the risk of investing in a single stock and also provide access to professionally managed portfolios.

5. Exchange-traded funds (ETFs): ETFs are similar to mutual funds, but they trade on stock exchanges like individual stocks. They provide a way to invest in a basket of stocks or a specific sector or index with the convenience of buying and selling shares like stocks.

6. Retirement accounts: Retirement accounts, such as 401(k) plans and individual retirement accounts (IRAs), are a way for individuals to invest in the stock market and save for retirement. These accounts have tax benefits and also come with restrictions and penalties for withdrawals before the retirement age.

7. Robo-advisors: These are digital platforms that use algorithms to manage portfolios of stocks and other investments. They provide a more affordable and automated way to invest in the stock market but also come with the risk of a lack of human expertise and guidance.

8. Private equity: Private equity is another way to invest in the stock market. It involves investing in private companies that are not publicly traded. Private equity investments can provide higher returns but also come with a higher level of risk and less liquidity.

Risks chat

It's important to note that investing in the stock market comes with different levels of risk and reward. It's important to consult with a financial advisor or investment professional to understand the options, the costs, and the risks involved and also to evaluate which one would best fit your individual needs and goals. It's also important to do your own research and stay informed about current market conditions and trends in the stock market. Additionally, it's important to have a well-diversified portfolio and not to put all your eggs in one basket by investing in one or a few stocks.

Diversification can help mitigate risk, and it's also important to have a long-term investment horizon.

Investing in the stock market can be a great way to build wealth, but it also comes with certain risks. Some of the risks associated with investing in the stock market include:

- Market fluctuations: The stock market is subject to fluctuations, and the value of individual stocks and the overall market can go up and down. This can result in losses for investors, especially if they have to sell their shares during a market downturn.
- Company-specific risks: The performance of a stock is closely tied to the performance of the company that issues it. If a company performs poorly, its stock value will likely decrease, resulting in a loss for investors.
- Interest rate risk: The stock market can be affected by changes in interest rates. When interest rates rise, the value of stocks may decrease as investors shift their money to fixed-income investments that offer higher returns.
- Inflation risk: Inflation can erode the value of stocks and other investments. As the cost of goods and services increases, the value of a company's earnings decreases and may result in a decrease in the value of the stock.
- Political and economic instability: Political and economic instability can affect the stock market and the performance of individual stocks. Wars, natural disasters, and other events can lead to market downturns and decreased stock values.
- Liquidity risk: Stocks can be difficult to sell in times of market stress, resulting in lower prices and losses for investors. This can be especially problematic for those who need to liquidate their investments quickly.
- Lack of diversification: Investing in a few stocks can make the portfolio more concentrated and increase the risk. It's important to have a diversified portfolio to mitigate the risk.
- Insider trading and fraud: There is a risk that a company's insiders, such as its executives, may use non-public information to trade its stock for personal gain; this is called insider trading. Additionally, some companies may engage in fraudulent activities,

such as cooking their books, which can result in significant losses for investors.

• Cybersecurity risks: Hackers can target online brokerage accounts, steal personal information, and use it for fraudulent activities. This can lead to financial losses and can cause a lack of trust in online platforms.

It's important to note that these risks can vary depending on the specific stock and the overall market conditions.

Biblical perspective

When the Bible was written, it was an agrarian economy. Wealth was created mainly by owning land and using it to grow crops or raise livestock. The Bible uses examples of investing in real estate because that was the common form of investing at that time. However, it is not an endorsement of real estate over other forms of investing.

At its most basic level, owning stock is owning a piece of a company. That ownership entitles you to vote on important issues facing the company, receive income from the company's operations (called dividends) and participate in the growth/decline of the company through the increase/decrease of the share price.

Investing in the stock market is not the right decision for everyone, but it can provide long-term growth.

Influence

Shareholders can influence company policy – they receive the company's accounts and statements; they can put forward motions and can vote at AGMs on the composition of the board and on the outcome of takeovers. If the company is involved in an unethical practice or product, the matter can be raised formally with the company, and the share can be sold if no change is forthcoming. It would seem, therefore, that shares are a more principled outlet for a Christian's savings than a bank deposit, especially if they are owned in a small local or family business where sufficient time can be devoted to be concerned with the management of the firm ('Business Angel' investment).

These ethical benefits are also enjoyed by workers who own shares in their company. Not only is return related to risk-taking, but employees are in a better position to know how their company is behaving and to object if this is immoral. (The one caution about employees owning a substantial part of their savings in the form of their company's shares is that they are very vulnerable if company bankruptcy means they lose their jobs, shares, and maximum pension rights.)

To help decide whether or not a Christian is justified in participating in the stock market, we can ask ourselves three questions. First, can we invest on a "limited liability" basis? Secondly, is the degree of risk involved in the stock market of such a nature that participants are, in fact, just legalised gambling? Third, could I support the separation of ownership and management?

1. Limited liability?

Although limited liability facilitates trading in shares and the growth of large corporations, it breaches one important ethical principle – the small matter of paying one's debts.

As business enterprises became more complex and needed increasing amounts of capital to operate, this organisational form was devised to allow a large number of investors to become part owners of a business without being involved in its daily operations. The stock market is merely a means for buying and selling these part-ownerships or shares in a corporation.

Christians have had, and rightly so, significant concerns about using incorporation as a legal device to escape from their debts. To show that Christians may incorporate their businesses would require a separate article. Let me merely observe that it now appears to be quite generally accepted among us. I believe that unless one incorporates with the intent to defraud or engage in ventures that are so risky that you would not do so without incorporation, this legal form is permissible.

However, if you believe that a Christian should not incorporate, it logically follows that you should also not buy shares in a corporation; by buying shares, you also accept the benefits of limited liability. If such a stand is necessary, consistency demands also that you take a close look at your pension and registered retirement savings plans. Many of us indirectly hold company shares through such plans.

Limited liability permits the separation of a firm's ownership from the exercise of managerial control. This allows shareholders to treat their shares as purely financial investments and take little interest in how their company is being run. Indeed, they will own so little of a large company that it is not worth their while making an effort to monitor the management.

Personally, I do not think such drastic action is required. However, I do believe that we do not limit our responsibilities when we buy shares in corporations. We are accountable for the actions taken by the companies in which we invest. Therefore, our choice of shares must be restricted to those of companies that, as far as we are aware, do not act against Biblical principles. As a minimum, this condition requires personal involvement and study of our investment choices. Not for us, investment based on an uninformed tip!

The market: The stock market performs a necessary role as one means of putting savings into productive use. Its participants indirectly assist businesses in developing world resources as good stewardship demands of us.

The primary market makes it possible for corporations to raise the necessary capital. An efficient market makes it possible to raise funds speedily and at a relatively low cost.

Secondary market: By providing a marketplace to allow one to sell shares virtually whenever one chooses, the secondary market provides "liquidity" and makes share-buying possible for many people or institutions that would otherwise not be able to invest. Money set aside for retirement, for example, could not be invested in shares because, eventually, that money will need to be available to live on

2. Gambling

Certain approaches to "playing the market," such as options and futures, can resemble gambling, though they can serve as hedges to mitigate risk. However, regular buying and selling of shares is not a gamble. Day-trading and other forms of investing dependent on luck rather than wise decisions and long-term planning should be avoided.

Speculating, on the other hand, is a normal aspect of the stock market, defined as buying and selling securities with the intention of capital gains based on market fluctuations unrelated to a company's earnings and dividends. Speculators may target stocks they expect to rise quickly, banking on positive news or changes in popularity.

Such speculative activities should be avoided by financial disciples since they often stem from greed and the "something for nothing" philosophy, leading to potential financial disaster in the long run. Nevertheless, professional speculators play a vital role in the market, providing liquidity, promoting price stability, and ensuring efficient market benefits for a diverse range of companies. Although even professionals can be susceptible to greed, their expertise and effort make such activities permissible from a Christian standpoint for those with the required skills and commitment.

3. Separation of ownership and management

When ownership and management are separated, decision-makers may prioritise profit maximisation over ethical considerations, leading to practices that exploit employees or harm the environment.

The separation of ownership and management can also lead to a lack of accountability in decision-making. Christian teachings emphasise the importance of integrity and honesty in all aspects of life, including business practices (Proverbs 11:3, Colossians 3:9-10). When management is not held accountable to the interests and values of shareholders or owners, there is a potential for conflicts of interest and decisions that prioritise personal gain over the well-being of the company and Its stakeholders.

When ownership demands short-term profits, there can be several consequences for the management of a company. These consequences can impact the overall performance, sustainability, and reputation of the business. Here are some possible outcomes:

- Focus on Immediate Results: Management may be pressured to prioritise short-term gains over long-term strategic planning. This can lead to decision-making that prioritises immediate profits, often at the expense of investing in research, development, and employee development for future growth.

- Reduced Investment in Innovation: When the emphasis is solely on short-term profits, management may cut back on investments in research, innovation, and development of new products or services. This lack of investment in innovation can hamper the company's ability to stay competitive in the long run.
- Neglect of Employee Welfare: Management might be driven to implement cost-cutting measures that negatively impact employees, such as layoffs, reduced benefits, or low wages. Neglecting employee welfare can result in reduced morale, decreased productivity, and higher employee turnover.
- Sacrificing Ethical Practices: To achieve short-term profits, management may be tempted to compromise on ethical principles. This can lead to practices that harm the environment, exploit workers, or engage in unethical business practices, ultimately tarnishing the company's reputation and public trust.
- Disregarding Corporate Social Responsibility: A focus on short-term profits may lead management to disregard corporate social responsibility initiatives, such as community engagement, environmental sustainability, and philanthropy. This can negatively impact the company's relationship with stakeholders and the community.
- Volatility in Stock Price: Overemphasis on short-term profits can lead to fluctuations in the company's stock price. Shareholders might react negatively to any deviations from expected short-term results, causing instability in the stock market.
- Decreased Customer Loyalty: Prioritising short-term profits may lead to decisions that prioritise cost-cutting over customer satisfaction and loyalty. This can result in reduced customer retention and diminished brand loyalty.

To mitigate the consequences of demanding short-term profits, a balanced approach is necessary. Management should be encouraged to prioritise long-term sustainable growth, ethical practices, employee well-being, and corporate social responsibility. This can lead to a more resilient and reputable company that serves the interests of both shareholders and the wider community.

The Christian case for integrating ownership with management in a company is rooted in principles of responsible stewardship, ethical leadership, and accountability.

Integrating ownership and management allows owners to actively participate in the decision-making process, ensuring that the company's operations align with Christian values and principles. Owners who are actively involved in management are more likely to prioritise the well-being of all stakeholders, including employees, customers, and the community, over short-term profit maximisation.

Integrating ownership with management also fosters a culture of ethical leadership and accountability within the company. Christian teachings emphasise the importance of integrity and honesty in all aspects of life, including business (Proverbs 11:3, Colossians 3:17). When owners are directly responsible for the management of the company, they are more likely to make decisions that align with their values and moral convictions. This sense of responsibility promotes transparency, encourages ethical behaviour, and ensures that the company's actions are in line with the principles of love, justice, and compassion advocated in the Christian faith. Ultimately, integrating ownership with management in a company allows for a more holistic approach to business that takes into account the spiritual and moral dimensions of leadership and decision-making.

Impact investing

Impact investing with stocks involves making investment decisions in publicly traded companies based not only on their financial performance but also on their social and environmental impact. The goal is to align investment choices with specific social or environmental causes while still seeking a financial return. Impact investors seek to support companies that are actively working towards positive change in areas such as sustainability, renewable energy, diversity and inclusion, community development, and other socially responsible initiatives.

When engaging in impact investing with stocks, investors carefully research and analyse companies to understand their practices, policies, and impact on various stakeholders. They may look for companies with strong environmental, social, and governance (ESG) performance, which indicates a commitment to responsible business practices.

Impact investors may actively seek out companies that are making strides in areas such as reducing their carbon footprint, promoting gender equality and diversity in leadership, supporting fair labour practices, and contributing positively to their local communities. These investors may also avoid companies involved in activities that conflict with their values, such as those contributing to environmental degradation or human rights violations.

There are several ways to practice impact investing with stocks:

- Direct Investment: Investors can directly invest in individual stocks of companies that align with their impact goals.
- Impact-Focused Funds: Many mutual funds and exchange-traded funds (ETFs) are specifically designed for impact investing. These funds target companies with strong ESG performance and align with specific impact themes.
- Shareholder Advocacy: Impact investors may use their influence as shareholders to advocate for positive change within companies. They can engage in dialogues with management, propose resolutions, and vote on important issues during shareholder meetings.
- Negative Screening: Some impact investors choose to apply negative screening, where they exclude certain companies or industries from their investment portfolio due to their involvement in harmful activities.
- Positive Screening: Conversely, positive screening involves actively seeking out companies with strong ESG practices and a track record of making a positive impact.

Impact investing with stocks allows investors to not only seek financial returns but also contribute to creating a better world by supporting companies that are making a difference in various social and environmental aspects. This approach empowers investors to use their financial resources to drive positive change and encourage businesses to prioritise sustainability, responsibility, and societal well-being.

Chapter 20: Real Estate

Investing in real estate in the car journey of investing is like choosing to take a scenic and rewarding route that offers both stability and potential for long-term growth. Real estate represents the diverse landscape of properties, each with its unique characteristics and investment potential, much like the various towns and attractions along a picturesque road trip.

Just as a road trip allows you to explore different locations, real estate investing offers a range of options, from residential properties such as houses and apartments to commercial properties like office buildings, retail spaces, and industrial complexes; each property is like a distinct destination on your investment journey, offering the opportunity to generate rental income and potential property appreciation over time.

Similar to how a well-located destination can become a tourist hotspot, investing in real estate involves carefully selecting properties in strategic locations. Factors such as proximity to amenities, transportation hubs, schools, and business centres can significantly impact the property's value and rental demand. Just as travellers look for desirable and convenient places to visit, real estate investors seek properties with the potential for strong rental demand and capital growth.

Moreover, real estate investing requires careful navigation and due diligence, much like driving through unfamiliar terrain. Investors must conduct thorough research, perform property inspections, and consider factors like market trends, local regulations, and property management to make informed decisions. Like using a GPS to plan your route, real estate investors create a sound investment strategy that aligns with their financial goals and risk tolerance.

Real estate investing also offers the potential for passive income, much like a rest stop along the way. Rental income from properties can provide a steady stream of cash flow, allowing investors to build wealth and achieve financial freedom over time. Additionally, real estate investments can act as a hedge against inflation, providing a sense of security and stability, much like finding a comfortable lodging during a road trip.

Investing in real estate

Real estate refers to the ownership, use, and development of land and buildings. It encompasses both residential and commercial properties, including houses, apartments, retail spaces, office buildings, and industrial facilities. It is often considered a tangible asset, as it involves the purchase of physical property, and can provide a stable source of income through rental income or appreciation in value over time.

Real estate investment can take several forms, including buying and holding properties for rental income, investing in real estate investment trusts (REITs), or participating in real estate crowdfunding or syndication.

There are several types of real estate investments, including:

1. Residential Properties: This includes single-family homes, multi-unit buildings, and condominiums.

2. Commercial Properties: This includes office buildings, retail spaces, and industrial properties.

3. Land: This includes undeveloped or agricultural land, as well as land for commercial or residential development.

4. Real Estate Investment Trusts (REITs): REITs are publicly traded companies that own and manage income-generating

properties and provide investors with access to a diversified portfolio of real estate assets.

5. Real Estate Crowdfunding: This allows individual investors to pool their money and invest in real estate projects, typically with lower minimum investment requirements compared to traditional real estate investments.

6. Real Estate Syndication: This is a form of partnership in which several investors pool their money to purchase a property, with the profits being shared among the partners.

7. Real Estate Development: This involves the acquisition of land and the construction of new properties or the renovation of existing properties for resale or rental.

Investing in real estate can be a great way to build wealth and create a steady stream of income. Some of the opportunities that come with investing in real estate include:

1. Appreciation: Real estate values can increase over time, providing investors with the potential for significant returns on their investment. As the value of the property increases, so does the equity in the property, which can be used to finance future investments or to provide a source of income through renting or flipping the property.

2. Income: Renting out a property can provide a consistent stream of income, which can be used to cover expenses and make mortgage payments. Investing in real estate can also provide a significant return on investment, especially if the property is located in an area with high demand for rental properties.

3. Tax benefits: Real estate investors can take advantage of tax benefits, such as deductions for mortgage interest, depreciation, and property taxes. These deductions can significantly reduce the overall cost of owning and renting out a property.

4. Leverage: Real estate investment allows investors to leverage their capital, meaning they can purchase a property worth much more than the amount of money they have on hand. This can be done by obtaining a mortgage loan, which can help to increase returns on investment.

5. Diversification: Investing in real estate can help diversify an investment portfolio, which can help to mitigate risk. Real estate investments can also provide a hedge against inflation, as the value of real estate tends to increase with inflation.

6. Control: As a real estate investor, you have more control over your investment compared to other types of investments, such as stocks or bonds. You can make repairs and upgrades and make decisions about the property management and rental rate.

7. Location: Location is one of the most important factors when it comes to real estate investment. Properties in desirable areas with strong job growth, good schools, and low crime rates tend to appreciate in value and attract tenants.

8. Rehabilitation: Real estate investors can purchase properties in need of repair or renovation and then make improvements to increase the value of the property. This can be a great way to increase returns on investment, especially if the property is located in an area with a high demand for housing.

9. Networking: Real estate investing can provide opportunities for networking and building relationships with other investors, real estate agents, and other professionals in the industry. This can lead to new investment opportunities and can provide valuable insights and advice.

10. Cash flow: Real estate can generate positive cash flow, meaning the rental income is greater than the expenses. This can provide a steady stream of passive income and can help to pay off the mortgage and other expenses associated with owning the property.

However, it's important to note that real estate investing also comes with certain risks, such as market fluctuations, property management and vacancy issues, and changes in the local economy. It's important to do your due diligence before investing in any property, and it's also important to have a clear plan for how you will finance and manage the property. It's also important to consult with a financial advisor or real estate professional to understand the options, the costs and the risks involved.

Building Societies

A building society is a financial institution that primarily focuses on providing financial services related to housing and mortgages. Here are some activities commonly associated with building societies:

• Mortgage Lending: Building societies offer mortgage loans to individuals and families for purchasing residential properties. They assess borrowers' eligibility, evaluate the value of the property, and provide funds to facilitate the purchase.

• Savings Accounts: Building societies typically offer a range of savings accounts designed to help individuals save money for various purposes, including home purchases. These accounts may provide competitive interest rates and may have specific features tailored to meet the needs of savers.

• Investment Services: Some building societies offer investment products, such as Individual Savings Accounts (ISAs) or investment funds, to help customers grow their savings or investments over time. These investment services may be aimed at providing options for long-term financial planning or retirement.

• Insurance Products: Building societies may offer insurance services related to homeownership, such as building and contents insurance, mortgage protection insurance, or life insurance. These products are designed to protect borrowers and their properties against unforeseen circumstances.

• Financial Advice: Building societies often provide financial advice to their customers. This can include guidance on mortgage options, savings strategies, investment choices, and other related financial matters.

• Community Support: Building societies often have a strong focus on community involvement and may engage in various initiatives to support local communities. This can include sponsoring events, supporting charitable organisations, or providing grants for community projects.

• Additional Services: Depending on the specific building society, they may offer additional services such as current accounts, credit cards, personal loans, or foreign currency exchange.

It is important to note that the activities of building societies can vary to some extent, as different societies may have unique offerings and areas of specialisation. However, the core activities generally revolve around providing mortgage lending, savings accounts, investment services, insurance products, financial advice, and community support.

Regulations ensure that societies can only lend to property-related activities and for consumer purchases. Also, societies are mutual organisations, so depositors are members with a stake in the reserves and assets of the society and voting rights at the AGM. Hence, a greater degree of stewardship can be exercised through a building society deposit, while there is less chance of involvement in 'unethical' business operations.

Biblical guidance on home ownership

Homeownership can be viewed as both a consumption item and an investment. On one hand, owning a home provides a place to live and brings emotional and psychological benefits. Additionally, it can appreciate in value over time, offering the potential for a capital gain when sold. Homeowners might also earn rental income by leasing out rooms or separate parts of the property.

However, it's essential to recognise that investing in a home doesn't guarantee returns like traditional investments such as bonds or stocks. The value of a home is influenced by local market conditions, economic trends, and changes in the housing market. Furthermore, homeowners bear ongoing costs like mortgage payments, property taxes, and maintenance expenses.

Careful evaluation of individual circumstances and goals is crucial before deciding whether it's the right investment choice. Seeking professional advice can help better understand the risks and benefits associated with homeownership.

From a retirement planning perspective, homeownership can be seen as an investment in the future. There are two types of retirement provision products: those aimed at increasing income in retirement, such as private pension insurance, and those focused on reducing costs during retirement. The latter seeks to enhance disposable income as a pensioner, and unlike the former, it is tax-free since reduced costs are not subject to income tax compared to additional income.

Risks chat

Investing in real estate can be a great way to build wealth, but it also comes with certain risks. Some of the risks associated with real estate investing include:

1. Market fluctuations: Real estate values can be affected by changes in the economy and the housing market. When the market is weak, property values can decrease, resulting in a loss of equity and income.
2. Vacancy: Real estate investors who own rental properties may face periods of vacancy, which can result in lost income and higher expenses.
3. Property management: Owning and managing rental properties can be time-consuming and can require a significant amount of effort and expertise. It's important to have a clear plan for how the property will be managed and to have a trusted property manager to oversee the property.
4. Maintenance and repairs: Owning real estate also comes with the responsibility of maintaining and repairing the property. This can be costly and can result in unexpected expenses.
5. Financing: Real estate investments often require financing, which can come with the risk of interest rate fluctuations and the potential for default. It's important to have a plan for how the property will be financed and to understand the terms and conditions of any loans.
6. Legal issues: Real estate investing can also come with legal risks, such as disputes with tenants or zoning issues. It's important to understand the legal requirements and regulations related to owning and renting out property.
7. Natural disasters: natural disasters such as floods, hurricanes, earthquakes, and wildfires can cause significant

damage to properties. This can lead to decreased property values, lost income, and higher expenses.

8.   Political and economic instability: Investing in real estate in countries with political and economic instability can come with a higher level of risk. It's important to research the current situation and the potential future developments in the country you're considering investing in.

9.   Limited liquidity: Real estate investments are not as liquid as stocks or bonds, meaning it can be difficult to sell the property quickly. This can make it harder to access cash when you need it.

10.   Limited diversification: Real estate investments can be costly, so for many people, it's not feasible to diversify their portfolio by buying multiple properties. Investing in one property can make the portfolio more concentrated and increase the risk.

It's important to note that these risks can vary depending on the specific property and the local market conditions. It's also important to consult with a financial advisor or real estate professional to understand the options, the costs and the risks involved.

Real estate is considered a classic tangible asset and, thus, an inflation-proof investment. This is because their value increases in the same proportion as inflation - that is the theoretical assumption.

It is true that in the case of inflation, the value of a property can be expected to rise, at least expressed in a currency. If, for example, a euro had only 50% of its original purchasing power, a property would not be worth less as a result because half a house would not be missing. The real value of the property would still be the same, but the value expressed in euros would have doubled.

In this simplified view, it should not be forgotten that inflation also increases the costs associated with a property. These are higher and less taxable for an investment property than for an owner-occupied home. The costs of properties in need of renovation also increase more due to inflation than those of newer properties.

At the same time, however, rent payments are not adjusted monthly to the level of inflation, so the surplus from rental income and operating costs decreases. Only in the medium term can the landlord adjust the rent and operating costs, whereby in many regions of Germany, there are legal limits to rent increases. Especially with older investment properties, one cannot automatically speak of an inflation-protected investment.

As already explained in the case of owner-occupied homes, the positive development of property prices in the recent past was triggered primarily by the low interest rate level. When central banks raise interest rates again, this development can also cause real estate prices to fall again, as the total cost of a property increases and thus demand is dampened.

Tension between renting and buying a home.

The financial tension between renting and buying a home arises from the different financial considerations and trade-offs associated with each option. Here are some key factors that contribute to this tension:
- Upfront Costs: Buying a home typically requires a significant upfront investment, including a down payment, closing costs, and potential fees associated with obtaining a mortgage. On the other hand, renting generally involves a more minor upfront cost, usually limited to a security deposit and possibly the first month's rent.
- Monthly Expenses: When renting, the monthly cost is generally fixed and includes rent and possibly utilities. However, homeownership involves ongoing expenses such as mortgage payments, property taxes, homeowner's insurance, maintenance, and repairs. These costs can vary and may fluctuate over time, potentially increasing financial burdens.
- Equity and Investment: Buying a home allows for equity accumulation as the mortgage is paid down and the property potentially appreciates in value. This can serve as a long-term investment and a source of wealth building. Renting, on the other hand, does not build equity, and monthly payments solely cover the cost of occupying the property.
- Flexibility and Mobility: Renting provides greater flexibility, allowing individuals to move and adapt to changing circumstances without the burdens of selling a property. Buying a home can limit

mobility and may require a more significant commitment to a particular location, potentially impacting career opportunities and lifestyle choices.

• Market Conditions and Risks: Housing markets can experience property values, interest rates, and rental price fluctuations. Buying a home exposes individuals to market risks, such as potential decreases in property value or difficulty in selling. Renting provides more flexibility to adjust to changing market conditions.

• Personal Financial Situation: Financial circumstances, such as income stability, creditworthiness, and long-term financial goals, play a crucial role in determining the feasibility and suitability of renting or buying a home. Individual financial situations can vary, and what may be a wise decision for one person may not be the same for another.

Ultimately, the financial tension between renting and buying a home depends on individual factors, including financial capabilities, personal goals, lifestyle preferences, and the local housing market. It is essential to carefully assess these factors, conduct thorough research, and consider long-term financial implications when deciding to rent or buy a home.

Biblical perspective

The Bible does not explicitly command or address owning one's own home. However, biblical principles can be applied to support the idea of homeownership. Although not directly comparable to contemporary conditions, Old Testament (OT) law provides helpful pointers for reform we should consider.

• Homeownership is a legitimate aspiration. Widespread homeownership incentivises responsibility for the property itself and involvement in the wider community and contributes to the putting down of roots in a locality. Urban property within Israelite cities could be owned freehold and was not subject to the periodic Jubilee (Leviticus 25:29-31).

- Debt may be necessary to relieve poverty but should not become a means of exploitation of the poor by the rich. While the OT law envisaged secured loans (Exodus 22:26,27; Deuteronomy 24:10–13) and regulated debt servitude, debts were to be cancelled and debt servants released every seven years (Deuteronomy 15:1-18). Jeremiah condemned the failure to cancel debts (Jeremiah 34:8-22); subsequently, Nehemiah re-instituted the practice of debt cancellation (Nehemiah 10:31).
- Interest was prohibited within Israel, but rents were allowed. Interest on loans to fellow citizens was not permitted (Deuteronomy 23:19) – a restriction reiterated in the OT (Psalm 15:5; Nehemiah 5:7,11; Ezekiel 18:8,13,17) and reinforced in Jesus' teaching (Luke 6:35). In contrast, a hire fee could be charged for the renting of oxen (Exodus 22:14,15) and the leasehold use of agricultural land. (Leviticus 25:15,16)

The Bible emphasises that God is the ultimate provider of our needs. (Matthew 6:25-34) Owning a home can be seen as a means of stewardship, responsibly managing the resources God has entrusted to us. It allows for the provision of shelter and a stable environment for ourselves and our families. It also encourages individuals to provide for their families (1 Timothy 5:8). Owning a home can offer family members stability, security, and a sense of belonging. It provides a place where love, support, and faith can be nurtured and passed down to future generations.

The Bible encourages wise planning and forethought (Proverbs 21:5). Owning a home can be considered part of a long-term financial strategy, allowing for stability and potential equity growth over time.

The Bible values community and hospitality (Hebrews 13:2, Romans 12:13). Owning a home can provide a space for welcoming and ministering to others, extending hospitality, and cultivating relationships within the community.

Owning a home can provide opportunities to use the space for God's purposes. It can be used for hosting Bible studies, fellowship gatherings, and ministry activities that contribute to the growth of God's kingdom and the sharing of the gospel.

While homeownership can bring numerous benefits, it is important to maintain a balanced perspective. Christians should not focus excessively on material possessions or view homeownership as the ultimate goal in life. Instead, they should prioritise their relationship with God, seek His guidance in financial decisions, and demonstrate generosity toward others.

Impact investing in real estate

Impact investing in real estate involves making investment decisions in properties or real estate projects that aim to achieve both financial returns and positive social or environmental outcomes. This approach focuses on creating a meaningful and lasting impact in local communities while generating competitive financial returns for investors.

Here's how impact investing in real estate typically works:

- Social and Environmental Objectives: Impact investors first identify specific social or environmental objectives they wish to address through real estate investments. These may include affordable housing, sustainable building practices, community development, historic preservation, or promoting green spaces.
- Property Selection: Investors seek real estate opportunities aligning with their impact objectives. This may involve investing in affordable housing developments, energy-efficient buildings, projects that revitalise underserved neighbourhoods, or properties with a strong focus on environmental sustainability.
- Impact Measurement: Measuring the impact of real estate investments is crucial. Impact investors use various metrics to assess their projects' social and environmental outcomes. They may track factors such as affordable housing units created, carbon emissions reduced, community engagement initiatives, and other relevant indicators.
- Community Engagement: Impact investors often prioritise community engagement and collaboration in their real estate projects. They work closely with local stakeholders, residents, and organisations to understand the community's needs and ensure that their investments align with the community's interests.

- Long-Term Perspective: Impact investing in real estate typically takes a long-term perspective. Investors understand that positive social and environmental outcomes may take time to materialise, and they are committed to staying involved with their investments for the long haul.
- Financial Viability: While impact is a significant investment aspect, financial viability remains essential. Impact investors aim to achieve competitive financial returns to ensure the sustainability of their investments and attract more capital to the impact real estate sector.
- Impact-Focused Real Estate Funds: Some impact investors choose to invest in real estate through impact-focused funds or real estate investment trusts (REITs). These funds pool together investments from multiple investors and deploy the capital into impact-driven real estate projects.

Impact investing in real estate offers a powerful way to address social and environmental challenges while contributing to the development and revitalisation of communities. By deploying capital in projects prioritising sustainability, affordability, and community well-being, impact investors can play a significant role in shaping a more inclusive, sustainable, and socially responsible real estate market.

Chapter 21: Precious metals

Precious metals, including gold, silver, and platinum, have been popular investments for centuries due to their perceived stability and value. Investing in precious metals can take various forms, including bullion coins, bars, exchange-traded funds (ETFs), and mining stocks.

Investing in precious metals in the car journey of investing is like choosing a reliable and time-tested classic car that retains its value and offers a sense of security during your financial journey. Precious metals, such as gold, silver, platinum, and palladium, have been regarded as stores of value for centuries and serve as a hedge against economic uncertainties and currency fluctuations.

Just as a classic car's value can be appreciated over time due to its rarity and historical significance, precious metals hold intrinsic value and are considered a safe haven in times of economic turmoil. Investing in precious metals provides a tangible asset that can weather market volatility and protect your wealth from potential economic downturns, much like a reliable classic car that remains valuable regardless of changing trends.

Moreover, just as a classic car can be easily traded or sold to collectors, investing in precious metals offers liquidity and flexibility. Precious metals are traded globally, and their value is widely recognised, allowing investors to convert them into cash when needed. This liquidity is like having a well-maintained car that can be sold at a fair price whenever you decide to part ways with it.

In addition, investing in precious metals is not limited by geographical boundaries. Just as a classic car can attract admirers and buyers from different parts of the world, precious metals have universal appeal and can be sought after by investors and governments worldwide. This global recognition ensures that precious metals can retain their value and serve as a valuable asset, regardless of the economic conditions in a particular region.

However, like any investment, there are considerations to bear in mind. Just as a classic car requires regular maintenance, investing in precious metals may involve storage and security costs, especially if you physically possess the metals. Additionally, the value of precious metals can be influenced by various factors, including supply and demand, economic conditions, and geopolitical events, much like how a classic car's value may fluctuate based on its condition, popularity, and historical significance.

Investing in precious metals

Investing in gold can be supported by several arguments:

1. Wealth Preservation: Gold has historically been considered a store of value and a hedge against inflation. Its limited supply and durable nature make it an attractive option for preserving wealth over the long term.

2. Portfolio Diversification: Including gold in an investment portfolio can help diversify risk. Gold often exhibits low or negative correlation with other asset classes, such as stocks or bonds, providing a potential safeguard during times of market volatility.

3. Safe-Haven Asset: Gold is often perceived as a safe-haven asset during times of economic uncertainty or geopolitical instability. Investors turn to gold as a perceived safe store of value, as it is not subject to the same risks as fiat currencies or other financial instruments.

4. Tangible Asset: Unlike many other investments, gold is a tangible asset that can be physically held and owned. This characteristic appeals to individuals seeking a physical representation of their investment and a sense of security.

5. Potential for Capital Appreciation: Gold has the potential for capital appreciation over time. Its value can rise due to factors such as increased demand, supply constraints, or changing market dynamics. Investors may benefit from price appreciation in gold over the long term.

6. Historical Track Record: Gold has maintained value and served as a medium of exchange for centuries. Its enduring appeal and historical track record provide a level of confidence to investors looking for a stable and reliable investment option.

7. International Acceptance: Gold is recognised and accepted globally as a form of currency and a valuable asset. Its universal appeal makes it highly liquid and easily tradable across international markets.

Ways to Invest:

Investing in metals can provide a hedge against inflation and a way to diversify an investment portfolio. Some of the ways to invest in metals include:

1. Physical metal: One of the most traditional ways to invest in metals is to purchase physical metal, such as gold or silver coins or bars. Physical metal can be stored in a safe deposit box or at a secure storage facility. The main advantage of owning physical metal is that it can be held as a tangible asset, but it does come with the risk of theft or loss.

2. Exchange-traded funds (ETFs): ETFs are a way to invest in a basket of metals without actually owning the physical metal. ETFs trade on stock exchanges and track the price of a specific metal or group of metals. ETFs provide the convenience of buying and selling shares but also come with the risk of fluctuation in the market.

3. Mining stocks: Investing in mining stocks is another way to gain exposure to metals. Mining stocks are shares of companies involved in the exploration, extraction, and production of metals.

When the price of metals rises, mining stocks tend to perform well, but they also come with the risk of fluctuation in the stock market.

4.   Futures contracts: Futures contracts are agreements to buy or sell a specific metal at a future date at a specified price. Futures contracts can be used as a way to hedge against price fluctuations or as a speculative investment. However, it's important to note that futures trading is considered a high-risk investment and requires significant capital and market knowledge.

5.   Options contracts: Similar to futures contracts, options contracts give investors the right, but not the obligation, to buy or sell a specific metal at a future date at a specified price. Options contracts can be used to hedge against price fluctuations, but they also come with a high level of risk.

6.   Metal-based mutual funds: Metal-based mutual funds are a way to invest in a diversified portfolio of metals companies, ETFs, and mining stocks. They offer diversification benefits but also come with the risk of stock market fluctuation.

7.   Collectible coins: Collectible coins can be a way to invest in metals, but it's important to note that their value is mainly based on rarity and historical significance rather than the intrinsic value of the metal. It's essential to do thorough research and consult with an expert before investing in collectable coins.

8.   Precious metal-based annuities: Precious metal-based annuities are insurance products backed by a pool of precious metals and can provide a steady income stream in retirement. However, it's important to note that these products have complex structures and come with high fees and commissions, so it's important to understand the terms and conditions before investing.

Investing in bullion coins or bars can be done through a dealer or a self-directed IRA. ETFs track the price of precious metals and can be bought or sold like stocks. Mining stocks give investors ownership in a precious metals mining company and offer exposure to the metal's price while offering the potential for dividends.

It is important to understand that investing in precious metals is not a guaranteed way to make money and can carry risks, including price volatility and the potential for fraud. As with any investment, conducting thorough research, consulting with a financial advisor, and having a well-diversified portfolio is crucial.

In conclusion, investing in precious metals can be a good addition to a diversified investment portfolio for those seeking to hedge against inflation and diversify their holdings. However, it is crucial to understand the risks and benefits thoroughly and to seek professional advice before making any investment decisions.

Risks Chat

It is important to note that investing in gold and other metals carries risks and uncertainties, and its performance can be influenced by various factors, including:

1. Price Volatility: Precious metal prices can be volatile and subject to sudden and substantial changes, leading to significant losses.
2. Lack of Income: Unlike other investments such as bonds, precious metals do not provide a regular income and rely solely on price appreciation for returns.
3. Counterparty Risk: When investing in exchange-traded funds (ETFs) or mining stocks, there is a risk of the issuer or the mining company defaulting or facing financial difficulties.
4. Market Illiquidity: Physical precious metals can be difficult to sell quickly, especially in large quantities, due to market illiquidity.
5. Storage Costs: Physical precious metals require secure storage, which can be expensive and add to the investment cost.
6. Fraud: Precious metals are often targeted by fraudsters, so it is important to only buy from reputable dealers and thoroughly research any investment before purchasing.

Investing in precious metals can be a good way to diversify a portfolio, but it is important to understand and carefully consider the risks involved before deciding. It is recommended to seek professional advice and consider your portfolio's specific goals and risk tolerance.

Biblical perspective

Objects acquired purely as a hedge against inflation or as a speculative gamble have few practical benefits. As such, we can question if they represent a good investment as a steward and look like hoarding. High inflation often encourages speculation in durables rather than investing in something productive.

Here are some reasons to invest in gold or silver.

Certainly, precious metals like gold possess universally recognised value. Throughout history, gold has served as a form of money, maintaining its worth over time. In contrast, fiat currencies, including the US dollar, tend to lose value and eventually become worthless. However, gold and silver will retain value until the return of Christ, as revealed in Revelation 18:12, 16.

During times of economic hardship and crisis, people seek stability in precious metals. In situations like hyperinflation, war, or disasters, paper money can lose its value entirely, but gold and silver can still retain purchasing power for essential goods, assuming they are available. Nevertheless, it is crucial to remember that ultimate certainty lies not in gold, silver, or any worldly possession but in the Triune God of Scripture and His infallible Word, the Bible.

Governments may attempt to manipulate gold and silver markets, but the value of precious metals does not solely depend on printed currencies like dollars, euros, yen, or pesos. Unlike paper money, which is susceptible to inflation, the value of gold and silver remains resilient against government actions.

In times of potential government confiscation or asset seizure, owning physical gold or silver can provide some protection from losing everything. Precious metals can serve as a hedge against such scenarios, safeguarding assets from potential government interventions.

Furthermore, if governments revert to a gold standard, the value of gold is likely to rise. As a result, investing in precious metals could present favourable opportunities if such a shift occurs.

Lastly, maintaining a diversified portfolio of investments reduces overall investment risk. By allocating a portion of assets to precious metals, individuals enhance protection against economic uncertainty compared to those solely invested in stocks or bonds.

Instead of investing in precious metals, you can choose to invest in Christian mutual funds or Biblically-based peer-to-peer lending, actively contributing to a positive impact in the world. By doing so, your money will support companies engaged in meaningful endeavours, such as researching cures for various types of cancer. Not only will you potentially achieve a better rate of return, but your investment will also make a tangible difference in the world, rather than merely sitting idle.

Investing in gold can be likened to moving a rare rock from one hole in the ground (a mine) to another (a vault). However, Christ's parable teaches a different approach to money management. The parable illustrates that the best use of money is to trade with it actively, similar to how companies operate, which yields the highest rate of return. The second-best option is to invest it through loans, such as investing in bonds, which earn interest. On the other hand, holding money without investment, represented by keeping it in the ground (a precious metal in the first-century context), is depicted as the least favourable approach. According to Christ's teaching, actively putting money to work and investing it wisely leads to greater rewards and impact. (Luke 19:15-16, 23; Matthew 25:27)

You could argue that in an emergency, such as government-instituted persecution of Christians or other times of severe crisis, precious metals are something that can be taken along when it is time to flee, avoid starvation, or deal in some other way with a crisis. However, Scripture states that all riches–even a stash of gold hidden somewhere–are "uncertain" (1 Timothy 6:17).
You should not think that your gold is some certain thing that you can always count on or trust in instead of in God. Perhaps a thief will break into your house and steal the gold. Maybe the government will issue a tyrannical decree confiscating all gold, as Franklin D Roosevelt did in America on April 5, 1933.

Christian objections to investing in gold and silver are not universal, and opinions may vary among different Christian denominations and individuals. However, some Christians may have reservations about investing in precious metals like gold and silver for the following reasons:

- Materialism and Greed: Investing in gold and silver can sometimes be driven by a desire for wealth accumulation, which may lead to materialism and greed. The Bible warns against the love of money and encourages contentment with what we have (1 Timothy 6:10, Hebrews 13:5).
- Worship of Wealth: Investing in precious metals may inadvertently lead to prioritising material possessions and financial security over faith and trust in God. Christians are called to serve God and not to worship earthly treasures (Matthew 6:24).
- Misplaced Trust: Putting too much trust in gold and silver as a form of security may lead to a misplaced focus on earthly wealth rather than relying on God's providence and guidance (Proverbs 11:28, Proverbs 23:4-5).
- Speculative Nature: Investments in gold and silver can be speculative and subject to market fluctuations. Christians may be cautious about engaging in speculative investments that carry higher risks and could lead to financial losses (Proverbs 21:5, Proverbs 13:11).
- Lack of Productive Purpose: Some Christians may view investing in precious metals as "hoarding" resources rather than using them productively to benefit others and advance God's kingdom (Matthew 25:14-30, Luke 12:33).

Not all Christians object to investing in gold and silver, and precious metals can serve as a legitimate part of a diversified investment strategy. Like any investment, the key is approaching it with a balanced perspective, mindful of the potential ethical and spiritual implications. Ultimately, Christians are encouraged to seek God's wisdom and discernment in all financial decisions, ensuring that their investments align with their values and are used to honour God and benefit others.

Impact investing in precious metals

Impact investing in precious metals is a relatively specialised approach that aligns the investment in precious metals, such as gold, silver, platinum, and palladium, with specific social or environmental objectives. While precious metals are traditionally viewed as a store of value and a hedge against economic uncertainties, impact investors aim to use these investments to contribute to positive change and address global challenges.

Here's how impact investing in precious metals can be approached:

- Responsible Mining Practices: Impact investors may focus on investing in precious metals sourced from mining companies that adhere to responsible and sustainable mining practices. They look for companies that prioritise environmental protection, worker safety, and ethical labour practices.
- Conflict-Free Sourcing: Some impact investors seek to invest in precious metals that are certified as "conflict-free," meaning they are sourced from areas that do not contribute to armed conflict or human rights abuses.
- Sustainable Supply Chain: Investors may support precious metal supply chains that are committed to reducing their environmental footprint and promoting social responsibility throughout the entire production process.
- Recycling and Circular Economy: Impact investors may explore opportunities in companies involved in recycling precious metals and contributing to a circular economy, thus reducing the demand for newly mined metals and minimising environmental impacts.
- Financing Sustainable Projects: Impact investors can use precious metals investments to finance projects that contribute to sustainability and social good. For example, investing in precious metals to support renewable energy initiatives or community development projects.
- Advocacy and Engagement: Impact investors in precious metals may engage with mining companies to advocate for responsible and sustainable practices. They may use their shareholder influence to encourage companies to improve their environmental and social performance.
- Blending with Other Impact Investments: Precious metals investments can be integrated into a diversified impact investment

portfolio, where investors allocate capital across various asset classes with the aim of achieving both positive impact and financial returns.

It's important to note that impact investing in precious metals may require a higher level of due diligence, as the extraction and mining processes associated with these metals can have significant environmental and social implications. However, by focusing on responsible and sustainable practices, impact investors can use precious metals investments as a means to drive positive change and contribute to a more sustainable and responsible global economy.

Chapter 22: Life Insurance

Investing in life insurance on the car journey of investing is like securing a reliable insurance policy to protect you and your loved ones during the trip of life. Just as a car insurance policy provides a safety net in case of unexpected accidents or damages on the road, life insurance offers financial protection and peace of mind for your family's future.

Life insurance serves as a valuable safeguard, much like fastening your seatbelt before embarking on a journey. By having a life insurance policy, you ensure that your loved ones will receive financial support in the event of your untimely passing. This can help cover expenses like outstanding debts, funeral costs, and daily living expenses, providing your family with the stability they need during a difficult time.

Moreover, life insurance can act as a navigation system, guiding you towards your financial goals and long-term planning. Just as a GPS helps you stay on course during your car journey, life insurance can be integrated into your overall financial strategy, helping you achieve various milestones like paying for your child's education or securing a comfortable retirement for your spouse.

Investing in life insurance requires thoughtful consideration, much like choosing the right route for your journey. You must assess your family's financial needs, your income, and your desired level of coverage to select the most suitable policy. Additionally, like periodic maintenance checks for your car, reviewing your life insurance coverage periodically ensures that it aligns with your changing circumstances and goals.

Furthermore, life insurance offers a unique form of investment, like filling up your car with fuel before starting a long journey. While life insurance does not generate traditional investment returns, it provides a safety net and financial security, allowing you to focus on pursuing other investment opportunities without worrying about the immediate impact on your family's financial welfare.

Is this an investment?

Putting money into a life insurance policy is not typically considered a traditional investment, but certain life insurance policies do have investment-like features. Life insurance primarily serves as a financial protection tool to provide a death benefit to beneficiaries in the event of the insured's death. However, some types of life insurance policies, such as whole life or universal life insurance, have a cash value component that can grow over time, similar to an investment.

The cash value in these policies accumulates based on the premiums paid and any potential earnings from the insurance company's investments. Policyholders may have the option to access the cash value through policy loans or withdrawals, making it function somewhat like a savings or investment account.

While life insurance can offer a measure of financial security and flexibility, it's essential to understand that the primary purpose of life insurance is protection, not investment. The returns on the cash value component of life insurance policies may be lower compared to other investment options like stocks, bonds, or mutual funds. Moreover, life insurance policies often come with fees and expenses that can reduce the growth potential of the cash value.

If you are considering life insurance as an investment or savings vehicle, it's essential to thoroughly understand the policy's terms and conditions, including any potential risks and costs. Consulting with a financial advisor can help you assess whether a life insurance policy is a suitable component of your overall financial plan, considering your specific financial goals and needs.

Investing in life insurance

There are several different types of life insurance, each with its own set of features and benefits. These types include:

1. Term life insurance: This type of insurance provides coverage for a specific period of time, such as 10, 20, or 30 years. If the policyholder dies during the term of the policy, the death benefit is paid to the beneficiaries. Term life insurance is typically the most affordable type of life insurance, but it does not accumulate cash value.

2. Whole life insurance: This type of insurance provides coverage for the entire lifetime of the policyholder. In addition to the death benefit, whole life insurance also accumulates cash value over time. This cash value can be used to pay premiums, or it can be borrowed against. Whole life insurance is generally more expensive than term life insurance, but it does provide the policyholder with lifelong coverage.

3. Universal life insurance: This type of insurance is similar to whole life insurance, but it offers more flexibility in terms of premium payments and death benefit amounts. Universal life policies allow policyholders to adjust their premium payments and death benefit amounts over time to meet their changing needs. This type of policy also has a cash value component that accrues over time.

4. Variable life insurance: This type of insurance is similar to universal life insurance, but it also allows policyholders to invest their cash value in a variety of sub-accounts, such as stocks, bonds, and mutual funds. The value of the policy and the death benefit can fluctuate based on the performance of the underlying investments.

5. Variable Universal Life Insurance: This type of insurance is a combination of variable life and universal life insurance. It offers the policyholder the flexibility of universal life insurance but also the investment options of variable life insurance. The cash value component of a variable universal life insurance policy can be invested in a variety of sub-accounts, and the value of the policy and the death benefit can fluctuate based on the performance of the underlying investments.

6.   Guaranteed universal life insurance: This type of insurance is similar to traditional universal life insurance, but it provides a guaranteed death benefit and premium payments for a specific period of time, such as to age 90 or 100. It is designed for people who want lifelong coverage but do not want to pay the higher premiums associated with whole life insurance.

7.   No-exam life insurance: This type of insurance is designed for people who do not want to go through the medical examination that is typically required for traditional life insurance policies. No-exam policies are generally more expensive than traditional policies, but they do offer coverage for people who may have health issues that would make them ineligible for traditional coverage.

8.   Return of Premium (ROP) life insurance: This type of insurance is a variation of term life insurance, which returns all the premiums paid by the insured if he/she survives the term of the policy. This type of policy is more expensive than traditional term life insurance, but it does provide the policyholder with a way to recoup some of their premium payments if they outlive the policy.

It's important to note that all these types of life insurance have different features and benefits, and it's important to evaluate which one would fit best to your individual needs, budget, and goals. It's also important to consult with a financial advisor or insurance agent to understand the options, the costs and the risks involved.

Risks chat

The risks involved in investing in life insurance include:

1.   Market Risk: The value of investments made through life insurance policies can be affected by market conditions and changes in interest rates, leading to potential losses.

2.   Insurer Risk: The financial stability and solvency of the insurance company that issues the policy are important, as the company's ability to pay out claims is crucial to the value of the policy.

3. Lapse Risk: If a policyholder does not pay their premiums, the policy may lapse, and the death benefit and any cash value may be lost.

4. Surrender Risk: If a policyholder decides to cancel their policy before it matures, they may be subject to surrender charges or other penalties that can reduce the value of the policy.

5. Interest Rate Risk: Policies that are linked to interest rates can be affected by changes in interest rates, leading to potential losses.

6. Policy Design Risk: The design of the policy, such as the amount of coverage, premium payments, and other features, can have a significant impact on the policy's value.

7. Financial reserve: Certain risks may be better handled by building up a personal financial reserve, such as saving for a wedding or possible theft of a laptop or smartphone, funeral expenses, or continued wage payment during illness. The insurance option, though, may be preferred if immediate payouts, irrespective of personal reserves, are needed.

8. Networks: In some cultures, financial risks are absorbed through networks like extended families or strong communities. In the early Christian communities, this sense of communal support was evident. In modern times, however, families and communities have moved away from this model, leading to the outsourcing of risks to institutional insurance companies.

9. Living with the risk: Sometimes, choosing to accept and live with certain risks is an option. Additionally, the probability of certain risks occurring can be reduced through lifestyle adjustments. However, such decisions require careful consideration, prayer, and conscious intention.

There are various, diverse reasons for individuals choosing to carry risks themselves:

- A pronounced willingness to take risks, with a mentality like "It won't happen to me!" reflects a bold and daring approach to life.
- An extremely optimistic outlook, believing that everything will turn out fine, regardless of potential risks involved.

- Strong cost awareness, where the cost of insurance is deemed too expensive, leads to a preference for self-assumption of risks.
- Financial constraints make insurance unaffordable and necessitate handling risks independently.
- Some individuals may rely on a concrete promise from God, choosing not to outsource risks to insurance carriers, believing in divine protection in their lives.

If God has not given you a specific individual promise, we should prayerfully consider which strategy is right for us and, if applicable, our family, at what risk. If we rely on networks such as family or church, it is also important to openly communicate our expectations and compare them with the view of the other party. For example, who in the family can concretely imagine providing financial support and in what amount if the worst comes to the worst?

When making our decision, we should consider two questions:

1. How likely is the occurrence of the risk?
2. How big would the financial consequences be if the risk were to materialise?

When faced with an unavoidable risk that could potentially overwhelm me and my support network, opting for an insurance solution may be the prudent choice.

However, this decision should not be solely based on personal assessment or human logic; it must also be weighed against biblical teachings. The responsibility of a main breadwinner to provide for their family and prepare for emergencies is emphasised by the Apostle Paul in the Bible (1 Timothy 5:8; NLT): "But those who won't care for their relatives, especially those in their own household, have denied the true faith. Such people are worse than unbelievers." Adequate financial protection against existential risks should not be seen as a lack of trust in God. Rather, it is a harmonious combination of trust in God and proactive action that complements each other.

While some isolated Bible verses may suggest divine protection, others remind us not to test God's providence. It is essential to maintain a relationship with Him, seek His guidance, and use our God-given intelligence to make informed financial decisions, free from the influence of fears. Seeking wisdom from other relevant Bible passages can further illuminate this perspective. In conclusion, life insurance can indeed be a valuable investment, but it requires careful consideration of risks and thorough comprehension of policy terms before committing. Seeking professional advice and evaluating specific investment needs and goals are recommended steps in building a well-rounded investment portfolio.

Biblical perspective

The Bible does not directly address the topic of life insurance since life insurance, as we know it today, is a relatively modern financial concept.

However, Christians can approach the decision to take life insurance from a biblical perspective by considering principles related to stewardship, provision for loved ones, and caring for one's family.

- Stewardship: The Bible emphasises responsible stewardship of the resources God has entrusted to us (1 Peter 4:10). Life insurance can be seen as a means of responsibly planning for the future and providing financial protection for one's family in the event of an untimely death.
- Provision for Loved Ones: The Bible encourages providing for one's family and ensuring their well-being (1 Timothy 5:8). Life insurance can be viewed as a way to fulfil this biblical principle by offering financial support to beneficiaries, such as a spouse, children, or dependents, in the event of the insured's death. Jesus taught the importance of caring for family members and loving others as ourselves (Mark 12:31, Matthew 15:4). Life insurance can demonstrate love and care for family members by alleviating potential financial burdens during difficult times, such as funeral expenses or loss of income.
- Wisdom and Prudence: Proverbs emphasises the value of wisdom and prudence in financial matters (Proverbs 21:5, Proverbs 27:12). Taking life insurance can be seen as a prudent financial decision to safeguard against unforeseen circumstances and provide peace of mind for the insured and their loved ones.

While life insurance can align with biblical principles of stewardship, provision, and care for family, it's essential for individuals to carefully assess their financial needs, budget, and long-term goals when considering life insurance.

Ultimately, the decision to take life insurance should be made prayerfully and thoughtfully, considering one's individual circumstances and the needs of those who depend on them, to honour God in their financial planning and provide for their family in a responsible and loving manner.

Whether putting money into a life insurance policy can be considered an investment for Christians depends on the type of life insurance policy and the individual's financial goals and values. Let's explore the two main types of life insurance and their implications for Christians:

- Term Life Insurance: Term life insurance provides coverage for a specific period, typically 10, 20, or 30 years. It is designed to offer financial protection to the beneficiaries if the insured passes away during the policy term. Term life insurance does not have a cash value component, and the premiums are generally lower than other types of life insurance. For Christians who prioritise pure protection and see life insurance as a way to care for their loved ones in case of an untimely death, term life insurance may be viewed as a valuable financial tool rather than an investment.

- Whole Life or Universal Life Insurance: Whole life and universal life insurance policies have a cash value component that accumulates over time. A portion of the premiums goes toward the insurance coverage, while the rest is invested by the insurance company. These policies provide a death benefit to beneficiaries and may offer the potential to build cash value over the long term. The cash value can be accessed through policy loans or withdrawals. Some Christians may view these types of life insurance policies as a form of forced savings or an additional investment vehicle with some tax advantages.

For Christians considering life insurance as an investment, it is essential to be mindful of the primary purpose of life insurance, which is financial protection for loved ones in the event of the insured's death. While whole-life and universal-life policies may have a savings component, the returns on the cash value are generally lower than other investment options. It's crucial to compare the potential returns, fees, and other features of life insurance policies with traditional investment options to make an informed decision.

Ultimately, whether life insurance is considered an investment for Christians should be evaluated based on individual financial goals, risk tolerance, and values. Consulting with a financial advisor who understands both insurance and investment products can help Christians navigate these decisions in alignment with their faith and overall financial strategy.

Impact investing in life insurance products

Impact investing in life insurance products involves using life insurance policies or products as a vehicle to achieve both financial returns and positive social or environmental outcomes. This approach seeks to align life insurance investments with specific impact objectives while still providing the benefits of life insurance coverage.

Here's how impact investing in life insurance products can be implemented:

- Social or Environmental Objectives: Impact investors define their social or environmental objectives, which may include supporting sustainable development projects, funding education initiatives, promoting healthcare access, or addressing other pressing social issues.

- Investing in Impact-Focused Policies: Impact investors can explore life insurance products that are specifically designed to support impact causes. These policies may allocate a portion of premiums or proceeds to fund impact projects or charitable endeavours.

- Socially Responsible Insurance Companies: Investors may choose to work with insurance companies that demonstrate strong environmental, social, and governance (ESG) practices. Such companies are committed to responsible business operations and contribute positively to society and the environment.

• Contributions to Non-profits: Some life insurance products offer the option for policyholders to direct a portion of their premiums or policy values to non-profit organisations or impact projects of their choice.

• Funding Social Impact Projects: Insurance companies can use the capital from life insurance policies to fund social impact projects or invest in impact-focused initiatives, contributing to positive change in communities and the environment.

• Impact Measurement: Measuring the impact of life insurance products is crucial. Impact investors may work with insurance companies or specialised organisations to track and evaluate the social and environmental outcomes of their investments.

• Engaging Policyholders: Impact-focused insurance companies may engage with policyholders to promote awareness of the social impact of their life insurance investments and offer opportunities for involvement in social or environmental initiatives.

• Supporting Sustainable Practices: Impact investors may choose to support insurance companies that prioritise sustainable practices, including reducing their carbon footprint, promoting diversity and inclusion, and advocating for ethical and responsible business conduct.

Impact investing in life insurance products provides investors with an avenue to integrate their financial goals with their desire to contribute positively to society and the environment. By selecting life insurance products that align with their impact objectives and collaborating with responsible insurance providers, investors can make a meaningful difference while securing financial protection for their families and loved ones.

Chapter 23. Pensions

Investing in a pension during the car journey of investing is like equipping your vehicle with a reliable and efficient engine, ensuring a smooth and comfortable ride towards retirement. Just as a powerful engine provides the necessary force to propel the car forward, a pension plan serves as a robust financial tool that powers your retirement journey.

A pension is akin to a long-term investment strategy, much like a well-maintained engine that supports you throughout the entire journey. It involves regular contributions made over your working years, steadily building a fund that will sustain you during retirement. Just as a car needs consistent fuel to keep running, contributing to a pension ensures a steady flow of funds into your retirement account.

Moreover, like a GPS guiding you on your car journey, a pension plan offers a clear roadmap to your retirement goals. It sets a path for your financial future, outlining the contributions required and the potential returns expected when you reach your retirement destination. Additionally, a pension plan may come with employer contributions or tax benefits, acting as extra gears that boost your retirement savings.

Investing in a pension involves planning for the long haul, much like preparing your car for a cross-country trip. It requires foresight, discipline, and a commitment to stay the course, just as you would make sure your car is well-maintained and prepared for a long journey.

During the journey of life, having a well-funded pension can provide financial security, allowing you to enjoy retirement with peace of mind. Just as a reliable engine ensures a smooth and enjoyable ride, a well-managed pension plan can lead to a comfortable and fulfilling retirement experience.

The pension plan.

A pension scheme is a retirement savings plan that is designed to provide you with a steady income stream once you reach retirement age. There are several different types of pension schemes, but the most common are defined benefit (DB) plans and defined contribution (DC) plans.

A defined benefit pension plan is a plan in which the benefits you receive in retirement are based on a formula that takes into account your years of service and your earnings. These plans are typically sponsored by employers and are funded by contributions from both the employer and the employee. The employer is responsible for making sure that there is enough money in the plan to pay out the promised benefits.

A defined contribution pension plan, on the other hand, is a plan in which the benefits you receive in retirement are based on the amount of money that you and your employer have contributed to the plan, plus any investment returns. These plans are typically less expensive for employers to set up and maintain, but the risk and responsibility for ensuring adequate retirement income falls on the individual.

When you participate in a pension scheme, you typically make regular contributions to the plan, either through payroll deductions or by making contributions directly to the plan. Your contributions are then invested, usually in a diversified portfolio of assets, to grow over time. The investment returns on the plan assets, along with any contributions made by your employer, are used to provide the benefits you receive in retirement.

There are different ways to save for retirement, such as individual retirement accounts and other types of investment accounts, but pension schemes offer certain advantages. For example, many pension schemes offer tax advantages, such as the ability to make pre-tax contributions or to defer taxes on the money you save until you withdraw it in retirement. Additionally, many pension schemes offer an option to take a lump sum, which can help you plan and manage your retirement.

When you're deciding whether to participate in a pension scheme, it's important to consider factors such as your age, your current income, and your retirement goals. It's also important to think about how much you can afford to contribute to the plan and how much you'll need to save to reach your retirement goals.

It's also important to consider the fees and expenses associated with the plan, as well as the investment options available. Some pension schemes may have higher fees and expenses than others, which can eat into your investment returns and reduce the amount of money you have available in retirement.

Private pension insurance offers flexible adaptability, provided that the tariff conditions are favourable. You can choose to make regular deposits, such as monthly contributions, or opt for a lump sum payment at the beginning or additional payments alongside your monthly savings. The contract typically begins with a deferment period, after which the pension payments start, usually coinciding with the end of your active working life. Immediate annuity insurance policies, however, begin the annuity payment right away without a deferment period, often through a one-time substantial premium payment.

The annuity insurance pay-out is usually structured as a lifelong annuity, but alternatives exist, such as an abbreviated life annuity, where the credit balance is paid over a defined period, or the lump-sum option, where the entire accumulated capital is paid out at once. In the accumulation phase, if the insured person passes away before the annuity payment begins, the contributions paid so far or the current credit balance is usually paid out to the heirs. Some providers offer the option to increase the death benefit individually, up to 100% of the premium sum. However, this mixed form is less of an investment, as the insurance company must set aside part of the premium to cover the risk of death.

In the pension phase, various death benefits are possible in the event of the insured's death after the annuity payments have started. The most common options include distributing the remaining balance not yet annuitised to surviving dependents and the annuity guarantee period. The annuity guarantee period ensures that the pension continues to be paid to surviving dependents for a specific guaranteed period of time.

A major advantage of annuity insurance is that it covers the risk of longevity. A lifelong pension is actually paid out to you by the pension insurer for life, no matter how old you get. This distinguishes annuity insurance from all other forms of investment.

Risks chat

The risks involved in investing in a pension scheme include:
1. Market Risk: The value of the investments made through a pension scheme can be affected by market conditions, leading to potential losses.
2. Interest Rate Risk: Changes in interest rates can impact the value of the pension scheme, particularly if it is invested in fixed-income securities.
3. Longevity Risk: The risk that the pensioner will outlive their savings and be unable to support themselves in retirement.
4. Inflation Risk: The risk that inflation will erode the purchasing power of the pensioner's savings over time.
5. Managerial Risk: The risk that the manager of the pension scheme will not perform as expected, either due to poor investment decisions or operational issues.
6. Regulatory Risk: Changes in laws and regulations affecting pension schemes can have a significant impact on the value of the pensioner's savings.
7. Solvency Risk: The risk that the pension scheme or its underlying investments may become insolvent, leading to a reduction in the value of the pensioner's savings.

Investing in a pension scheme can be an important part of planning for retirement, but it is important to understand and carefully consider the risks involved. It is recommended to seek professional advice and carefully evaluate the specific needs and goals of your investment portfolio.

Biblical perspective

The Bible does not specifically address pensions, as the concept of pensions as we know it today did not exist in biblical times. The only biblical mention of retirement exists in Numbers 8:24-26, which says that priests responsible for the backbreaking work of placing the sacrificed bulls and rams on the altar were directed to do this type of work only from ages 25 to 50. However, the Scriptures never said that after age 50, these priests were to suddenly find a place by the Dead Sea with a hammock and engage in a life of leisure. They were to continue 'assisting.'

However, the Bible does provide principles and teachings that can be applied to the concept of pensions and retirement planning. For example, Proverbs 6:6- 8 advises people to be diligent and save for the future: "Go to the ant, you sluggard; consider its ways and be wise! It has no commander, no overseer or ruler, yet it stores its provisions in summer and gathers its food at harvest." This passage emphasises the importance of saving and planning for the future, which can be seen as a principle that can be applied to retirement planning.

Proverbs 21:20 states, "In the house of the wise are stores of choice food and oil, but a foolish man devours all he has." This passage points to the importance of being wise with one's resources and saving for the future, which can be seen as applicable to retirement planning and pensions.

Additionally, 1 Timothy 5:8 says, "If anyone does not provide for his relatives, and especially for his immediate family, he has denied the faith and is worse than an unbeliever." This verse highlights the importance of taking care of one's family, which can include saving for retirement and providing for one's future needs through a pension plan or other retirement savings vehicle.

Retirement from a traditional career does not mean a Christian should stop serving God and others. The Bible emphasises the importance of using our gifts and talents to bless others (1 Peter 4:10-11). In retirement, Christians can find new avenues for service, whether through volunteering, mentoring, sharing their wisdom, or supporting charitable causes. Retirement can be a new opportunity to focus on God's calling and invest time and resources into meaningful pursuits that align with their faith and values.

Let's revisit the subject of pension insurance and responsible investment. Similar to banks, we have the option to choose life insurance providers who not only prioritise returns but also consider the ecological and social impact of their investments. While Christian providers may be absent in the life insurance sector, unlike banks, we can ensure that sustainable investment funds are available within the portfolio of unit-linked annuities.

However, for classic annuity insurance, only a limited number of life insurers currently establish firm sustainability criteria for all their protection assets. Nonetheless, we anticipate that the number of such providers will grow significantly in the years to come.

When choosing a retirement plan fund as a Christian investor, there are several factors to consider, aligning your investments with biblical principles and your financial goals. Here are some key things to look for:

- Ethical Investment Options: Seek retirement plan funds that offer ethical or socially responsible investment options. These funds screen out companies involved in activities that go against Christian values, such as gambling, tobacco, alcohol, or industries that harm the environment.

- Transparent Fees and Expenses: Look for funds with transparent and reasonable fees and expenses. High fees can erode your returns over time, so it's essential to understand the cost structure of the fund.

- Diversification: Choose funds that provide diversification across different asset classes (e.g., stocks, bonds, real estate) and industries. Diversification helps spread risk and can improve overall portfolio performance.

- Long-Term Performance: Evaluate the historical performance of the fund over the long term rather than focusing solely on short-term returns. Look for funds with consistent performance that aligns with your risk tolerance and financial goals.
- Financial Stability of the Fund Manager: Assess the financial stability and reputation of the fund manager or investment company. A reputable and financially sound manager is more likely to make prudent investment decisions.
- Alignment with Your Risk Tolerance: Consider your risk tolerance and choose funds that match your comfort level with market fluctuations. Retirement plan funds generally offer a range of risk profiles to accommodate various investor preferences.
- Investment Philosophy: Understand the investment philosophy and approach of the fund. Ensure it aligns with your values and beliefs as a Christian investor.
- Low Turnover: Look for funds with low turnover, as frequent buying and selling of securities can lead to higher costs and potential tax implications.
- Positive Impact: Consider funds that prioritise environmental, social, and governance (ESG) factors and aim to make a positive impact on society. These funds often invest in companies with strong ethical practices and corporate responsibility.
- Pray for Guidance: Seek God's wisdom and guidance in your decision-making process. Pray for discernment and direction in choosing retirement plan funds that align with your faith and financial goals.

It's crucial to research and carefully evaluate the investment options available within your retirement plan to ensure they are in line with your Christian values and contribute to your long-term financial well-being. Consulting with a financial advisor who understands both investing and ethical considerations can also provide valuable insights and help you make informed choices for your retirement planning.

Impact investing in pensions

Impact investing in pensions involves incorporating environmental, social, and governance (ESG) factors into the investment decisions made within pension funds. The aim is to achieve positive social or environmental outcomes alongside the financial objectives of the pension plan.

Here's how impact investing can be integrated into pension strategies:

- ESG Integration: Pension fund managers consider ESG factors when selecting and managing investments. They evaluate companies based on their environmental impact, social practices, and governance standards. By investing in companies with strong ESG performance, pension funds can support sustainability and social responsibility.

- Impact-Focused Funds: Pension funds may invest in impact-focused funds that target specific social or environmental goals. These funds actively seek opportunities that align with the pension plan's impact objectives, such as renewable energy projects, affordable housing initiatives, or sustainable infrastructure developments.

- Engagement and Advocacy: Pension funds can engage with companies in their investment portfolio to advocate for better ESG practices. They may use their shareholder influence to promote transparency, responsible business conduct, and positive impact initiatives.

- Divestment from Harmful Activities: Some pension funds choose to divest from companies involved in activities that conflict with their values or contribute to environmental or social harm. This may include divestment from fossil fuels, tobacco, or firearms industries, among others.

- Impact Measurement and Reporting: Pension funds measure and report on the social and environmental impact of their investments. They track progress toward impact objectives and communicate the outcomes to pension plan members, stakeholders, and beneficiaries.

- Sustainable Asset Allocation: Pension funds may implement a sustainable asset allocation strategy, ensuring that a portion of their portfolio is allocated to impact investments that align with the plan's values and objectives.
- Member Engagement: Pension funds can involve plan members in the impact investing process, seeking input on impact priorities and sharing information on the positive effects of their investments.
- Long-Term Perspective: Impact investing in pensions often takes a long-term perspective, considering the potential effects of investment decisions on future generations and the broader community.

By integrating impact investing principles into pension strategies, pension funds can contribute to a more sustainable and responsible economy while still fulfilling their financial obligations to plan members. This approach enables pension funds to align their investments with the values and concerns of their beneficiaries, leading to positive social and environmental change and securing a more resilient and prosperous future.

Chapter 24: Hedge Funds

Investing in a hedge fund during the car journey of investing is like joining a group of skilled drivers who take alternate routes to reach their destinations efficiently. Just as these expert drivers employ various strategies and shortcuts to navigate the roads effectively, a hedge fund employs a diverse range of investment techniques to potentially achieve higher returns and manage risks.

A hedge fund is like a team of experienced drivers with fast cars having a keen sense of direction, using their knowledge to seek out opportunities in the financial markets. They may take advantage of market trends, employ leverage, or engage in short selling, allowing them to adapt to changing market conditions, much like drivers rerouting their journey based on real-time traffic updates.

Furthermore, just as a carpool of skilled drivers can pool their resources for mutual benefit, a hedge fund can pool money from multiple investors. This collective approach enables the fund to access larger investment opportunities that may not be available to individual investors, much like carpooling, which saves on fuel and toll costs.

Investing in a hedge fund is like entrusting your journey to a team of seasoned drivers who aim to optimise your financial gains. However, it is essential to be aware that this approach also comes with certain risks, as driving alternative routes may not always lead to the intended destination.

Similarly, hedge funds may involve higher risks due to the complexity of their strategies and the potential use of leverage.

Investing in hedge funds

A hedge fund is a type of investment fund that pools together capital from a number of investors and uses it to invest in a wide range of assets and strategies, often with the goal of generating high returns while minimising risk. Hedge funds are typically only available to accredited investors, such as high-net-worth individuals and institutional investors and are not subject to the same regulatory requirements as mutual funds or other types of investment vehicles.

Hedge funds employ a variety of investment strategies, such as long-short equity, global macro, and event-driven, among others. Long-short equity funds, for example, invest in stocks while simultaneously taking short positions in other stocks in order to hedge against market risk. Global macro funds, on the other hand, invest in a wide range of assets based on macroeconomic trends and events. Event-driven funds, meanwhile, invest in companies that are undergoing significant changes, such as mergers or acquisitions.

One of the key characteristics of hedge funds is the use of leverage, which allows them to invest more capital than they have on hand. This can increase the potential for high returns but also increase risk. Hedge funds also employ a wide range of derivatives and other complex financial instruments to manage risk and generate returns.

Hedge funds are typically managed by a professional investment manager or team, who make investment decisions on behalf of the fund's investors. These managers often receive a performance fee, which is a percentage of the fund's returns, in addition to a management fee, which is a percentage of the fund's assets under management.

One of the main benefits of investing in a hedge fund is the potential for high returns. Hedge funds have historically delivered returns that are higher than those of traditional investments such as stocks and bonds. Additionally, hedge funds can provide diversification benefits, as they often invest in a wide range of assets and strategies, which can reduce overall portfolio risk.

However, hedge funds also come with a number of risks. Because of the use of leverage and complex financial instruments, hedge funds can be highly volatile and may experience significant losses in a short period of time. Additionally, hedge funds are not subject to the same regulatory requirements as other types of investment vehicles, which can make them more susceptible to fraud and mismanagement.

It's also worth noting that hedge funds are considered as high-risk, high-return investments. They are not suitable for all investors, particularly for those who are risk-averse or are looking for a more stable investment. Additionally, hedge funds can have high fees, which can eat into returns. They also have lock-up periods, which means that investors can't withdraw their money for a certain period of time, sometimes several years.

Hedge funds are not suitable for all investors and should be approached with caution.

Risks chat

Investing in a hedge fund comes with a number of risks, which investors should be aware of before deciding to invest in one. Here are some of the most common risks associated with hedge funds:

- Lack of transparency: Hedge funds are not subject to the same regulatory requirements as other types of investment vehicles, which means that they are not required to disclose as much information about their investments and strategies. This can make it difficult for investors to understand the risks involved and to assess the fund's performance.
- High volatility: Hedge funds often use leverage and complex financial instruments, which can result in high volatility and significant losses in a short period of time. Additionally, hedge funds are not always fully transparent about their investment strategies, which can make it difficult for investors to understand the risks involved.
- Lack of liquidity: Hedge funds often invest in illiquid assets, such as private companies or real estate, which can make it difficult for investors to cash out their investments when they want to. Additionally, hedge funds may have lock-up periods, during which investors are not allowed to withdraw their money.

- High fees: Hedge funds typically charge higher fees than other types of investment vehicles, such as mutual funds. These fees can eat into returns and make it more difficult for hedge funds to generate positive returns for investors.
- Counterparty risk: Hedge funds often use derivatives and other complex financial instruments, which can expose investors to counterparty risk or the risk that the other party to the transaction will default on its obligations. This can result in significant losses for investors.
- Managerial risk: Hedge funds are typically managed by a professional investment manager or team, but they are not always successful. If the manager or team makes poor investment decisions, it can result in significant losses for investors.
- Operational risk: Hedge funds are complex and can be subject to operational risks, such as fraud, mismanagement, or cyber-attacks. These risks can result in significant losses for investors.
- Geopolitical risk: Hedge funds often invest in a wide range of assets and markets, which can expose investors to geopolitical risks, such as currency fluctuations, trade tariffs, and political instability. These risks can result in significant losses for investors.
- Regulatory risk: Hedge funds operate in a largely unregulated environment, but regulatory changes can occur that could negatively impact the hedge fund's operations or returns.
- Credit risk: Hedge funds may also invest in debt securities, which carry credit risk. This means that if the issuer of the debt security defaults on its payments, it can result in significant losses for investors.

It's important to note that hedge funds are considered as high-risk, high-return investments. They are not suitable for all investors, particularly for those who are risk-averse or are looking for a more stable investment. Additionally, hedge funds can have high fees, which can eat into returns. They also have lock-up periods, which means that investors can't withdraw their money for a certain period of time, sometimes several years.

Biblical perspective

The Bible does not mention hedge funds specifically, but one important point to mention is the level of debt incurred. Proverbs 22:7 says, "The rich rule over the poor, and the borrower is slave to the lender." This verse highlights the importance of avoiding becoming dependent on debt, as hedge funds most often involve high levels of risk and leverage.

While the Bible does not directly address hedge funds, certain biblical principles and values may raise objections to investing in hedge funds for some Christians:

- Risk and Greed: Hedge funds often involve higher risks and speculative investment strategies to achieve potentially higher returns. The Bible warns against the love of money, greed, and pursuing wealth at all costs (1 Timothy 6:10, Proverbs 28:20). Christians may be cautious about engaging in investment practices that emphasise excessive risk-taking and financial gain over responsible stewardship and contentment.
- Lack of Transparency: Hedge funds are known for their limited transparency and disclosure requirements. The Bible emphasises the importance of honesty and integrity (Proverbs 11:1, Ephesians 4:25). Christians may have reservations about investing in vehicles that lack transparency and could potentially engage in practices contrary to biblical principles.
- Ethical Concerns: Some hedge funds may invest in industries or practices that go against Christian values, such as gambling, alcohol, or other businesses that may harm individuals or communities. The Bible encourages believers to avoid participation in activities that conflict with their faith and values (Ephesians 5:11, 2 Corinthians 6:14).
- Concerns About Wealth Inequality: Hedge funds are often associated with catering to high-net-worth individuals, which can contribute to wealth inequality. The Bible speaks about the responsibility to care for the poor and vulnerable (Proverbs 14:31, Luke 12:33). Christians may question whether investing in hedge

funds aligns with the call to love and serve others, especially those in need.
*   Speculation and Gaming: Hedge funds' strategies may involve speculative and market-timing approaches that resemble gambling. The Bible discourages gambling and instead encourages diligence, hard work, and prudent planning (Proverbs 14:23, Ecclesiastes 11:6).

It's important to note that investment decisions are subjective and can vary among individuals based on their understanding of the Bible and their personal convictions. Christians considering investments in hedge funds should prayerfully seek discernment and consider how such investments align with their faith, values, and overall financial goals.

Impact investing in hedge funds

Impact investing in hedge funds involves incorporating environmental, social, and governance (ESG) factors into the investment decisions made within hedge fund strategies. The aim is to achieve positive social or environmental outcomes alongside the financial objectives of the hedge fund.

Here's how impact investing can be integrated into hedge fund strategies:
*   ESG Integration: Hedge fund managers consider ESG factors when selecting and managing investments. They evaluate companies based on their environmental impact, social practices, and governance standards. By investing in companies with strong ESG performance, hedge funds can support sustainability and responsible business practices.
*   Impact-Focused Hedge Funds: Some hedge funds are specifically designed as impact funds, targeting investments that align with specific social or environmental goals. These funds actively seek opportunities that create positive change and contribute to sustainable development.
*   Shareholder Engagement: Hedge funds can engage with the companies they invest in to advocate for better ESG practices.

Through shareholder engagement, hedge fund managers can influence corporate policies and practices, promoting transparency and responsible conduct.

- Divestment and Negative Screening: Impact-focused hedge funds may choose to divest from companies involved in activities that conflict with their values or contribute to environmental or social harm. Negative screening involves excluding certain industries or companies from the investment universe.
- Impact Measurement and Reporting: Hedge funds measure and report on the social and environmental impact of their investments. They track progress toward impact objectives and communicate the outcomes to investors and stakeholders.
- Sustainable Strategies: Hedge funds may employ sustainable investment strategies, such as incorporating environmental considerations into their long-short equity positions or utilising sustainable debt instruments.
- Impactful Private Investments: Some hedge funds invest in private companies or projects that have a direct and measurable impact on society or the environment. These investments may focus on sectors such as renewable energy, affordable housing, or healthcare.
- Collaborative Initiatives: Hedge funds can participate in collaborative initiatives that address global challenges and promote sustainable business practices. These collaborations may involve partnerships with other investors, organisations, or governments.

Impact investing in hedge funds allows investors to align their financial goals with their desire to make a positive contribution to society and the environment. By selecting hedge funds that prioritise ESG considerations and impact objectives, investors can support sustainable and responsible investment practices while seeking competitive financial returns.

Chapter 25: Cryptocurrency

Investing in cryptocurrency during the car journey of investing is like embarking on an exciting road trip with an innovative, high-performance vehicle. Cryptocurrency represents a new and dynamic form of investment, akin to driving a cutting-edge electric car that promises thrilling speed and ground-breaking technology.

Cryptocurrencies, like the electric car's advanced features, rely on blockchain technology—a decentralised and secure system that records transactions. This technology acts as the engine driving the cryptocurrency market, providing speed, efficiency, and transparency in transactions.

Just as an electric car can revolutionise transportation, cryptocurrency has the potential to transform the financial landscape. It offers opportunities for high returns, much like an exhilarating acceleration on a fast, open road. Moreover, cryptocurrency operates 24/7, allowing investors to experience a continuous journey of investment possibilities.

However, similar to driving an innovative vehicle, investing in cryptocurrency also comes with risks. The cryptocurrency market can be highly volatile, akin to navigating through unpredictable weather or unfamiliar terrains. Just as sudden weather changes can impact a car journey, cryptocurrency prices can experience rapid fluctuations, leading to potential gains or losses.

Investing in cryptocurrency requires a careful understanding of the digital market, much like mastering the intricacies of a state-of-the-art vehicle. Proper research and risk management are essential to ensure a smooth journey and avoid potential pitfalls.

Investing in Cryptocurrency

Cryptocurrency is a digital or virtual currency that uses cryptography to secure its transactions and control the creation of new units. Transactions are recorded on a decentralised public ledger, called a blockchain, and each currency has its own underlying technology, such as the blockchain of Bitcoin, Ethereum, etc. Cryptocurrency operates independently of a central bank, and transfers are made directly between users through the use of public and private keys. Miners verify transactions and add them to the blockchain, and they are incentivised with small amounts of the currency they are mining.

It's important to note that investing in crypto is highly speculative and comes with a high degree of risk. It's not suitable for all investors, particularly for those who are risk-averse or are looking for a more stable investment. All investments carry some level of risk, and there are ways to mitigate the risks of investing in cryptocurrency. It is important to diversify your portfolio, investing in a range of different assets, including stocks, bonds, and real estate, in addition to cryptocurrency. This can help to reduce the impact of any losses in one area on your overall financial situation.

One financial advisor gave this excellent advice. "There are three main considerations. One, your ability. Do you have the ability to learn and understand it? Two, your liquidity. Do you have money in the bank so you won't fall into debt? Third, your suitability. This is a very high-risk profile. Cryptocurrency also has the 'VUCA' element – Volatility, Uncertainty, Complexity and Ambiguity. So, you need to take a lot more time to learn about it instead of jumping into it."

Investing in cryptocurrency can be a complex and highly speculative endeavour, but it also has the potential for high returns. Here are some of the options for investing in crypto:

1. Buying and holding: One of the simplest ways to invest in crypto is to buy and hold a specific currency, such as Bitcoin or Ethereum. You can buy crypto on a variety of exchanges, such as Coinbase, Binance, and Kraken, using fiat currency or other cryptocurrencies. Once you have purchased the crypto, you can store it in a digital wallet and wait for the value to increase.

2. Trading: Another option for investing in crypto is to trade it on a cryptocurrency exchange. This involves buying and selling crypto in order to take advantage of price fluctuations. Trading can be a high-risk, high-reward endeavour, as prices can be highly volatile. It's important to have a good understanding of the market and technical analysis before attempting to trade.

3. Mining: Mining is the process of creating new crypto by solving complex mathematical problems. It is a way for people to earn crypto by contributing their computing power to the network. It requires specialised hardware, and it's becoming increasingly difficult to mine Bitcoin and other crypto as the network becomes more secure.

4. Staking: A newer option for investing in crypto is staking, which allows holders of certain currencies to earn a return by holding and "staking" their coins in order to validate transactions on the blockchain. Staking is becoming increasingly popular as more and more currencies adopt proof-of-stake consensus mechanisms.

5. Lending and borrowing: Some exchanges offer lending and borrowing platforms, which allow you to lend or borrow crypto to earn a return. This can be a high-risk option, as there is a risk of default or price fluctuations.

6. Initial Coin Offerings (ICOs): An ICO is a fundraising mechanism in which a new cryptocurrency project sells a percentage of its tokens to early backers of the project in exchange for fiat or cryptocurrency. It is a high-risk, high-reward option as it's a fundraising process, and you should be aware of the risks associated with investing in an ICO.

7.   Crypto-funds: A crypto-fund is a type of investment fund that pools together capital from several investors and uses it to invest in a wide range of cryptocurrencies and blockchain-based projects. These funds are similar to hedge funds and offer investors exposure to a diverse portfolio of crypto assets, but they also come with similar risks.

8.   Decentralised Finance (DeFi): This is a new type of financial system that is built on blockchain technology. DeFi offers a wide range of financial products and services, such as lending, borrowing, trading, and insurance, all built on top of smart contracts. It's an emerging field, and you should be aware of the risks associated with investing in DeFi.

It's important to note that investing in crypto is highly speculative and comes with a high degree of risk. Prices can be highly volatile, and there is a risk of fraud, hacking, and other types of fraud. Additionally, cryptocurrency is not legal in all countries, and the regulations can change quickly. Before investing in crypto, it's important to do your own research and consult a financial advisor.

To sum up, investing in crypto can be a complex and highly speculative endeavour, but it also has the potential for high returns. Some options for investing in crypto include buying and holding, trading, mining, staking, lending, borrowing, initial coin offerings (ICOs), crypto-funds, and decentralised finance.

Risks chat

Investing in cryptocurrency comes with several risks that investors should be aware of before deciding to invest. Here are some of the most common risks associated with investing in crypto:

• Volatility: Cryptocurrency prices are highly volatile and can fluctuate dramatically in a short period of time. This can make it difficult to predict the value of your investment and can result in significant losses if you're not careful.

• Lack of regulation: Cryptocurrency is not yet widely regulated, which can make it difficult to protect your investment.

Additionally, regulatory changes can occur that could negatively impact the value of your investment.

• Hacking and fraud: Cryptocurrency exchanges and wallets are vulnerable to hacking and fraud. If you store your crypto on an exchange or in a digital wallet, it's important to make sure that the platform is secure and that you have strong passwords and two-factor authentication.

• Lack of understanding: Cryptocurrency can be difficult to understand, especially for those who are new to the market. It's important to do your research and to consult with a financial advisor or other expert before investing.

• Security risks: The blockchain technology that underlies most cryptocurrencies is still relatively new, and there may be unknown security risks that have yet to be discovered. Additionally, the security of smart contracts, used in decentralised finance, is still in the early stage of development and could have vulnerabilities.

• Lack of adoption: Cryptocurrency is still not widely accepted as a form of payment, which can make it difficult to use your crypto in real-world transactions. This lack of adoption could also limit the potential for growth in the value of your investment.

• Scams: Scammers may use the hype around crypto to trick investors into sending money to fake projects or exchanges. It's important to be vigilant and to only invest in projects that have a strong track record and a solid team.

• Limited track record: Cryptocurrency is a relatively new asset class, and the market is still in its early stages. This means that there is a limited track record to draw upon when assessing the potential of an investment.

• Lack of insurance: Unlike traditional investments, cryptocurrency is not typically insured. This means that if an exchange or wallet is hacked or if you lose your private key, there is often no way to recover your investment.

• Illiquidity: Some crypto assets can be illiquid, meaning it can be hard to find buyers or sellers for the assets you wish to trade, making it difficult to cash out your investment.

It's important to note that investing in crypto is highly speculative and comes with a high degree of risk. It's not suitable for all investors, particularly for those who are risk-averse or are looking for a more stable investment. Before investing in crypto, it's important to do your own research and consult a financial advisor. It's also important to be aware of the risks and to invest only what you can afford to lose.

Biblical perspective

It is interesting to note that the meaning of Crypto comes from the ancient Greek 'κρυπτός' *(kruptós)*, which means "hidden, secret."

Therefore, before investing in cryptocurrency, the Christian must understand this form of money and approach this, as with any investment opportunity, with wisdom and discernment. The Bible teaches us to be good stewards of the resources God has given us, and this includes our finances. "The plans of the diligent lead to profit as surely as haste leads to poverty." (Proverbs 21:5)

This means that we should take the time to educate ourselves about what crypto is, what its risks and potential rewards are, and seek the guidance of wise and trusted advisors.

The diligent Christian with surplus money to invest will seek God's wisdom as He reveals it to us. "For nothing is hidden that will not be made manifest, nor is anything secret that will not be known and come to light." (Luke 8:17)

The Christian view on Bitcoin and other cryptocurrencies can vary and is often influenced by individual interpretations of scripture and theology. Some Christians may view it as a positive development in the financial world, as it operates outside of traditional banking systems and has the potential to empower people in countries with weaker currencies or limited access to traditional banking. Others may be more sceptical and view it as promoting materialism and greed or view it as incompatible with Christian values around stewardship and the responsible use of money. There is no single "Christian view" on Bitcoin, and individuals and communities may hold differing opinions on its use and morality.

Investing in cryptocurrencies is not illegal, and a Christian should be free to hold cryptocurrencies. However, there are some compelling reasons why it is prudent for the Christian to stay away from this type of investment, for example;

1. Environmental cost

Mining crypto consumes a huge amount of energy. It has been calculated that the amount of electricity needed to maintain Bitcoin is more than the annual consumption of The Netherlands. [22]

2. Potential for illegal activities

There is clear evidence that crypto is being widely used to finance drug deals, weapon trading and other criminal activities. It was estimated that in 2019, over 46% of all Bitcoin transactions were involved with illegal activities. [23]

3. The temptation for speculation

As Christians, we want to invest rationally and responsibly. We cannot give explanations for its radical swings in price. The temptation to take extraordinary risks to make money is high.   "A faithful man will abound with blessings, but whoever hastens to be rich will not go unpunished." (Proverbs 28:20) We want to invest in building wealth, not merely accumulate riches.

4. The risk is extremely high

Although a certain amount of risk-taking is inherent in investing, as Christians, we want to take a calculated risk based on known factors. This is not the case with cryptos. "here is another serious problem I have seen under the sun. Hoarding riches harms the saver. Money is put into risky investments that turn sour, and everything is lost. In the end, there is nothing left to pass on to one's children." (Ecclesiastes 5:14,15)

As Christians, we are called to act ethically and with integrity in all areas of our lives, including our financial dealings. This means that we should carefully consider the ethical implications of investing in cryptocurrency and ensure that our investments are aligned with our values and beliefs.

Ultimately, the decision to invest in cryptocurrency is a personal one, and there is no one-size-fits-all answer. As with any investment opportunity, it's important to approach cryptocurrency with wisdom, discernment, and a strong ethical compass. By doing so, Christians can ensure that their investments are aligned with their values and beliefs and that they are using their resources to further God's kingdom on earth.

A footnote: Due to the high risk, it would be wise to only invest what you can afford to lose. If you could afford to lose some money – why not invest this in God's Kingdom work? It has been said that the bellies of the poor are a safer investment than any other because it is guaranteed by God Himself! "Whoever is generous to the poor lends to the LORD, and he will repay him for his deed." (Proverbs 19:17)

Impact investing in crypto

Impact investing in cryptocurrencies involves using digital assets to achieve both financial returns and positive social or environmental impact. While cryptocurrencies are known for their volatility and speculative nature, impact investors aim to leverage these assets for social good and sustainable initiatives.

Here's how impact investing in crypto can be approached:

- Supporting Social Impact Projects: Impact investors may use cryptocurrencies to support social impact projects and charitable organisations. Cryptocurrencies offer a fast and cost-effective way to transfer funds globally, enabling donations to reach those in need quickly and efficiently.

- Investing in Blockchain Solutions: Blockchain technology, which underpins most cryptocurrencies, has the potential to drive positive change in various sectors, such as supply chain transparency, renewable energy trading, and identity verification. Impact investors may invest in cryptocurrencies that are powering these blockchain solutions.

- Financing Sustainable Development: Impact investors can direct their crypto investments toward projects that promote sustainability, environmental conservation, or renewable energy initiatives. This could involve investing in cryptocurrencies that are linked to green energy projects or carbon-offsetting initiatives.

- Financial Inclusion: Cryptocurrencies have the potential to provide financial services to the unbanked and underbanked populations worldwide. Impact investors may support projects that aim to foster financial inclusion and empower marginalised communities through crypto-based solutions.

- Blockchain for Social Impact: There are initiatives and platforms focused on using blockchain and cryptocurrencies to address social challenges, such as poverty, education, and healthcare. Impact investors can contribute to these projects and support their development.

- ESG Considerations: Impact investors may assess the environmental, social, and governance aspects of cryptocurrencies they choose to invest in. They may avoid cryptocurrencies with significant negative environmental impacts or weak governance structures.

- Transparency and Accountability: Impact investors may seek projects and cryptocurrencies that prioritise transparency, providing clear information on how funds are used and their social impact.

- Advocacy and Education: Impact investors can advocate for the responsible and ethical use of cryptocurrencies and blockchain technology. Education about the potential benefits and risks of cryptocurrencies can also promote informed decision-making within the crypto community.

It's important to note that investing in cryptocurrencies carries inherent risks due to their price volatility and the evolving regulatory landscape. Impact investors must carefully research and select crypto projects that align with their impact objectives and risk tolerance.

Impact investing in cryptocurrencies provides an innovative way to contribute to positive change while navigating the fast-paced world of digital assets. By leveraging the transformative power of blockchain and cryptocurrencies, impact investors can play a role in advancing sustainability, financial inclusion, and social good on a global scale.

Chapter 26: Crowdfunding

Investing in crowdfunding during the car journey of investing is like embarking on a collaborative road trip with a group of fellow travellers. Crowdfunding represents a unique investment approach, similar to pooling resources and experiences with other passengers to collectively reach a destination.

In this metaphorical car, the crowdfunding platform serves as the vehicle, providing a space for investors to come together and contribute towards a shared goal. Just as each passenger brings their unique perspectives and resources to the trip, crowdfunding allows individuals to invest smaller amounts collectively, making it accessible to a broader range of investors.

As the journey progresses, each investor's contribution adds up, much like the collective efforts of passengers fuel the car's progress. This pooling of resources enables crowdfunding to finance projects or ventures that may have been difficult to achieve individually, creating opportunities for innovative ideas and small businesses to take flight.

However, like any road trip, there are potential risks and uncertainties. The success of the journey depends on the chosen destination and the collaboration between travellers. Similarly, investing in crowdfunding requires careful consideration of the project or business being funded, as well as the terms and conditions of the investment.

Additionally, crowdfunding often involves early-stage ventures, making it akin to exploring new territories. Investors should be prepared for a range of outcomes, understanding that some ventures may flourish while others may face challenges along the way.

Investing in crowdfunding

Crowdfunding is a method of raising capital by soliciting small investments from a large number of people, typically through online platforms. Here are some ways to invest in crowdfunding:

1. Rewards-based crowdfunding: In this type of crowdfunding, investors receive a reward, such as a product or service, in exchange for their investment. This is a popular method for start-ups and small businesses to raise capital for product development or other projects.
2. Equity crowdfunding: This type of crowdfunding involves investing in a company in exchange for equity, or ownership, in the company. This is a popular method for start-ups and small businesses to raise capital for growth and expansion.
3. Debt crowdfunding: This type of crowdfunding involves investing in a company or project in exchange for a return on the investment in the form of interest payments. This can be a good option for investors looking for a steady return on their investment.
4. Real estate crowdfunding: This type of crowdfunding involves investing in real estate projects, such as the development of a new property or the renovation of an existing one. This can be a good option for investors looking for a tangible asset and a steady return on their investment.
5. Community investing: This type of crowdfunding is focused on raising capital for projects that have a social or environmental impact. It's a popular option for investors who are interested in making a positive impact on their community or the world.
6. P2P lending: This is a type of crowdfunding in which individuals can lend money directly to borrowers, bypassing traditional financial institutions. It can be a good option for investors

looking for higher returns than those offered by traditional savings accounts or bonds.

7. Crowdfunding platforms: These platforms are websites that connect investors with projects or businesses that are seeking funding.

Risks chat

Investing in crowdfunding can come with some risks that investors should be aware of before deciding to invest. Here are some of the most common risks associated with investing in crowdfunding:

1. Lack of regulation: Crowdfunding is not yet widely regulated, which can make it difficult to protect your investment. Additionally, regulatory changes can occur that could negatively impact the value of your investment.

2. Lack of information: Crowdfunding campaigns often provide limited information about the project or business being funded, making it difficult to fully evaluate the investment opportunity. Additionally, financial statements and other disclosures may not be required, making it hard to assess the financial health of the company.

3. Lack of control: As a crowdfunding investor, you may have little control over how the funds are used or how the project or business is run.

4. High risk of failure: Crowdfunded projects and businesses are often start-ups, which have a higher risk of failure. Additionally, the projects may not be fully developed or may not have a proven track record.

5. No secondary market: Crowdfunding investments are not typically traded on secondary markets, which can make it difficult to sell your investment if you need to raise cash.

6. Potential fraud: There have been cases of fraud in the crowdfunding industry, with individuals or companies using the platform to raise money for fraudulent projects or schemes. It's important to do your research and to only invest in projects that have a strong track record and a solid team.

7.   Illiquidity: Some crowdfunding investments may be illiquid, meaning it can be hard to find buyers or sellers for the assets you wish to trade, making it difficult to cash out your investment.

8.   Lack of diversification: Investing in crowdfunding may involve putting a significant portion of your investment in a single project or business, which can be risky if the project or business fails.

9.   Lack of investor protection: Crowdfunding investors may not have the same level of protection as investors in other types of investments, such as stocks or bonds.

Biblical perspective

Some Christians may view crowdfunding as a way to support and empower individuals and communities, particularly in areas where traditional financial systems may not be easily accessible. Crowdfunding can also provide a way for people to pool resources and work together towards a common goal, aligning with Christian values of community and collaboration. It has been said that crowdfunding is the place where Christian love and solidarity intersect with online fundraising.

The earliest Christian example of crowdfunding was right at the start of the Church in Jerusalem. "There were no needy people among them, because those who owned land or houses would sell them and bring the money to the apostles to give to those in need." (Acts 4:34,35) For the Christian community, this should be a general practice: to support one another with our resources. For basic needs, this should be done by donation and not by investing as such, expecting nothing in return.

Others may be more wary of crowdfunding and view it as promoting greed or taking advantage of people's generosity. There may also be concerns about the ethics of investment and the potential for fraudulent activity.

Ultimately, the Christian view of crowdfunding will depend on how it is perceived and used and whether it aligns with the values of responsibility, fairness, and generosity that are often central to the Christian faith. Crowdfunding sites are not regulated, and accountability might be a problem. It may be that you don't get your money back, and the Christian should only be willing to invest what s/he is willing to lose.

• The Bible does not directly address crowdfunding as an investment option since crowdfunding is a relatively modern concept. However, Christians can approach crowdfunding as an investment with biblical principles and values in mind. Here are some considerations from a biblical perspective:

• Ethical Considerations: Crowdfunding campaigns may involve various projects and ventures. Christians should assess the ethical implications of the project they are supporting through crowdfunding. Investing in ventures that promote positive values, contribute to the common good, and avoid harmful practices is consistent with biblical principles (Philippians 4:8).

• Discernment and Diligence: Christians are encouraged to exercise discernment and diligence in their financial decisions (Proverbs 21:5, Proverbs 4:7). Before investing in a crowdfunding project, it's essential to research and evaluate the feasibility, credibility, and potential risks associated with the venture.

• Love and Generosity: The Bible encourages believers to be generous and to love their neighbours as themselves (Mark 12:31, 2 Corinthians 9:6-7). Crowdfunding can be an opportunity for Christians to support projects that align with their values and contribute to the well-being of others.

• Caution with High-Risk Ventures: Some crowdfunding opportunities may involve high-risk ventures, such as start-up businesses or innovative projects. While taking risks can be appropriate in certain circumstances, Christians should exercise caution and consider their risk tolerance and overall financial goals.

• Prayerful Consideration: Before investing in crowdfunding campaigns, Christians are encouraged to seek God's wisdom and guidance through prayer (James 1:5). Seeking God's direction can help believers make sound investment decisions aligned with their faith and values.

As with any investment, Christians should exercise discernment, seek wise counsel, and consider the potential ethical and financial implications of crowdfunding campaigns.

Impact investing

Impact investing in crowdfunding involves using online crowdfunding platforms to support projects and ventures that align with specific social or environmental impact objectives. Crowdfunding allows individuals to pool their financial resources to fund projects, businesses, or initiatives that they believe in while also contributing to positive change in society or the environment.

- Here's how impact investing in crowdfunding can be approached:
- Impact-Focused Projects: Impact investors can browse crowdfunding platforms to find projects or ventures that are specifically focused on addressing social or environmental challenges. These projects may include sustainable agriculture, renewable energy initiatives, clean water access, social enterprises supporting marginalised communities, educational programs, and more.
- Socially Responsible Crowdfunding Platforms: Some crowdfunding platforms specialise in impact investing and prioritise projects with clear social or environmental benefits. Investors can choose platforms that have a track record of promoting responsible and sustainable projects.
- Equity Crowdfunding: Impact investors can participate in equity crowdfunding, where they invest in a stake in the business or project in exchange for financial returns. This allows them to support companies with impact-driven business models and share in their potential success.
- Rewards-Based Crowdfunding: Impact investors may also engage in rewards-based crowdfunding, where they contribute funds to a project in exchange for non-financial rewards, such as products, experiences, or acknowledgements. This approach enables investors to back projects that resonate with their values without seeking financial returns.

• Peer-to-Peer Lending: Some crowdfunding platforms facilitate peer-to-peer lending, where investors lend money directly to individuals or businesses in need of capital. Impact investors can use this approach to support responsible borrowers and projects with social or environmental missions.

• Impact Measurement: Impact investors may evaluate the potential social or environmental impact of crowdfunding projects before making their investment decisions. They can look for projects that have clear goals, transparency, and a commitment to measuring and reporting their impact outcomes.

• Diversification: As with any investment strategy, diversification is essential. Impact investors may spread their investments across multiple crowdfunding projects to reduce risk and increase the potential for positive impact.

• Community Engagement: Crowdfunding allows impact investors to be part of a community of like-minded individuals supporting projects that align with their values. Engaging with project creators and fellow investors can enhance the sense of collective impact.

Impact investing in crowdfunding empowers individuals to make a difference in areas that matter to them personally, whether it's environmental conservation, poverty alleviation, education, or social empowerment. By leveraging the power of online crowdfunding platforms, impact investors can support a wide range of projects and initiatives that contribute to a more sustainable and equitable world.

Chapter 27: Micro-financing

Investing in micro-financing during the car journey of investing is like taking a detour to visit local communities and provide a helping hand to small businesses and entrepreneurs. Micro-financing represents a unique and impactful approach to investment, similar to stopping at roadside stalls or small shops to support the local economy.

In this metaphorical car, micro-financing acts as a bridge, connecting investors with individuals or small businesses in need of financial assistance. Just as exploring off-the-beaten-path destinations offers a chance to engage with local cultures, micro-financing allows investors to connect with entrepreneurs who may not have access to traditional banking services.

As the journey progresses, investors' contributions directly impact the lives of these entrepreneurs, much like the support from travellers benefits the local communities they visit. Micro-financing provides crucial capital for small businesses, enabling them to grow and thrive and contributing to the economic development of the regions they operate in.

However, just like exploring new places, micro-financing may involve risks and uncertainties. Some businesses may face challenges, and investors should be prepared for varying outcomes. Nevertheless, the potential rewards go beyond financial gains, as MICRO-FINANCING allows investors to be part of positive change and social impact.

Investing in micro-financing

Investing in micro-financing requires a willingness to engage with the stories and aspirations of the entrepreneurs, much like travellers who immerse themselves in the local cultures they encounter. It demands empathy, understanding, and a long-term perspective to support sustainable growth and development.

Micro-finance, often referred to as "banking for the poor," is a powerful financial tool that aims to provide financial services to individuals and small businesses who lack access to traditional banking services. It is a concept that has gained significant recognition and popularity over the past few decades due to its potential to alleviate poverty and promote economic development in underserved communities around the world.

At its core, micro-finance focuses on offering small loans, savings accounts, insurance, and other financial services to individuals who are often excluded from the formal financial sector. These individuals typically reside in low-income areas, lack collateral or credit history, and face numerous barriers when attempting to secure financial support from traditional banks.

The key principle of micro-finance is to empower the underserved population by promoting financial inclusion, fostering entrepreneurship, and enabling individuals to create sustainable livelihoods. By providing access to credit and financial tools, micro-finance institutions (MFIs) seek to enable borrowers to start or expand their businesses, invest in education, improve their living conditions, and break the cycle of poverty.

One of the distinguishing features of micro-finance is the emphasis on building social capital and promoting social responsibility. MFIs often operate as mission-driven organisations, focusing not only on financial returns but also on the social impact of their activities. They aim to create positive changes in the lives of their clients and the communities they serve by offering financial literacy training, promoting gender equality, and encouraging responsible financial practices.

Micro-finance has demonstrated its effectiveness in numerous countries, particularly in developing regions. By providing financial resources and support to those who lack access to conventional banking services, micro-finance has proven to be a catalyst for economic growth, poverty reduction, and women's empowerment. It enables individuals to seize opportunities, improve their income-generating activities, and build resilience against unexpected financial shocks.

In recent years, micro-finance has also witnessed innovation and adaptation to changing technologies. The rise of mobile banking and digital financial services has allowed for more efficient and cost-effective delivery of micro-finance products, enabling wider outreach and reducing operational barriers.

While micro-finance has experienced notable success, it also faces challenges and criticisms. Critics argue that high-interest rates and aggressive lending practices by some MFIs can lead to over-indebtedness among borrowers. Additionally, there are ongoing debates about the long-term impact of micro-finance and the need for comprehensive poverty alleviation strategies that address structural issues.

Overall, microfinance continues to play a vital role in expanding financial inclusion and fostering economic development. By providing access to financial services for the unbanked and underserved populations, micro-finance contributes to creating a more equitable and inclusive society where individuals and communities have the opportunity to thrive.

Risks chat

Investing in micro-finance, like any other form of investment, carries certain risks. While micro-finance has proven to be an effective tool for poverty alleviation and economic development, it is important to consider the potential risks involved. Here are some key risks associated with investing in micro-finance:

1. Credit Risk: Micro-finance institutions (MFIs) primarily lend to individuals and small businesses with limited or no credit history and often operate in high-risk environments. There is a possibility of loan defaults or delinquencies, which can impact the repayment of principal and interest to investors. Credit risk is inherent in micro-finance due to the vulnerable nature of the borrowers and the absence of traditional collateral.

2.   Operational Risk: MFIs face operational risks such as inadequate risk management systems, insufficient governance structures, or inadequate monitoring of borrowers. Inefficient operations and poor portfolio management can lead to financial losses, affecting the returns on investments.

3.   Political and Regulatory Risks: Micro-finance is influenced by political and regulatory environments in the countries where it operates. Changes in government policies, regulations, or legal frameworks can impact the operations and profitability of MFIs. Political instability, corruption, or regulatory restrictions can pose risks to investments in microfinance.

4.   Market Risk: Micro-finance investments can be exposed to market risks, including fluctuations in interest rates, exchange rates, and macroeconomic factors. Economic downturns, currency devaluations, or interest rate volatility can affect the financial performance of MFIs and, consequently, the returns on investments.

5.   Currency Risk: Investing in micro-finance in countries with different currencies exposes investors to currency risk. Exchange rate fluctuations can impact the value of investments, particularly when repatriating funds or converting returns into the investor's home currency.

6.   Reputation and Social Risk: Micro-finance operates within a social context, and negative incidents or controversies related to MFIs can harm their reputation and social standing. Issues such as aggressive lending practices, high-interest rates, or inadequate client protection can lead to public scrutiny and potential backlash, affecting investor confidence.

7.   Liquidity Risk: Micro-finance investments, particularly in the form of funds or vehicles, may have limited liquidity. It can be challenging to quickly convert investments into cash when needed, as secondary markets for micro-finance investments may be illiquid or limited.

8.   External Shocks: Micro-finance can be vulnerable to external shocks such as natural disasters, political unrest, or economic crises. These events can disrupt the operations of MFIs

and affect the ability of borrowers to repay loans, leading to potential losses for investors.

Investors need to conduct thorough due diligence, assess the risk-reward trade-off, and diversify their portfolios to mitigate the risks associated with microfinance investments. Investing through reputable and well-regulated institutions, monitoring the performance of investments, and staying informed about the local context is crucial in managing these risks effectively.

Biblical perspective

A Christian approach to micro-financing is guided by principles and values derived from Christian teachings and ethics. It emphasises the importance of economic justice, compassion, and stewardship in addressing poverty and empowering marginalised individuals and communities. Here are some key aspects of a Christian approach to micro-financing:

1. Dignity and Empowerment: A Christian approach recognises the inherent dignity of every person as being created in the image of God. Micro-financing seeks to empower individuals by providing them with the means to create sustainable livelihoods, start businesses, and improve their standard of living. It aims to restore a sense of dignity and self-worth to those who have been marginalised or excluded from traditional financial systems.

2. Social Justice and Fairness: Christian teachings emphasise the pursuit of justice and fairness in economic relationships. Micro-finance institutions operating from a Christian perspective strive to ensure that their practices are fair and transparent, with interest rates and terms that are reasonable and not exploitative. They are committed to promoting economic opportunities for the poor and combating systemic inequalities.

3. Compassion and Solidarity: Christianity emphasises the importance of compassion and care for those in need. A Christian approach to micro-financing recognises the vulnerability of

marginalised individuals and seeks to meet their financial needs with empathy and compassion. It goes beyond financial assistance by providing support services, mentoring, and training to help borrowers succeed and achieve long-term self-sufficiency.

4.   Responsible Stewardship: Christian principles emphasise responsible stewardship of resources. Micro-finance institutions with a Christian approach encourage borrowers to use their loans wisely and responsibly, promoting financial literacy and entrepreneurship training. They also advocate for sustainable business practices that consider environmental and social considerations, aligning economic activities with Christian values of stewardship and care for creation.

5.   Values-Based Decision Making: Christian micro-finance institutions often make decisions based on values rather than purely financial considerations. They prioritise the well-being of individuals and communities over profit maximisation, considering the social impact of their actions. They may prioritise lending to vulnerable groups, such as women or marginalised communities, to address systemic inequalities and promote social justice.

6.   Holistic Development: A Christian approach to micro-financing recognises that poverty is multi-dimensional, encompassing not just financial poverty but also social, spiritual, and relational poverty. It seeks to address the holistic needs of individuals and communities, providing access to not only financial services but also education, healthcare, and spiritual support. This approach acknowledges that true transformation involves addressing the root causes of poverty and fostering a sense of hope and purpose.

A Christian approach to micro-financing combines financial services with Christian values of justice, compassion, stewardship, and holistic development. It seeks to empower individuals, promote social justice, and foster sustainable economic growth while embodying the love and care that Jesus Christ taught and exemplified.

Impact investing in micro-financing

Impact investing in micro-financing involves providing financial resources to micro-finance institutions or directly to micro-entrepreneurs and individuals in underserved or low-income communities. The goal is to empower and uplift disadvantaged populations by promoting economic inclusion, fostering entrepreneurship, and supporting sustainable development.

Here's how impact investing in micro-financing can be implemented:

1. Supporting Micro-finance Institutions (MFIs): Impact investors can invest in micro-finance institutions that provide financial services to low-income individuals and small businesses. These institutions offer micro-loans, savings accounts, insurance, and other financial products tailored to the needs of the economically vulnerable.

2. Enabling Entrepreneurship: Impact investors can fund micro-loans for micro-entrepreneurs who lack access to traditional banking services. These loans help them start or expand small businesses, creating income-generating opportunities and fostering economic growth in local communities.

3. Empowering Women: Micro-financing often prioritises supporting women entrepreneurs and economically disadvantaged women. Impact investors can direct their investments to initiatives that specifically focus on empowering women and enhancing their economic participation.

4. Social Impact Bonds: Some impact investors engage in social impact bonds, where they provide upfront funding to support micro-finance projects that aim to achieve specific social outcomes, such as improved healthcare, education, or poverty reduction.

5. Environmental and Social Performance: Impact investors assess the social and environmental performance of micro-finance institutions to ensure they operate ethically, transparently, and responsibly, aligning with the investors' impact objectives.

6. Monitoring and Impact Measurement: Impact investors track and measure the social and economic impact of their micro-financing investments. This involves assessing the success of funded projects in terms of poverty alleviation, job creation, income generation, and improvements in livelihoods.

7. Financial Inclusion: By investing in micro-financing initiatives, impact investors contribute to expanding financial inclusion, enabling marginalised individuals to access financial resources, build assets, and improve their overall economic stability.

8. Collaborative Partnerships: Impact investors often collaborate with other organisations and governments to scale up micro-financing efforts and create lasting change in communities.

Impact investing in micro-financing not only provides individuals with much-needed access to financial resources but also helps break the cycle of poverty by fostering economic self-reliance and resilience. By supporting micro-finance initiatives, impact investors play a significant role in promoting social and economic development, empowering communities, and advancing sustainable livelihoods for vulnerable populations.

Chapter 28: Business Equity

Investing in business equity during the car journey of investing is like becoming a co-driver in a dynamic and growing business. Business equity represents a share of ownership in a company, similar to being a trusted partner sitting beside the driver, contributing to the journey's success.

In this metaphorical car, the business represents the vehicle driven by the entrepreneur or management team. As an equity investor, you become an integral part of the journey, sharing in the company's successes and challenges. Just as a co-driver brings valuable insights and support to the driver, an equity investor provides capital, expertise, and guidance to the business.

As the journey progresses, your investment in the business is closely tied to its performance, much like a co-driver's contribution directly impacts the car's direction and speed. If the business thrives and grows, the value of your equity investment increases, providing potential financial rewards.

However, just like a co-driver assumes risks during the journey, investing in business equity comes with inherent uncertainties. Business performance, market conditions, and other external factors can influence the value of your investment, much like unforeseen circumstances can impact a road trip.

Investing in business equity requires careful due diligence and a strong belief in the company's vision and leadership, akin to choosing the right co-driver for a long and challenging journey. As an equity investor, you have a vested interest in the company's growth and profitability, and your active involvement may also contribute to the business's success.

Investing in business equity

Investing in a (start-up) business can be one of the highest areas of impact investing. Private equity is a high-impact investment strategy that involves investing in privately held companies or taking direct ownership stakes in businesses with significant growth potential. Through private equity investments, institutional investors and high-net-worth individuals provide capital and strategic support to companies, fostering innovation, expansion, and operational improvements. As these investments often target non-public firms in their early or growth stages, private equity can have a profound impact on job creation, technological advancements, and economic development, driving transformative changes in industries and contributing to long-term value creation for both investors and the broader economy.

One of the key attractions of investing in a start-up is the potential for high returns. Start-ups are often in their early stages of development, and as they grow and achieve success, their value can increase significantly. If you invest wisely in a promising start-up, you could see your initial investment multiply several times over. Some of the most well-known start-up success stories, like Airbnb and Uber, have generated extraordinary returns for their early investors.

Another advantage of investing in a start-up is the opportunity to support and be part of innovative ideas and disruptive technologies. Start-ups are typically founded by passionate entrepreneurs who are eager to bring their visions to life. By investing in their ventures, you become a stakeholder in their journey, and your support can help them overcome hurdles and reach their full potential.

Diversification is a key strategy when investing in start-ups. Since the failure rate is high, spreading your investment across multiple start-ups can help mitigate the impact of potential losses. Angel investor groups and venture capital funds often adopt this approach, investing in a portfolio of start-ups to increase the likelihood of discovering the next big success.

Timing is crucial in start-up investing. Getting in early can mean access to a lower valuation and a larger equity stake. However, it also means taking on more risk. On the other hand, joining a start-up at a later stage may offer a more proven concept and market traction but could lead to a higher initial investment cost.

Building a strong relationship with the start-up's founders and management team is paramount. Transparent communication and a shared vision are essential for the success of the investment. As an investor, your knowledge, experience, and network can add value to the start-up beyond just financial backing.

Start-up investing is a long-term commitment. It may take years before a start-up realises its full potential and provides a return on investment. Patience, resilience, and a willingness to stay invested through ups and downs are essential traits for successful start-up investors.

In recent years, various crowdfunding platforms and online angel investor networks have made it easier for individuals to invest in start-ups. However, it's crucial to understand the risks and conduct proper research before committing funds.

In conclusion, investing in a start-up business can be a thrilling and potentially rewarding experience. It offers the chance to support innovation and entrepreneurship while seeking high returns. Nevertheless, it is not without risks, and due diligence, diversification, and a long-term perspective are crucial for navigating the dynamic world of start-up investing. If approached thoughtfully, investing in a start-up can be a gratifying addition to a well-rounded investment portfolio.

Risks chat

However, investing in start-ups also comes with inherent risks. The majority of start-ups fail, and as an investor, you must be prepared to accept the possibility of losing your entire investment. Start-up ventures face numerous challenges, including fierce competition, changing market dynamics, and operational hurdles. Thorough due diligence and a keen understanding of the industry and the start-up's business model are essential to minimise risks.

When investing in a start-up business opportunity, it's crucial to approach the process with careful consideration and due diligence. Start-ups are inherently risky, but with thorough research and evaluation, you can increase your chances of making a wise investment. Here are some key factors to look for when considering a start-up business opportunity:

1. Unique Value Proposition: Evaluate the start-up's product or service and assess its uniqueness and potential market demand. Look for innovations that solve a real problem or address an unmet need in the market. A strong value proposition is essential for the start-up's growth and success.

2. Experienced and Committed Team: The team behind the start-up is a critical factor in its success. Look for a team with relevant industry experience, a clear vision, and a commitment to execute the business plan. Assess their track record, expertise, and ability to adapt to challenges.

3. Market Potential: Analyse the size and potential growth of the target market. Consider the competitive landscape and the start-up's ability to differentiate itself and capture market share. A large and expanding market can provide a favourable environment for growth.

4. Scalability: Assess the start-up's potential for scalability, meaning its ability to grow rapidly without incurring disproportionately higher costs. A scalable business model can attract additional investors and lead to higher returns.

5. Traction and Validation: Look for evidence of early traction and validation, such as customer testimonials, sales figures, or partnerships. A start-up that has already gained some market validation may have a higher likelihood of success.

6. Financial Health: Review the start-up's financials, including revenue projections, expenses, and funding requirements. A clear and realistic financial plan is crucial for assessing the viability and sustainability of the business.

7. Intellectual Property: Evaluate the start-up's intellectual property rights, such as patents, trademarks, or copyrights. Intellectual property can provide a competitive advantage and protect the start-up's innovations.

8. Exit Strategy: Consider the start-up's exit strategy, such as potential acquisition opportunities or plans for an initial public offering (IPO). An established exit strategy can provide a roadmap for potential returns on your investment.

9. Risk Mitigation: Be aware of the risks associated with start-up investments and assess the start-up's strategies for mitigating those risks. Understand the potential challenges and have a clear understanding of your risk tolerance.

10. Legal and Regulatory Compliance: Ensure the start-up complies with all legal and regulatory requirements. Review contracts, agreements, and potential legal issues that may affect the business.

11. Investor Protection: Evaluate the terms and conditions of the investment, including equity ownership, valuation, and shareholder rights. Seek legal counsel if necessary to protect your interests.

12. Alignment with Your Values: Consider whether the start-up's mission, values, and practices align with your personal beliefs and investment principles.

By thoroughly examining these factors, seeking expert advice when needed, and aligning your investment with your risk tolerance and financial goals, you can make an informed decision when investing in a start-up business opportunity. Remember that start-up investing involves risk, and diversifying your portfolio across various asset classes is essential for managing overall risk exposure.

Biblical perspective

Jesus, in his parable of the Ten Minas, said, "A nobleman went into a far country to receive for himself a kingdom and then return. Calling ten of his servants, he gave them ten minas, and said to them, 'Engage in business until I come.' (Luke 19:12,13)

Engaging in business is a worthy calling for disciples who want to honour God with their resources and talents.

The Bible does not directly address the concept of investing money in a business as we understand it in modern financial terms. However, the Bible does provide principles and wisdom that can be applied to business activities and financial decisions. A further discussion is out of the scope of this book.

Investing in a business can have a positive impact on people in several ways:

1. Job Creation: One of the most significant ways that starting a business helps others is by creating job opportunities. As a business grows, it requires a workforce to operate, leading to the creation of new employment opportunities for individuals in the community. Providing jobs can contribute to reducing unemployment rates and improving the economic well-being of individuals and families.

2. Economic Growth: Successful businesses contribute to the overall economic growth of a region or country. They pay taxes, purchase goods and services from other businesses, and stimulate economic activity. This increased economic activity can lead to a healthier and more vibrant local economy, benefiting the entire community.

3. Product or Service Innovation: Entrepreneurs often start businesses to address unmet needs in the market or to introduce innovative products and services. These innovations can enhance the quality of life for consumers, making their lives more convenient, efficient, or enjoyable.

4. Community Development: Businesses can play a vital role in community development. They may actively engage in supporting local charities, sponsoring events, or participating in community projects. By being involved in community development, businesses can positively impact the well-being of the people they serve.

5.   Transfer of Knowledge and Skills: Entrepreneurs and business owners often share their knowledge and expertise with their employees, helping them develop valuable skills and experience. This transfer of knowledge can empower individuals, enabling them to take on more significant roles within the company or even start their own ventures in the future.

6.   Supplier and Vendor Support: Businesses rely on suppliers and vendors for the goods and services they need to operate. By engaging with these suppliers, businesses contribute to the economic growth and sustainability of other businesses within their supply chain.

7.   Social Impact Initiatives: Some businesses incorporate social impact initiatives as part of their core values. They may commit to environmentally friendly practices, fair labour standards, or support social causes. Such initiatives can positively impact society and inspire others to do the same.

8.   Inspiration and Entrepreneurship: Successful entrepreneurs and business owners can serve as role models, inspiring others to pursue their own entrepreneurial dreams. Their stories of resilience, innovation, and hard work can motivate aspiring entrepreneurs to take risks and contribute to the economy.

Starting a business has the potential to make a meaningful and lasting impact on the lives of many people, ranging from employees and customers to the wider community and beyond. It's an opportunity to create something of value, provide jobs, and contribute positively to society's economic and social fabric.

Impact investing

Impact investing in business equity involves making investments in companies with the dual objective of achieving financial returns and generating positive social or environmental impact. Impact investors seek out businesses that align with their values and have a clear commitment to sustainability, social responsibility, and ethical practices.

Here's how impact investing in business equity can be implemented:

1.   Impact-Focused Business Selection: Impact investors actively seek out businesses with impact-driven missions and strategies. These businesses may be dedicated to environmental sustainability, social inclusion, diversity and equality, renewable energy, healthcare access, or other positive social and environmental outcomes.

2.   Engagement and Advocacy: Impact investors may engage with the businesses they invest in to advocate for better ESG practices (Environmental, Social, and Governance). They use their shareholder influence to encourage ethical behaviour, transparency, and responsible business conduct.

3.   Long-Term Perspective: Impact investing in business equity often takes a long-term perspective, as creating meaningful impact and sustainable change may require time and commitment.

4.   Impact Measurement: Impact investors assess and measure the social and environmental impact of the businesses they invest in. They use relevant metrics to track progress toward impact objectives and to ensure accountability.

5.   Supporting Social Enterprises: Impact investors may focus on supporting social enterprises, which are businesses with a primary mission of creating a positive social impact while also generating revenue.

6.   Diversity and Inclusion: Impact investors consider diversity and inclusion in their investment decisions, supporting businesses that prioritise diversity in their leadership and workforce and promote inclusive practices.

7.   Sustainable Business Practices: Impact investors favour companies that demonstrate sustainable business practices, including reducing their environmental footprint, promoting fair labour practices, and fostering positive community relationships.

8.   Collaborative Partnerships: Impact investors often collaborate with other stakeholders, such as other investors, NGOs, or governmental organisations, to leverage resources and maximise impact.

Impact investing in business equity allows investors to align their financial interests with their desire to contribute to positive change in the world. By directing capital to businesses that prioritise sustainability and social responsibility, impact investors can drive meaningful progress toward a more inclusive, equitable, and sustainable global economy.

Chapter 29: Collectables

Investing in collectables during the car journey of investing is like embarking on a thrilling treasure hunt to discover and acquire unique and valuable artefacts. Collectables represent rare and coveted items, similar to hidden gems waiting to be unearthed along the road of investment.

In this metaphorical car, the world of collectables serves as an exciting landscape full of diverse and fascinating treasures. Just as travellers venture into uncharted territories to find hidden treasures, investing in collectables involves exploring niche markets and unique pieces that have the potential to appreciate over time.

As the journey progresses, each collectable you acquire becomes a precious souvenir, much like the cherished memories travellers bring back from their expeditions. Collectables can hold sentimental value and evoke nostalgia, making them not only a potential investment but also a source of joy and fascination.

However, like any treasure hunt, there are risks and uncertainties along the way. The value of collectables can be influenced by various factors, such as market demand, authenticity, and condition, akin to the challenges of assessing the true worth of undiscovered artefacts.

Investing in collectables requires a discerning eye and specialised knowledge, much like the expertise needed to identify genuine treasures amidst replicas. Understanding market trends and historical significance can be crucial in making informed investment decisions.

Moreover, just as travellers need to protect their findings from damage or loss, preserving and caring for collectables is essential to maintain their value over time. Collectables can be delicate and require proper handling and storage to retain their allure and investment potential.

Investing in collectibles

There are many types of collectables. They are often sorted into categories and subcategories as they come in different shapes, sizes, and price ranges. Some of the common types of collectables include:

1. Coins
2. Stamps
3. Fine art
4. Timepieces and vintage jewellery
5. Classic automobiles
6. Antique furniture and houseware

Investing in collectables is a pursuit that not only brings immense pleasure to collectors but also offers the potential for extraordinary gains. Those engaged in collecting acknowledge the following benefits associated with this activity:

1. Personal Fulfilment: Collecting allows individuals to follow their passions, especially those who may not have had the opportunity to indulge in such interests during their working years or in retirement. Whether it's completing a set of baseball cards or acquiring a collection of designer bags from different brands, the process can be deeply satisfying.

2. Social Networking Opportunities: Collectors often become part of niche groups with shared interests, fostering social connections. Regular meetups and collective travel to auctions provide opportunities for interaction, assistance in locating missing items for their collections, and a sense of camaraderie among like-minded enthusiasts.

3. Portfolio Diversification: Including collectables as unique assets in an investment portfolio can contribute to diversification. This diversification can be especially advantageous during periods of inflation or market downturns, as collectables often move independently of traditional stock market trends, potentially mitigating losses.

4. Confidentiality: The transfer of collectables generally occurs without public records or strict regulation, offering a degree of confidentiality. For collectors with rare and valuable items, this discretion can be particularly appealing, as they can maintain privacy regarding the value of their collection.

5. Potential Financial Returns: Investing in collectables with the anticipation of appreciation over time can yield significant financial rewards. For instance, remarkable stories of collectors acquiring items for relatively modest prices and later selling them for astronomical sums in auctions exemplify the potential for lucrative returns.

Investing in art and antiques involves purchasing valuable artworks, collectables, and historical artefacts with the expectation that their value will appreciate over time, leading to potential financial gains. Unlike traditional financial assets, investing in art and antiques is considered an alternative investment that can offer diversification and potential hedging against market volatility.

Here are some key aspects of investing in art and antiques:

1. Unique Assets: Art and antiques are tangible, unique assets with intrinsic historical, cultural, and aesthetic value. Investors often appreciate the opportunity to own and preserve valuable pieces of art or rare collectables.

2. Potential for Appreciation: The value of art and antiques can appreciate significantly over time, driven by factors such as artistic significance, rarity, provenance, and demand from collectors and museums. However, it's important to note that the art market can be highly subjective and influenced by trends and tastes.

3. Diversification: Including art and antiques in an investment portfolio can provide diversification benefits, as these assets have a

low correlation with traditional financial markets like stocks and bonds. During economic downturns, the art market may behave differently from traditional assets, potentially reducing overall portfolio risk.

4. Long-Term Investment: Investing in art and antiques typically requires a long-term investment horizon. The art market can be illiquid, and finding the right buyer for a particular piece may take time. Patience and a willingness to hold onto assets for an extended period are essential for art investors.

5. Expertise and Research: Successful art and antique investing often involves a deep understanding of the market and individual artists or collectables. Conducting thorough research, seeking expert advice, and building relationships with reputable art dealers and auction houses are crucial for making informed investment decisions.

6. Preservation and Storage: Proper preservation and storage of art and antiques are critical to maintaining their value. Factors such as temperature, humidity, and protection from damage play a vital role in preserving the condition of these assets.

7. Risk Factors: Art and antiques are illiquid assets, meaning they cannot be easily converted to cash. Additionally, the art market can be speculative and subject to fluctuations, making it challenging to predict future returns accurately.

8. Non-Financial Benefits: Beyond potential financial gains, investing in art and antiques can offer non-financial benefits, such as cultural enrichment, personal enjoyment, and the satisfaction of preserving and contributing to the art world's heritage.

Investing in art and antiques can be a rewarding and fascinating endeavour for those with a passion for culture and history. However, it's essential to approach this type of investment with careful consideration, research, and a long-term perspective.

Risks chat

Investing in art and antiques carries several risks, which potential investors should carefully consider before committing their resources:

1.   Market Volatility: The art and antique market can be highly volatile, with prices fluctuating based on trends, demand, and economic conditions. Prices for specific artists or collectables can experience significant ups and downs, leading to unpredictable investment returns.

2.   Lack of Liquidity: Art and antiques are illiquid assets, meaning they cannot be easily and quickly converted to cash. Finding the right buyer for a specific piece can take time, and selling the investment may require engaging with specialised auction houses or art dealers.

3.   Value Subjectivity: The value of art and antiques is subjective and can vary significantly based on individual opinions, expert assessments, and prevailing market sentiments. Determining an accurate value can be challenging, leading to potential discrepancies between the perceived and actual worth of an investment.

4.   Limited Diversification: Investing in art and antiques can be capital-intensive, potentially limiting an investor's ability to diversify their portfolio across different asset classes. Over-concentration in one type of asset may expose the investor to higher risks.

5.   Art Market Speculation: The art market can be influenced by speculative behaviour, with investors buying and selling based on anticipated short-term price changes rather than long-term intrinsic value. Speculation can exacerbate price volatility and contribute to price bubbles.

6.   Lack of Information Transparency: Unlike publicly traded stocks, art and antique markets may lack transparency, with limited publicly available information on sales, valuations, and overall market conditions. Investors may face challenges in obtaining reliable and comprehensive data.

7.   Artwork Condition and Authenticity: The condition of art and antiques significantly impacts their value. Damage or restoration can affect the artwork's authenticity and historical significance, potentially diminishing its investment value.

8.   Storage and Maintenance Costs: Investing in art and antiques requires proper storage, maintenance, and insurance to

preserve their value. These costs can be substantial, especially for valuable or delicate pieces.

9. Counterfeiting and Forgery: The art market is not immune to counterfeiting and forgery, and investors must take precautions to ensure the authenticity of the pieces they acquire.

10. Changing Tastes and Trends: Art and antique values can be influenced by changing tastes and trends, which may cause certain artists or collectables to fall out of favour with collectors and investors.

Given these risks, potential investors in art and antiques should approach their investment decisions with caution, conduct thorough research, seek expert advice, and carefully assess their risk tolerance and long-term investment objectives. Additionally, investors may choose to complement their art and antique investments with a well-diversified portfolio that includes traditional financial assets to mitigate overall risk.

Biblical perspective

A Christian critique of investing in art and antiques raises several considerations based on biblical principles and values:

1. Stewardship and Priorities: Christianity emphasises the concept of stewardship, acknowledging that all resources, including money, belong to God. Investing in art and antiques may divert financial resources from more direct and impactful ways of helping others in need or supporting missions and charitable causes.

2. Materialism and Greed: Christianity warns against the dangers of materialism and the love of money. Investing in art and antiques solely for potential financial gain may lead to a focus on material possessions rather than on spiritual growth and serving others.

3. Ethical Concerns: The art market, like any other market, can involve unethical practices, such as trafficking in stolen artefacts or supporting artworks that promote values contrary to Christian

beliefs. Christians should carefully consider the ethical implications of investing in certain art pieces or antiques.

4.   Risk of Idolatry: The appreciation of art and antiques can sometimes border on idolatry, placing undue value on material objects rather than on God and spiritual matters. Christians should guard against developing an unhealthy attachment to such investments.

5.   Inequality and Wealth Distribution: The art market can perpetuate economic inequality, as high-value artworks and antiques may be primarily accessible to the wealthy. Investing in these assets may contribute to widening wealth gaps rather than promoting economic justice and equality.

6.   Long-Term Focus: Investing in art and antiques typically requires a long-term perspective, which may divert attention from more immediate needs, such as supporting ministries or helping the disadvantaged.

7.   Uncertain Returns: While art and antiques can appreciate in value, their market can be unpredictable and speculative. Relying on these investments for financial security may not align with the biblical call to trust in God's providence.

8.   Proper Motivations: Christians are encouraged to do all things, including investing, with pure motivations and a focus on glorifying God. Investing in art and antiques should not be driven solely by greed or the desire for personal gain.

It's important to note that not all Christians would share the same critique, and individual beliefs and interpretations of biblical principles may vary. Some Christians may find ways to engage in art and antique investing responsibly, such as by using profits for charitable purposes or investing in pieces that align with their values and contribute positively to society. Ultimately, a Christian critique of investing in art and antiques should consider both financial and ethical aspects and be grounded in a prayerful and discerning approach.

There are potential dangers of collecting and the risks of idolatry within the Christian context. Motivations behind collecting can inadvertently lead to idolising material possessions, diverting one's focus from God.

Collecting, when approached with a healthy perspective, can be a gratifying hobby. However, an innocent hobby can turn into a consuming obsession, leading individuals to prioritise material possessions above their relationship with God.

Impact investing

From a Christian viewpoint, investing in art holds the potential for a significant impact on both personal and societal levels. On a personal level, investing in art can foster a deeper appreciation for God's creativity and beauty in the world. Art has the power to inspire and uplift the human spirit, evoking emotions and reflections on spiritual themes. By investing in art that aligns with Christian values and messages, individuals can surround themselves with visual representations of faith, hope, love, and other biblical virtues. The presence of spiritually meaningful art in one's surroundings can serve as a constant reminder of God's presence and teachings, nurturing a closer relationship with Him.

On a societal level, investing in art can support and uplift artists who use their talents to create works that celebrate humanity and reflect God's glory. Art can transcend cultural boundaries and communicate universal truths, making it a powerful tool for promoting understanding, compassion, and unity among people of diverse backgrounds. By investing in art that promotes positive values and messages, Christians can contribute to a cultural landscape that fosters beauty, goodness, and truth. Additionally, investing in art can also facilitate the preservation and promotion of Christian heritage, ensuring that artistic expressions of faith from different eras and cultures continue to inspire and inform future generations. Ultimately, investing in art from a Christian viewpoint can have a transformative impact on individuals' spiritual lives and the broader cultural fabric, contributing to a world that reflects God's love and creativity.

Chapter 30: Your Eternity Portfolio

Just as a wise traveller plans for the final destination, for a Christian investor, it is of paramount importance to focus on their eternal destination. While earthly investments are essential for our financial well-being in this journey called life, setting our sights solely on temporal gains would be like fixating on roadside attractions while neglecting the ultimate destination.

Investing in an eternity portfolio encompasses investments not only for this life but also for the life to come. It involves stewarding our resources and talents in a way that aligns with our eternal values and God's purposes. This means prioritising investments that contribute to the advancement of God's kingdom, supporting causes that reflect His love and compassion, and seeking opportunities to impact lives for eternity. By keeping an eternity portfolio in mind, we maintain a balanced perspective, acknowledging the significance of temporal needs while understanding that true wealth lies in investing in the treasures of heaven.

A portfolio is generally an overview or collection of our achievements and possessions, which we have gained through life on the basis of which we desire meaningful rewards.

We have a work portfolio of our work experience, which we use when we're looking for a new job. Artists would have a portfolio of things they have designed, which they would show to prospective customers. Students would have a portfolio of their achievements and their grades, which they have achieved throughout their time in college. We have our financial investment portfolio in which we put in different things like stocks and shares, real estate, unit trusts or whatever.

And then we also have an eternity portfolio, something that will last beyond our life today and have an eternal impact, And last, basically forever.

This is the privilege of the disciple of Christ - to build an eternity portfolio. Why eternity? Well, because we are designed for eternity. We find the meaning of our life and that our life does not consist merely of our short life span here on earth, but that it continues after our physical death. We were made for eternity! In Ecclesiastes 3:11, Solomon said, "He has made everything beautiful in its time. Also, he has put eternity into man's heart."

Investing in treasures in heaven.

Paul gave some very specific investment advice to those with surplus funds to invest.

"As for the rich in this present age, charge them not to be haughty, nor to set their hopes on the uncertainty of riches, but on God, who richly provides us with everything to enjoy. They are to do good, to be rich in good works, to be generous and ready to share, thus storing up treasure for themselves as a good foundation for the future, so that they may take hold of that which is truly life." (1 Timothy 6:17-19)

He is asking investors not to be proud, thinking that they can increase their capital, living off its return, because this is so uncertain in any economic situation. Instead, they are to trust in God as their Source of provision. When investing, they would, first of all, do good work - investing in the sustainability and promotion of quality of life. Secondly, they should be generous and share, not expecting economic return. By doing this, they will build up an eternity portfolio of 'treasures in heaven' which will help them to enjoy abundant and meaningful life, as God intended.

Jesus Himself spoke many times of rewards or something great that we could look forward to – especially these rewards of "treasures in heaven." What are these "treasures in heaven"?

When Jesus spoke to a very rich young man, he gave an unexpected answer to the question, "Master, what must I do to inherit eternal life?" The young man was exemplary in keeping the law, but one thing was missing!

"Jesus said to him, 'If you want to be perfect, go and sell your property and give it to the poor, and you will have a treasure in heaven, and come here, follow me" (Luke 8:18-30)

Paul thanked the believers from Philippi for their gifts and said, "Not that I seek the gift, but I seek the fruit that increases in your account." (Philippians 4:19) Could it indeed be that investing in 'treasures in heaven' opens a kind of account from where we can then 'reap rewards'?

Treasures in heaven represent all which is invested into God's economy. When we use money to help the poor, widows, orphans, and oppressed; when we invest in sustaining and promoting life; when we invest money in projects for God's Kingdom; whenever we give out of love for our Heavenly Father, we are building up treasures in heaven.

The fruit of the 'treasures in heaven' has two dimensions. First of all, the many rewards that are described in the Bible await us as we enter into eternity with Jesus. But also today's fruit, such as an intimate relationship with Christ, the fruit of the Spirit and the provision of daily needs that Jesus spoke about when he said, "But first seek the Kingdom of God and His righteousness, and all these things will be given to you." (Matthew 6:33)

Those who know Jesus have received a wonderful perspective on eternity in heaven. Every time you send treasures to heaven, your heart moves in that direction, taking you ever closer to heaven.

Furthermore, it refers to the place where those treasures are kept – the actual storehouse. We have to ask ourselves, Are we storing up precious things that will amount to something only on earth (temporary), or are we storing up real treasures that matter to God in heaven (forever)?

Buried treasure.

It's a hot day. A traveller walks across sun-burned fields toward his business in the city. He carries a staff to help him on the long journey. All of a sudden, he pokes his staff into some softer earth and hits something hard. A box! *I wonder what's in there,* he thinks. He furtively looks around, sees no one there and pokes some more. He starts digging and unearths the box. His heart is pounding as he pries open the rusty lock and looks inside the chest. Treasure! Gold and precious jewels – a fortune!

Overjoyed at finding such treasure, he wonders who owns the land. Can I afford to buy it? The man buries the treasure again and travels on to the city.

He decides to liquidate all his assets in order to buy the field containing the box of treasure. It's a risk, but one worth taking, he thinks to himself. He sells his farm and livestock, and with the proceeds, he negotiates a good price with the owner of the field. It costs him everything he owns to gain everything that matters!

Jesus tells this parable in two sentences. "The kingdom of heaven is like treasure hidden in a field, which a man found and covered up. Then in his joy he goes and sells all that he has and buys that field" (Matthew 13:44).

The parable could signify Jesus giving up all He had to gain the "treasure" of you and me. It could also be a reference to the immeasurable treasures in heaven that await us, making it more than worthwhile to sell all we have to gain them.

Realising that I can lay up for myself *"treasures in heaven"* drives me to re-evaluate my investments in the light of eternity. What is most important to me?

Investing in treasures in heaven.

We are invited to invest in an 'eternity portfolio.' A portfolio is an overview or collection of your achievements and possessions which you have gained through life on the basis of which you desire meaningful rewards. A portfolio of investments will give you financial rewards; a portfolio of your experiences and works will get your desired employment. A student portfolio is a collection of your work to gain a degree, and a design portfolio will get you assignments. An eternity portfolio will get you rewards.

What could an 'eternity portfolio' look like? Considering the aspects of the Great Commission and the Great Commandment, we could identify five areas of investment potential. To love God and love your neighbour. To make disciples in all nations, teaching them and baptising them. Here are five eternal funds to invest in!

1. Treasury Fund

Investing in loving God could be a Treasury Fund - investing in the Church, God's storehouse.

So I have provided for the house of my God, so far as I was able, the gold for the things of gold, the silver for the things of silver, and the bronze for the things of bronze, the iron for the things of iron, and wood for the things of wood, besides great quantities of onyx and stones for setting, antimony, coloured stones, all sorts of precious stones and marble. 3 Moreover, in addition to all that I have provided for the holy house, I have a treasure of my own of gold and silver, and because of my devotion to the house of my God I give it to the house of my God: (1 Chronicles 29;2,3) David invested a huge amount in the building of the temple because of His love for God and His house.

We invest in God's treasury fund in heaven when we use our money to express worship to God. According to modern-day calculations, David gave roughly $20 billion to the construction of the temple.

God doesn't need money. But when people give an offering to God, they're saying, "God, I love you, and I'm thinking of you, and I want you to be first in my life." Worship-giving is undesignated. We offer it as a sacrifice with no strings attached and no controls placed on it. And we offer it when and where we worship in our local congregation or during special gatherings.

2. Service Fund

Investing in the command to love your neighbour could be developing a Service Fund - helping the poor and needy.

"Sell your possessions and give to the needy. Provide yourselves with moneybags that do not grow old, with a treasure in the heavens that does not fail, where no thief approaches and no moth destroys. For where your treasure is, there will your heart be also." (Luke 12:33,34)

The church should develop a reputation for responding to crises financially, and it should happen in behind-the-scenes ways as well when members of a small group help another member during a difficult season.

The Bible tells of a church in Greece that did this. They heard about another church that was in trouble and going through a famine, so they gave them some money. The Bible says in 2 Corinthians 8:3-4(NCV), "They gave as much as they were able and even more than they could afford. No one told them to do it. They pleaded with us to let them share with us in this service [that's the Service Fund] for God's people,"

3. Global Fund

Investing in the commission to 'go and make disciples in all nations' could be your Global Fund, supporting missions and evangelism.

"The master commended the dishonest manager for his shrewdness. For the sons of this world are more shrewd in dealing with their own generation than the sons of light. And I tell you, make friends for yourselves by means of unrighteous wealth, so that when it fails, they may receive you into the eternal dwellings." (Luke 16:9)

4. Growth Fund

Investing in the command to teach people to obey all Jesus' commands could be your Growth Fund, investing in teaching opportunities.

"Do not lay up for yourselves treasures on earth, where moth and rust destroy and where thieves break in and steal, but lay up for yourselves treasures in heaven, where neither moth nor rust destroys and where thieves do not break in and steal. For where your treasure is, there your heart will be also. "The eye is the lamp of the body. So, if your eye is healthy, your whole body will be full of light, but if your eye is bad, your whole body will be full of darkness. If then the light in you is darkness, how great is the darkness!" (Matthew 6:19-22)

5. Mutual Fund

Investing in the command to baptise people into the life of the Trinity, to be part of the fellowship in the Body, could be your Mutual Fund.

"They are to do good, to be rich in good works, to be generous and ready to share, thus storing up treasure for themselves as a good foundation for the future, so that they may take hold of that which is truly life." (1 Timothy 6:17)

When money and possessions are spent on heavenly treasure, the equation changes radically. The investment takes on eternal value. Since God, his Word, and people are eternal, what will last is what is used wisely for God, his Word, and his people.

Risks Chat

There are no risks involved when investing in treasures in heaven. However, Jesus talked about three scenarios involving risks involved in investing in 'treasures on earth.' These are not valid for 'treasures in heaven.' He said, "Do not lay up for yourselves treasures on earth, where moth and rust destroy and where thieves break in and steal, but lay up for yourselves treasures in heaven, where neither moth nor rust destroys and where thieves do not break in and steal." (Matthew 6:20)

Jesus employs three powerful symbols – moths, rust, and thieves – to illustrate the inherent dangers associated with accumulating material wealth. Let's break down each of these risks.

Firstly, Jesus warns about the danger of moths. Moths are insects known for their ability to damage clothing, particularly wool and other natural fibres. By referencing moths, Jesus highlights the vulnerability of earthly possessions to gradual decay and destruction. No matter how valuable or precious our possessions may be, they are still subject to the passage of time and the wear and tear of everyday life.

In economic terms, the reference to moths made by Jesus regarding treasures on earth can be understood as a representation of inflation or the erosion of purchasing power over time.

Inflation is the general increase in prices of goods and services over a period of time, leading to a decrease in the real value of money. When inflation occurs, the same amount of money can buy fewer goods and services, reducing the purchasing power of that money. This phenomenon is akin to moths gradually eating away at the value of material possessions, causing them to lose their worth over time.

Just as moths can slowly destroy clothing, inflation can diminish the value of cash and other financial assets held by individuals or investors. The more one relies on holding significant amounts of money or low-yielding assets, the greater the risk of losing purchasing power as inflation erodes the value of those holdings.

To counteract the impact of inflation on financial assets, investors can seek investments that can outpace inflation, such as stocks, real estate, or commodities. These assets have historically provided returns that tend to outstrip the rate of inflation, helping to protect the investor's purchasing power over the long term.

Second, Jesus mentions rust as a symbol of danger. Rust is a form of corrosion that affects metals, causing them to weaken and lose their original lustre. In today's economic terms, the "rust" that Jesus referred to regarding treasures on earth can be understood as the concept of depreciation or obsolescence.

Depreciation is the decrease in the value of tangible assets over time due to wear and tear, ageing, or changes in market demand. For example, vehicles, machinery, and buildings often experience depreciation as they are used and become less valuable with age. Similarly, certain consumer goods may lose value quickly as newer and more advanced models are introduced.

Obsolescence, on the other hand, refers to the loss of value of an asset or product due to it becoming outdated or irrelevant in the market. In today's rapidly changing technological landscape, many electronic devices and gadgets can quickly become obsolete as newer, more advanced versions are released.

Both depreciation and obsolescence result in the decline of an asset's value over time, much like rust corrodes metals and weakens their original form. In economic terms, this means that the purchasing power or utility of assets or possessions can decrease, and they may no longer be as valuable or useful as they once were.

Jesus's warning about rust can be interpreted as a reminder that material possessions, despite their initial value, are subject to the forces of depreciation and obsolescence. In today's consumerist society, where constant upgrades and replacements are common, people may find themselves investing heavily in possessions that eventually lose their value, both in monetary terms and in practical utility.

To counteract the effects of rust on one's financial well-being, individuals may consider investing in assets that can appreciate in value or maintain their relevance over time. For instance, long-term investments in real estate, quality businesses, or valuable collectables might withstand the effects of depreciation and obsolescence, providing a more stable store of value.

Third, the "thieves" that Jesus referred to regarding treasures on earth can be understood in today's economic terms as the risk of loss or theft of financial assets due to various factors. Just as physical thieves can break into homes or establishments to steal valuable possessions, in the modern context, there is still a risk of theft of tangible assets, such as cash, jewellery, or valuable items. Burglaries and robberies can result in the loss of material wealth, leaving individuals or businesses financially vulnerable.

With the increasing reliance on digital transactions and online financial activities, the risk of cybercrime has become prevalent. Cyber thieves use various tactics, such as hacking, phishing, or malware attacks, to gain unauthorised access to personal or financial information. They can steal funds from bank accounts, compromise digital wallets, or commit identity theft, leading to significant financial losses.

In the world of finance and investing, there are various investment scams and fraudulent schemes that promise high returns but are, in reality, designed to deceive and swindle unsuspecting individuals. Ponzi schemes, pyramid schemes, and fake investment opportunities are examples of such fraudulent activities that can lead to the loss of hard-earned money.

Financial markets are subject to fluctuations and volatility, which can impact the value of investments. Market downturns, crashes, or economic crises can result in significant losses for investors, affecting their overall wealth.

As mentioned earlier, inflation can act as a "thief" by eroding the purchasing power of money and reducing the value of financial assets over time. This steady loss of value can lead to a diminished ability to maintain the same standard of living or achieve financial goals.

Jesus's warning about moths, rust and thieves serves as a reminder of the uncertainties and risks associated with accumulating earthly treasures. It encourages individuals to be cautious and not place excessive trust in investment wealth alone. Instead, seeking eternal and spiritual treasures, such as acts of kindness, love, and generosity, can provide a more meaningful and lasting form of wealth and fulfilment.

Impact investing

Impact investing in eternity for the Christian entails directing financial resources and efforts toward investments that not only yield positive returns in this life but also have a lasting impact in the kingdom of God. It involves making intentional choices to support businesses, organisations, and projects that align with biblical values, promote social justice, and contribute to the well-being of others.

Impact investing goes beyond financial gains; it seeks to be a channel of God's love, mercy, and compassion in the world. By focusing on eternity, the Christian impact investor aims to leave a legacy that reflects their faith and values, impacting lives not just for a fleeting moment but for all eternity.

This form of investing is about being a good steward of God's resources, recognising that true wealth lies not in personal accumulation but in making a meaningful difference in the lives of others and in advancing God's purposes on earth. Impact investing in eternity is a powerful way for Christians to use their financial influence to bring about positive and lasting change in this world and the world to come.

Chapter 31: Accountability

Just as a responsible driver is accountable for their actions and decisions on a car journey, being accountable as a Christian investor is of utmost importance. When navigating the intricate world of investing, it is essential to align our choices with our values and principles rooted in faith.

Being accountable means acknowledging that our financial decisions impact not only our well-being but also the well-being of others and the environment. Just as a driver follows traffic rules and respects the safety of fellow travellers, a Christian investor should prioritise ethical investments that contribute positively to society, uphold social justice, and honour God's creation. It involves being transparent in our investment practices, seeking wise counsel, and evaluating the potential consequences of our choices. Embracing accountability in investing enables us to honour God with our resources and serve as faithful stewards of His blessings, ensuring that our financial journey aligns with our Christian values and bears fruit for the greater good.

Everyone is ultimately accountable to God. He is the Creator of all things. "And there is no creature hidden from His sight, but all things are open and laid bare to the eyes of Him with whom we have to do" (Hebrews 4:13, NASB1995).

Accountability is extremely important to God, and the Bible teaches a lot about the topic with examples of those who were accountable and those who were not.

The definition of accountability as expressed in the Bible comes from Romans 14:12, "So then each of us will give an account of himself to God." When we die, we will all arrive at the Judgement Seat of Christ and give an account of what we did with the life we have been given. If we are found faithful and have used what we have been given in His way, we will hear the blessed recognition from Jesus, "Well done, good and faithful servant" (Matthew 25:23).

Jesus talked about accountability in Matthew 12:36: "I tell you, on the day of judgment people will give account for every careless word they speak, for by your words you will be justified, and by your words you will be condemned."

What we say and how we say it can make or break others and ourselves. On the day of judgment, we will be reminded of these words. We should not think that we will automatically be fine when we stand before God.

Judgement

When visiting the ancient city of Corinth, I would say the most moving spot of all is the raised stone platform called the '*bema*.' In ancient Greece, the *bema* was typically located at the centre of the forum or marketplace where officials gave public addresses and heard legal cases. It was a raised platform in the assembly where speeches were given, and crowns were awarded to winners of the games. In ancient Rome, the Caesars sat on a '*bema*' to reward those who had been victorious in battle.

As I stood there, the awesomeness of the moment overtook me, and I saw myself on a future day standing at Christ's throne. The Bible says, "For we must all appear before the judgment seat (bema) of Christ, so that each one may receive what is due for what he has done in the body, whether good or evil" (2 Corinthians 5:10).

All other courts or tribunals pale into insignificance before the bema of Christ. There, we will be judged by a righteous Judge who knows and sees everything. "And no creature is hidden from his sight, but all are naked and exposed to the eyes of him to whom we must give account."

(Hebrews 4:13)

The judgment seat of Christ will take place after Christ returns and gathers believers to be with Him. Christ will evaluate our works and will reward us for faithfully serving Him. This is not a judgment to determine our eternal destination. That has been settled when we come to faith in Christ, accept Him and are born again by the Holy Spirit.

Jesus told his beloved John in Revelation 22:12, "Behold, I am coming soon, bringing my recompense with me, to repay each one for what he has done." Believers are judged at the judgment seat of Christ (see Romans 14:10-12). Every believer will give an account of himself, and the Lord will judge the choices we have made. This judgment does not determine salvation, which is by faith alone, but is the time when believers have to give an account of their lives in service to Christ.

The basis for judgement

What is the reference point by which we shall be judged at the bema? Jesus commended the stewards who had done well with the funds they had been given to work with: "Well done, good and faithful servant."
From the commendation Jesus gave to the stewards who had used the funds well, we can detect two criteria on which we will be judged. The first criterion is goodness, and the second is faithfulness.

A friend of mine, a financial adviser, tells the story of the 'fourth steward' as an extension of Jesus' parable of the tenets from Matthew 25. I think this makes a good point. Two of the servants were above to double their resources. One servant was afraid and did nothing with the resources given to him to use, making the Master angry. He imagined a fourth, fictive servant who invested money in fitting out and provisioning a ship to a faraway port to pick up goods which were needed in his marketplace. A storm arose, and the ship floundered. The investment was lost. Do you think the Master would have been as angry as he was with the third servant? I don't think so. He did good work and was faithful.
Jesus has given us resources to invest - but not all endeavours will be successful. We will not be judged on our success but on the goodness and faithfulness we showed.

Paul uses the metaphor of a building in his first letter to the Corinthians. "For we are God's fellow workers. You are God's field, God's building" (1 Corinthians 3:9). He explains that the foundation of the building is Jesus Himself. We have been given the privilege of working together with God to build the kingdom. God encourages His fellow workers, "Let each one take care how he builds upon it" [the foundation] (1 Corinthians 3:10). We must not take this privilege lightly.

Then Paul goes on to explain that we will be evaluated on how we build and with what kinds of materials. "Now if anyone builds on the foundation with gold, silver, precious stones, wood, hay, straw – each one's work will become manifest, for the Day will disclose it, because it will be revealed by fire, and the fire will test what sort of work each one has done. If the work that anyone has built on the foundation survives, he will receive a reward. If anyone's work is burned up, he will suffer loss, though he himself will be saved, but only as through fire" (1 Corinthians 3:12-15).

Building with gold, silver, and precious stones is the work I believe God has prepared for us to do. "For we are his workmanship, created in Christ Jesus for good works, which God prepared beforehand, that we should walk in them" (Ephesians 2:10). This foundation has little to do with quantity (you can hold these gems and minerals in the palm of your hand) but more with quality: that which is done in obedience to Christ and out of love for Him.

John Bunyan, writing The Pilgrim's Process from a prison cell, stated, "Whatever good thing you do for Him, if done according to the Word, is laid up for you as treasure in chests and coffers, to be brought out to be rewarded before both men and angels, to your eternal comfort."[24]

Building with an impressive pile of combustible materials, however good they may look in the eyes of the world, will not last a few seconds in the holiness of the fire. These represent "treasures on earth," which Jesus tells us not to store up for ourselves.
David Livingstone, the Scottish explorer and missionary to Africa, said, "I place no value on anything I possess, except in relation to the kingdom of God."[25]

- Our thoughts and intentions will be judged: ". . . discerning the thoughts and intentions of the heart. And no creature is hidden from his sight, but all are naked and exposed to the eyes of him to whom we must give account" (Hebrews 4:12-13).
- Our spoken words will be judged. "I tell you, on the day of judgment people will give account for every careless word they speak, for by your words you will be justified, and by your words you will be condemned" (Matthew 12:36-37).
- Our motives will be judged. "Therefore do not pronounce judgment before the time, before the Lord comes, who will bring to light the things now hidden in darkness and will disclose the purposes of the heart. Then each one will receive his commendation from God" (1 Corinthians 4:5).

At the judgment seat of Christ, justice will be done and truth revealed.

When I think about this judgment, it really motivates me to take my responsibility seriously to steward all God has entrusted to me. I want to ask the Spirit daily to produce the fruits of righteousness in me, including my responsibility to pour Christ's love into the lives of others.

Earl Rademacher says, "The person I am becoming today is preparing me for the person I shall be for all of eternity." We should be all that we can be on earth so that we can be all that we could be in heaven!"

The apostle John was given a vision of the end times. He wrote, "And I heard a voice from heaven saying, 'Write this: Blessed are the dead who die in the Lord from now on.' 'Blessed indeed,' says the Spirit, 'that they may rest from their labours, for their deeds follow them!'" (Revelation 14:13). Our deeds on earth will not be lost or forgotten; they follow us, even after death, into eternal life.

Rewards

Your faith determines your eternal destination, but your behaviour determines your eternal rewards. As a believer, you are guaranteed an inheritance based on your adoption into God's family as His child: it is eternal life with the Trinity! Your rewards are based on your actions.

Salvation is a free gift given by God. Rewards are given for faithfulness in the Christian life, or rewards can be withheld for unfaithfulness. Eternal rewards should be one of the great motivators of the Christian's life!!

The great Bible teacher Ray Fowler writes, "Your reward will correspond to what you have been building in this life. If you have been living for God and Christ and His kingdom, then what you have built will survive into the next life."

I like what N.T. Wright says about this in his book, "Surprised by Hope." [26] He writes, "It isn't a matter of calculation, of doing a difficult job in order to be paid a wage. It is much more like working at a friendship or a marriage to enjoy the other person's company more fully."

He goes on to say that it's somewhat like practising golf when you experience the joy of a good shot that results from the time put in at the practice range. "The 'reward' is organically connected to the activity, not some kind of arbitrary pat on the back, otherwise unrelated to the work that was done. And it is always abundantly beyond any sense of direct or equivalent payment…. The resurrection means that what you do in the present, in working hard for the gospel, is not wasted. The rewards we will be given serve to equip us for the responsibilities we will be given in eternity when we are to "rule with Christ."

Most Christians have never thought much about life in eternity. This is surprising because the Bible gives us wonderful glimpses of what it will be like. Of course, we cannot fully grasp the enormity of it. I have found that having a clear view of what our "treasures in heaven" will include is a strong motivating factor to live for Christ in tough times and a reason to forego the "treasures on earth" that seem so very attractive.

Think of the biblical saints who were driven to serve God because of the prospect of a reward.

Abraham was willing to leave the security of Ur and live in tents without knowing where he was going because "he was looking for the city which has foundations, whose architect and builder is God" (Hebrews 11:10, NASB). This promise motivated him to obey God even though he died without the promise being fulfilled. He was rewarded in the life to come.

Moses was willing to leave the treasures of Egypt and defy the Pharaoh, "choosing rather to be mistreated with the people of God than to enjoy the fleeting pleasures of sin. He considered the reproach of Christ greater wealth than the treasures of Egypt, for he was looking to the reward" (Hebrews 11:25–26).

We are rewarded out of His generosity, not as an obligation. His grace permeates our whole life; without His grace, we would be utterly lost. However, after showering us with His unmerited favour, He does expect us to respond. As Augustine said, "Without God, we cannot; without us, He will not." The initiative and work come entirely from God, and we react in response to and in cooperation with Him. Augustine continued, "He who created you without your help will not save you without your cooperation."

God expects us to work alongside Him to "work out your own salvation with fear and trembling, for it is God who works in you, both to will and to work for his good pleasure" (Philippians 2:12-13). That is grace: not only does He save us from ourselves, but also empowers us to work in such a way that He can say, "Well done!"

Rewards are not based on a day's pay for a day's work. God will reward us completely out of proportion to the work we have done. He has placed Himself under a loving obligation to reward us. If He didn't reward us, the author of Hebrews says, He would be *"unjust." "For God is not unjust so as to overlook your work and the love that you have shown for his name in serving the saints, as you still do"* (Hebrews 6:10).

Our relationship with Him is not just between master and servant but between a Father who delights in sharing His inheritance and His obedient child. In the end, we shall receive much more than we have merited; in fact, as we have already learned, we "deserve" nothing. God will give us rewards that are totally out of proportion to the work we have done. Since no one "earns" rewards anyway, we shall receive the benefits of a gracious wage. We will have hearts of gratitude for all of eternity.

What rewards?

God grants rewards for many things, including doing good works, (Ephesians 6:8; Romans 2:6, 10) denying ourselves, (Matthew 16:24-27) and showing compassion to the needy, (Luke 14:13-14) and treating our enemies kindly. (Luke 6:35) He also grants us rewards for sacrificial and generous giving: "Go, sell your possessions and give to the poor, and you will have treasure in heaven." (Matthew 19:21)

What should we think of when considering eternal rewards?

I believe the most important thing is enjoying a perfect relationship with Jesus in heaven. It is said that all life is a treasure hunt for a perfect person in a perfect place! What better reward to receive than to hear from Jesus, "Well done, good and faithful servant, enter into the joy of your master!"

In several places, the Bible also mentions a position of authority, reigning with Jesus Himself. Some will be put "in charge of many things." (Matthew 25:21-23) Christ spoke of granting some followers rulership over cities—in proportion to their faithful service in managing his assets. (Luke 19:17-24)) Endurance to the end is a necessary qualification. "To him who overcomes and does my will to the end, I will give authority over the nations . . . just as I have received authority from my Father. I will also give him the morning star." (Revelation 2:26-28)

The list is almost too long to detail and out of the scope of this book, but here are some indications of what awaits the faithful. The Bible also names 'crowns' as rewards. The crown of life for being faithful in losing your life for His sake; an incorruptible crown for victory in your Christian life; a crown of joy over the people you have influenced with the gospel; a crown of glory for faithfully carrying out leadership tasks, and a crown of righteousness given for getting ready for Christ's return in holy and pure living. The greatest joy will be to be able to lay all these crowns at Jesus' feet, giving Him the glory and honour!

We are promised other rewards, such as 'hidden manna,' a white stone,' and a pillar in God's temple.'

We will be allowed to eat from the tree of life in Paradise, receive praise from the angels and be given new, white robes, a new name, and a new home in a new city where justice and love reign – shalom and provision for all!

C.S. Lewis said in the opening of his remarkable sermon "The Weight of Glory": [27] "Indeed, if we consider the unblushing promises of reward and the staggering nature of the rewards promised in the Gospels, it would seem that Our Lord finds our desires, not too strong, but too weak. We are half-hearted creatures, fooling about with drink and sex and ambition when infinite joy is offered us, like an ignorant child who wants to go on making mud pies in a slum because he cannot imagine what is meant by the offer of a holiday at the seaside. We are far too easily pleased."

The Author

Peter Briscoe is an Englishman, born in 1950, and studied Industrial Chemistry and Management at Loughborough University of Technology. He moved to The Netherlands in 1974 and was asked by his company to set up a subsidiary in Holland to sell chemical specialties to the aerospace and food processing industries. From 1986 to 2002, Peter was Executive Director of CBMC, Christian Businessmen's Committees, in Holland.

In 1990, Peter set up "Synthesys". a consulting company specialising in chemical product development. When the Berlin Wall collapsed in 1990, Peter developed Europartners, a movement dedicated to reaching European business and professional leaders for Christ. He was co-founder of the Dutch National Prayer Breakfast and the European Economic Summit.

In 2002, Peter took an assignment as Managing Director of HE Space Operations, serving European Space institutions and specialising in providing professional services for spaceflight activities. He was co-founder of the International Association for the Advancement of Space Safety.

In 2008, Peter retired from business to develop a movement of Biblical stewardship in Europe, first of all through Crown Financial Ministries and then Compass - finances God's way.

At home, Peter is a member of the Baptist Church of Leiden in Holland and has served twelve years as chair of the elder board.

He has been married to his Dutch wife, Didie, since 1972. They are blessed with three daughters, three sons-in-law, and six grandchildren.

About Compass

Compass - finances God's way is a global, non-denominational movement teaching financial discipleship and generosity. The purpose is to serve churches, businesses, ministries, schools and other organisations by providing biblically-based solutions for handling money and possessions. Our vision is to see everyone, everywhere, faithfully living by God's financial principles in all areas of their lives.

Compass's mission is to help people everywhere learn, apply, and teach God's financial and business principles. We are looking for three major outcomes.
- To know Christ more intimately.
- To become free to serve the Lord and our neighbours.
- To help to fulfil the Great Commission

The Compass Global Team is comprised of local leadership on six continents – Europe, Asia, South America, North America, Africa and the Indian subcontinent. Our continental offices serve more than 90 nations around the world. Compass is active in over 80 nations over the globe and has resources in many languages.

To see specific English language resources, please visit the US shop at **www.compass1.org** or the EU shop at **www.compass1.eu**

Endnotes

1. T. Aldworth, Letter to E. India Co., 1613. http://www.sabrizain.org/malaya/library/letterseic2.pdf

2. Strong's Hebrew Dictionary, nr. H3533

3 Strong's Hebrew Dictionary, H3498

4. Al Wolters, Creation Regained: Biblical Basics for a Reformational Worldview (Eerdmans, 2005).

5 www.fbcdurham.org/wp-content/uploads/2012/02/Stewardship-Money-Possessions-Eternity-5-Lessons-from-the-Stewardship-Parables.pdf

6. Jacques Ellul in Money and Power, InterVarsity Press, page 97.

7. "The Touch of the Master's Hand" attributed to Myra "Brooks" Welch

8. https://reasonsforhopejesus.com/only-one-life-twill-soon-be-past-by-c-t-studd-1860-1931/

9. Elisabeth Elliot, Passion & Purity, published by Fleming Revell, p. 43

10. Strong's Hebrew Dictionary, g3126

11. Logan Pearsall Smith, Afterthoughts, 1931, 'Other people.' Published by Isha, 201.

12. The Large Catechism by Martin Luther Translated by F. Bente and W.H.T. Dau. Published in: Triglot Concordia: The Symbolical Books of the Ev. Lutheran Church (St. Louis: Concordia Publishing House, 1921) page 565

13. C.S. Lewis, "The Screwtape Letters."published by Paper One, edition 2015 , page 143

14. In - Following the Equator, Mark Twain. 1897.

14. https://www.firstlinks.com.au/warren-buffett-letter-speculation

16 https://www.inspireinvesting.com/post/the-duty-of-a-christian-investor

17 https://together.nbcuni.com/wp-content/uploads/sites/ 3/2023/03/Rise-of-the-Finfluencer-.pdf

18 https://universonline.nl/nieuws/2023/04/24/finfluencers-are-popping-up-everywhere-who-protects-the-investor/

19 Dr. Paul Mills, Cambridge Papers, vol 5, nr. 2. June 1996

20 https://www.kingdom.bank/about/why-bank-with-us/

21 https://www.adelfibanking.com/giveback

22 Bitcoin Electricity Consumption Index

23 https://academic.oup.com/rfs/article-abstract/ 32/5/1798/5427781?redirectedFrom=fulltext

24. https://generositymonk.com/meditations/page/374/

25. https://dtbm.org/ownership/

26 http://www.rayfowler.org/sermons/real-answers-about-heaven/judgment-and-eternal-rewards/

27 The Weight of Glory, by C.S. Lewis. Published by Harper One, 2001.

www.ingramcontent.com/pod-product-compliance
Lightning Source LLC
Chambersburg PA
CBHW070533310726
48976CB00002BA/614